Going Underground

For Dave

Going Underground

How to Rob the Bank of England

Andrew Clark and Jon Charters-Reid

First published in Great Britain in 2024 by
Pen & Sword Crime
An imprint of Pen & Sword Books Limited
Yorkshire – Philadelphia

ISBN 978 1 03612 189 1

A CIP catalogue record for this book is
available from the British Library.

Typeset by Mac Style
Printed in the UK by CPI Group (UK) Ltd, Croydon, CR0 4YY.

Pen & Sword Books Limited incorporates the imprints of After
the Battle, Atlas, Archaeology, Aviation, Discovery, Family History,
Fiction, History, Maritime, Military, Military Classics, Politics,
Select, Transport, True Crime, Air World, Frontline Publishing, Leo
Cooper, Remember When, Seaforth Publishing, The Praetorian Press,
Wharncliffe Local History, Wharncliffe Transport, Wharncliffe True
Crime and White Owl.

For a complete list of Pen & Sword titles please contact

PEN & SWORD BOOKS LIMITED
47 Church Street, Barnsley, South Yorkshire, S70 2AS, England
E-mail: enquiries@pen-and-sword.co.uk
Website: www.pen-and-sword.co.uk
or
PEN AND SWORD BOOKS
1950 Lawrence Road, Havertown, PA 19083, USA
E-mail: uspen-and-sword@casematepublishers.com
Website: www.penandswordbooks.com

Contents

Chapter 1

Jack peered through the darkness, inhaled deeply and sprinted towards the flat rooftop ledge before him. Breath held, he hit, pushed and swung his arms high, leaping into the night.

Cool air encompassed his body as he fell, the shadow of a building looming into view. His feet hit concrete as he pushed his body sideways, rolling to soften the impact, and a small grunt was forced from his mouth. His arms reached out, his hands grasping a masonry ledge, halting his fall. Shoulder muscles strained as he steadied his body with his legs dangling below.

"Can't believe that worked!" he said aloud. Looking down he could see the still bustling streets of Soho; the public wending their way from theatres, restaurants and pubs to their homes, or further on into the morning where they could party until the early hours.

Jack adjusted his grip and, in a well-practised move, reached out with his right leg and secured his foot in a crevice. Releasing one arm, he gently shook it, freeing the pooled lactic acid from his limb into his body. Switching arms he repeated the move and, looking up, identified his route to the window. He climbed with ease, reaching a small balcony where he rested, raised the balaclava from his lower face, and checked his watch. *One o'clock. Plenty of time.*

Two windows now faced him, replacing the position of once resplendent doors which had led to the balcony. He examined the locks, took his picks from his trouser pocket, and easily defeated one lock. Balaclava now pulled down, he gently opened the window. His research had identified that these particular windows had not been alarmed but, taking nothing for granted, Jack waited, prepared to flee if he needed to. The window now fully open, he gracefully slid his body through the open gap and dropped silently onto an upper floor balcony. The hall remained quiet. No persons present except for Jack. Defeating the lock and entry had taken two minutes.

Holding the shadows, he sidled along the wall, noting the security camera placement towards the lower hall. Jack knew the system, was aware of the movement sensors, and knew that he would trigger them. Looking down he could see mannequins lined up on either side of the hall. They wore various costumes depicting the different houses within the country's freemasonry guilds.

At the front of the hall, resolutely guarding a glass case, stood two fully armoured Knights Templar, their longswords resting point down to the oak flooring. They stood, silently, as witnesses to the crime to be committed. Jack reached between his shoulder blades, where an empty leather scabbard lay positioned down the centre of his back. Under his mask he smiled. *Here we go.*

Jack moved swiftly to the balustrade, climbed up and balanced as he moved to a pillar which led to the oaked hall floor. He positioned his arms around the column, grasped it, and slid slowly to the floor. Feet now on the floor, he moved with swift feline grace towards the glass case sitting upon a marble table. *The silent alarm will have triggered,* he thought, fleetingly. Jack's gloved hand reached to either side of the case, his forefingers pressing two small indentations on the wooden sides. He lifted the glass, revealing the true sword of King Arthur, in all its glory. Reaching in, he removed the weapon, sliding it into the sheath between his shoulders. Jack looked towards one of the Templars.

"Don't mind if I do, Sir." He removed a knife from the Knight's belt and placed it where King Arthur's sword had been, placing a rectangular card underneath the knife. Jack spotted a small compartment at the right side of the case and, lifting the lid, pulled a small, heavy velvet bag from within. *Never miss an opportunity,* he thought, as he placed the soft bag in his pocket. Jack turned to the room and, with arms wide, gave a courtly bow before he sprinted and leapt for the pillar. Reaching high, he grabbed a stanchion and, aiding his body up, grasped a lintel, pulling himself up and over the interior balcony. He raced for the window, an alarm siren now wailing from the building. Sliding through, he pushed the window closed behind him, hearing the click of the window as it locked. Jack moved, traversed the balcony, and climbed towards the roofline. Deftly moving along the apex he headed to one end, gaining speed as he reached the precipice. He leapt and tucked his legs in tight to his body as he dropped towards a further building. He hit, rolled and continued sprinting, a determined grimace now on his face. Jack melted into the night.

With Big Ben chiming one a.m., Jack strolled around a rooftop bar in Soho. The journey from St Anne's churchyard had not taken him long. Now dressed in a smart white shirt and black trousers, he chatted to other customers in the bar and enjoyed the ambience of the light music. Jack moved comfortably around the room, slipping in and out of conversations, ensuring that he was seen. Regular attendees at the venue recognised him, although in reality, none of them really knew him. He was just a known face in the crowd. Jack moved to a quieter area, taking a burner mobile phone from his pocket to text his buyer.

Your item is ready for collection.
Location?

Money transfer. He waited. Two minutes later he received a reply.
Complete.
Kick.museum.tones 9 am. Keith will meet you.

Jack was confident that half of his fee for the job would now be in his account. He had worked for the customer before and neither party had any reason to distrust the other. The buyer was aware that 'what3words' would reveal the location of the sword. Jack placed his phone back in his pocket and moved back into the gathering. He would await his buyer's text confirming receipt of the sword, then he would receive the second half of his fee for obtaining the item. Once the transfer was complete, Jack would dispose of the burner phone and sim card. He walked towards the bar.

"Tom Collins, please." The barman prepared the drink and placed it on the bar. "Cheers." Jack raised his glass and took a congratulatory sip. He'd had a good night.

* * *

Simeon Fortescue groaned as he was pulled from his sleep by the ringing of his mobile phone. He reached wearily to the side table, lifting the telephone to his ear.

"Hello," he mumbled.

"Terribly sorry to disturb you, Sir. Jones here. I'm afraid the hall's been burgled."

"The hall?"

"The Grand Lodge."

"What? Impossible!" Fortescue sat bolt upright, his grey wispy hair on end, grasped for the bedside light and switched it on. His wife next to him stirred, peeling back her eye mask.

"What's happening, Simeon?"

"Oh, be quiet woman. Can't you see that I'm on the phone. Now repeat that, Jones."

"I said that there's been a burglary at The Grand Lodge."

"How do you know, man? Explain! Explain!"

"I'm there now, Sir. I'm one of the keyholders that they ring when …"

"Never mind that," interrupted Fortescue. "What's been taken?"

"The sword."

"The sword!" Fortescue had now climbed out of bed, forgetting that he had removed his pyjama bottoms before falling asleep as they had been twisting around his legs. Mrs Fortescue looked at him, replaced the mask and turned over, not wishing to cope with the sight of Simeon's bare buttocks.

"Order me a taxi, Jones."

"Already on its way, Sir. An Uber. It will be with you in five minutes."

"An Uber! A bloody Uber! Oh well, it will have to do. I'll meet you there Jones. Don't say anything to anyone."

"Of course not, Sir."

"I mean anyone," repeated Fortescue.

"Stum, Sir. My lips are sealed."

Fortescue ended the call and walked towards his chair where he had laid all his clothes out for the morning. Realising he was half naked, he grabbed his pants (white Y-fronts of course) and began dressing. Within minutes he was standing, looking smart and pristine in his three piece suit. He combed his greying, and slightly curly hair into a neat side parting and headed to the front door.

Stepping out to the street he spotted a white Toyota Prius parked outside of his neighbour's house with its engine running. He walked forward and tapped on the driver's window, which slowly lowered.

"Evening, guv. Mr Fortesue is it?" asked a young spotty male with cropped blond hair.

"That's right. Yes it is."

"Hop in then," replied the driver. Fortescue opened the rear door and climbed in, pleasantly surprised with the cleanliness of the car, which had an aroma of alpine forest.

"Good morning, Sir. My name's Barry and I'll be your driver." *Seems obvious*, thought Fortescue, Barry being the only other person in the car. "Please feel free to give me a good review once I've got you to your destination. Now where is that to be?"

"Soho, please, and can you make it quick."

"Of course, Sir. If you could just buckle up then I'll have you there in a jiffy." Barry turned and looked at Fortescue's attire before turning around and addressing Fortescue in the rear view mirror. "Dressed to impress the ladies, are we?" He winked in the mirror as he slowly pulled the car away.

"Not at all. I have a business meeting." Barry looked at his wrist watch and gave Fortescue a knowing smile.

"Course you have, Sir. Secret's safe with me." Barry accelerated the vehicle, forcing Fortescue's body back into the seat, giving him no chance to reply. He gripped the passenger door handle as the Uber swiftly took him through the city to Soho, halting on Queen Street.

"There you go, Sir."

"How much?"

"Already covered by the gent who booked it, Sir."

"Thank you, eh…Bernie was it?" questioned Fortescue climbing out of the car and straightening his now ruffled jacket and hair.

"Barry, Sir. Barry." The vehicle pulled away from the kerb.

"Dirty bastard," said Barry to himself, "No chance of a review from you. Business meeting my arse." He checked his rear view mirror, observing his passenger, who was walking in the direction of Freemasons' Hall.

* * *

Jones met Fortescue at the main entrance of the building and allowed him through the doors.

"That was quick, Sir."

"Yes, a horrible little Uber but he could drive. Anyway, what's the situation here?"

"Only me here, Sir. I rang the police switchboard and advised them that it was an alarm fault."

"Good man."

"I haven't touched anything, Sir. Everything is as I found it."

"Do we know how they got in?"

"No, Sir. No sign of any forced entry. Windows and doors are all closed and locked."

"Yet the sword is missing?"

"Yes, Sir. The alarms wouldn't have sounded unless an intruder had entered the building. They were only serviced two weeks ago." The men walked towards the hallway and entered. Fortescue surveyed the room. All appeared as normal. He walked towards the table at the head of the room and looked upon one of the templar's daggers which sat where the sword had been.

"What about the CCTV?"

"I haven't checked it yet?" Fortescue turned his head, stopped and returned to look again at the dagger.

"What's that?" He pointed to a white corner of a card poking out from under the dagger.

"I don't know, Sir!" Jones removed a clean kerchief from his pocket and, using it to cover his fingers, gently pulled on the corner, revealing a white business card with a black hare imprinted thereon. "What the devil!"

Five minutes later and not without technical problems, the men watched the burglar slide down the hall column and commit the theft. The male was dressed entirely in dark clothing with gloved hands and balaclava. They watched as he bowed to the camera.

"The cheeky bastard!" both exclaimed in synchronism. They watched open-mouthed as he acrobatically left with the prize. Fortescue pressed the stop button on the recording, annoyance now clear on his face.

"Time to mobilise the troops, Jones. He's not getting away with this." He snatched up his mobile phone and dialed.

In his office, within the Metropolitan Police Control Room, Chief Superintendent Robert Harrison lifted his personal mobile phone and answered.

"Good morning, Grand Master. Unusual for you to call at this time in the morning. Is everything OK?"

"No, Robert, it is not. We have a problem."

* * *

Keith sat on a bench near St Anne's Church, enjoying the peaceful haven within London. Usually clients would travel to one of his shops but this was a special case. The item to be fenced was unusual to say the least, and for the money he was getting paid, he needed to ensure that everything went smoothly. The park was empty at this time, it being a weekday, with commuters' concentration focussed on work. The ceaseless drone of traffic in the background was a constant with city life.

"Bollocks!" he said aloud, as he missed his mouth whilst taking a sip from his take out coffee. He leaned forward, wiped his chin and dabbed at the coffee stain on his top. Keith was an anomaly, a purveyor of popular antiques, with a unique sense of fashion. Today he was sporting a bright red jacket, tight blue jeans and black trainers. His most prominent feature being his black dyed thinning quiff. 'Keith the Quiff' was a facilitator/organiser who could get what you needed, get rid of what you didn't and pocket the change. He was connected. If it's people you need, he would probably know them. If he didn't then just give him twenty-four hours and he wouldn't let you down. He wiped some sprayed coffee from the Harrods suit carrying case positioned next to him on the bench. Keith looked up as he saw a tall male dressed in a black suit enter the Dean Road entrance.

"Here we go," he said quietly to himself. The male, checking his phone, was walking directly in Keith's direction. Keith stood up as he approached, scanning his surroundings. Two young ladies pushing prams now walked along slowly as they chatted. Otherwise, the park was empty.

"Alright, son," said Keith, his cockney accent clear in his timbre. The male stopped and looked at him, clearly confused with his attire.

"Keith?" asked the male in a thick European accent.

"The one and only." Keith smiled. "It's there on the bench, mate. I'm off." Keith strolled away as the male reached for the Harrods case. With a quick glimpse over his shoulder, before leaving the grounds, he saw the suited male with bag in hand talking on his mobile phone. Keith walked on to Dean Street and blended in with the crowds, making his way from the drop off.

* * *

Tommy lay back on his sunlounger, looking from the sea towards the Bay of Cannes on the French Riviera. An iced tea in hand, he watched a small dinghy carve the waters towards his Manhattan 52. He was expecting his son, Terry, who he was aware had flown into Cannes Mandelieu airport. He felt relaxed but this was an important meeting. Tommy had enjoyed his life of crime, enjoyed the risk and the danger, but had retired a number of years ago, having been involved in one of the biggest heists ever committed. As a younger man he had thrived on the excitement and the danger, but now approaching seventy he lived a sedentary lifestyle, enjoying the fruits of his criminal endeavours. An Englishman through and through, he now cruised around in his large yacht (when it suited him) or stayed at his private villa. The challenge currently facing him was that he was painfully aware his funds were drastically depleting. He needed more cash. At his age, he was too old to go 'grafting' and that was where Terry came in. Although a successful criminal in his own right, Tommy knew that Terry lived in his father's shadow. He just never quite pulled off the quality jobs that Tommy had in his youth. Tommy had called him here for a meeting. A proposal. An idea. Something that would put Terry ahead and make Terry's name revered amongst his criminal peers. Tommy just hoped that he would go for it.

Tommy stood up, with hand raised in greeting. As the dinghy approached, he recognised the stocky outline of his son. Terry waved in response as the outboard motor slowed and the dinghy approached the Sunseeker. The tender pulled up towards the aft deck at the bathing ladder.

"Permission to come aboard, Captain." Tommy laughed.

"Get up here you daft idiot." He watched as Terry nervously stood up in the dinghy and grabbed hold of the ladder, pulling himself onto the craft. He climbed up, where Tommy waited with arms wide.

"Good to see you, Father." Terry hugged his dad.

"Father! We're a bit beyond that. Tommy will do, mate." Terry released his hug and held his father at arms length, one eyebrow raised. *What are you after then?*, he thought.

"You got a cold beer... Tommy?"

"Of course, my boy. Follow me to the flybridge." Terry followed his father to the starboard side, ascended the side deck, listening to the sounds of the dinghy heading back to shore. He held tightly to the rail as he followed his father's footsteps towards the front of the yacht. They climbed the stairs to the main entertainment area and walked across the teak flooring, towards the wet bar.

"Grab a seat, son." Terry walked to the U seating, surrounding a central table, as Tommy produced two bottles of Peroni from the cooler. He popped the lids and walked over to Terry, handing him a bottle, and sat down opposite him. "How are you doing then?"

"I'm fine and obviously you're doing fine. Why have you dragged me all the way out here?"

"Is this not better than London?"

"Well, the air smells cleaner. The water looks better than the Thames but the beer's the same. Cheers." He raised his bottle and took a drink. "Now what are you after, old man?" Tommy placed his bottle on the table.

"Do you think you can be better than I was?" He leaned forward.

"What?"

"I'm one of the best that there is. Do you think you can do better?"

"What are you on about, you old fool?"

"Come on, son. You've been itching to outdo me. You can't wait." Tommy looked directly at his son. "And I've got the job to prove that you can." Terry sat up, gripped by the infectious delivery of his father's dialogue.

"Go on."

"The Bank of England."

"The Bank of England?"

"Yes, The Bank of England."

"What about it?"

"It's never been screwed."

"And?"

"If you wanna outdo me son, then that's the job."

"Are you serious?"

"As serious as a heart attack." Terry was intrigued. *Why are you touting this then?*

"And how do you suggest I do that?"

"Well, I know it's not an easy one."

"Bloody right it's not"

"Just reach into the compartment under your seat. You'll find the blueprint for the bank…" Terry stood up, raised the seat cover and recovered a plastic tube. Unscrewing it, he unrolled the architectural plans for the Bank of England. He looked at his father who smiled confidently at him "… and I already have an inside man." Terry's interest was piqued. Tommy could read it in his son's face. He smiled.

"So we have a way in?"

"Sure do."

"Getting away with it though. The cops will be all over us."

"Not if the bank doesn't report it."

"And why wouldn't they?"

"We steal just enough gold so that it doesn't push the country into economic decline and crash the stock market. If we aren't greedy, my insider is confident that the bank won't dare to tell a soul."

"How much is too much?"

"That's for you and your team to work out. That's part of the challenge. Come on, it's got to be worth a shot." Terry took a swig of beer. The temptation to outshine his father was too much.

* * *

Jane Swithens walked on to Cannon Street, having taken the tube into work. Dressed smartly in a navy suit and clutching her handbag tightly, she checked her watch and headed for Walbrook.

"I've got time to grab a coffee," she mumbled to herself as she matched the pace of the pedestrians walking in her direction. The city commuter traffic dominated the area, spouting cloudy fumes to the skies, which added to the smog enveloping the city. The atmosphere was humid. Jane could already feel perspiration building on her lower back as she navigated the crowds. Ahead she could see the Magistrates Court, with Mansion House sitting regally adjacent to it, and a Starbucks positioned invitingly on the corner. Jane went in and ordered a flat white. Strong enough to stimulate her senses, with the luxury of velveteen milk. Ordered "to go" she collected her disposable cup, Jane now written on the side, and headed towards Threadneedle Street where the Bank of England awaited her arrival.

Jane had been working at the bank for several years and, having progressed through various roles now, held a senior position on the security team. A team which was responsible for the integrity of all of the systems which protected the gold within the vault. It was Jane's responsibility to ensure her part of the team maintained the bank's high standards. She approached the staff entrance, where a security guard waited to allow staff into the building. Handing over her handbag to be searched, she showed her identity pass and walked confidently through the metal detector.

"Morning, Jane," said a man wearing a blue uniform.

"Morning, Jim. How's Mary doing?"

"She's doing just fine," he beamed at her, happy that she'd recalled his wife's name.

"That's good to hear," she returned his smile, collected her handbag and strode towards the corridors which led to her office. Employees passed her en route to their stations, carefully studying paperwork or texting messages to loved ones before the day's work started. Jane turned into a further corridor, aware of the internal CCTV cameras which recorded all activity in the building. She reached a secure door and pressed her pass onto the Bora lock, which restricted access to required personnel only. The light sensor on the lock turned from red to green.

With a click, Jane knew it was safe to push the door, which opened inwards. She walked into a small room which housed four desks and computers. Only two desks were currently occupied, with two bespeckled faces looking over their screens as she entered.

"Morning, gents," said Jane, the door shutting automatically behind her with an audible 'click'. Both smiled in greeting but silently dipped their heads back towards their screens, mesmerised with their content. Used to their behaviour, Jane walked through the room to another door which opened up to the nerve centre. Reminiscent of a NASA control room, CCTV screens covered one wall, with an array of computer desks opposite, all occupied by staff members completing various tasks. Cooled to an ambient temperature, Jane welcomed the atmosphere as she strolled towards her private office, the faint buzzing of conversations brushing her consciousness. She left the room, crossed a corridor and entered her office, leaving her door open. Jane placed her coffee on her desk and entered her passwords into her computer, watching it come to life. The room was sparse, with only one enlarged photograph of St. Mark's Square, taken from the Dome of St. Peter's Basilica, dominating a wall. She looked at it wistfully, remembering the wonders of Italy which she had recently discovered with her family. The rest of the room was sparsely furnished. A desk and computer. No adornments and no windows. Uplighters illuminated the room, providing comfort to the eyes but, with a 'clear desk, clear room' policy, any frivolities were frowned upon. She unlocked her desk and lifted out her desk tidy and diary, items which she would return to the drawer at the end of the day. Jane was indifferent about her job but knew why she was there. She was comfortable in her role, knowing that one day her prospects would improve. Jane knew that she was destined for better things and that her days of purgatory would soon end. Her mobile phone buzzed in her handbag. She retrieved it and read the message sent from a number that she didn't recognise.

I'll ring you in 2

Jane stood up and walked to her office door, gently closing it, and placed her phone on the desk. Now sitting back down, looking at her phone, she quickly answered it as her screen displayed a blocked number. Jane accepted the call and lifted the phone to her ear.

"Jane, can you speak?" she smiled, recognising the familiar tones of her Great Uncle Tommy.

"Yes, I'm on my own." Jane's stomach flipped and fluttered as she barely controlled her excitement.

"We're on, love. It's gonna happen." She clenched a fist in celebration. "Firstly, you need to meet Terry. He's got your number, he'll be in contact." Jane listened as Tommy recounted his meeting with Terry.

* * *

Jones stood waiting patiently outside the Guild Hall as he watched a black cab pull up outside. The tall figure of Robert Harrison exited the vehicle, wearing a dark waist-length jacket, black trousers and black shoes which were highly polished. He walked stiffly towards the steps and looked every bit of the copper that he was. His arrogant gait and stiff-armed posture portrayed a man on a mission. Harrison climbed the steps.

"Andrew," Harrison addressed Jones, "how's he been?"

"Robert," in reply, "to be honest, bloody awful. Brace yourself." Jones opened the building doors allowing Harrison to enter first. Jones followed, quickly scanned the street outside and pulled the doors closed, locking them securely. The clip of Harrison's soles echoed on the parquet flooring as he headed to the main hall. He walked in.

"You took your bloody time," stated Fortescue, turning towards Harrison.

"Well I had to cancel some meetings, Sir. It's not always easy at short notice."

"Some things are more important than your meetings, Robert. Your meetings can wait. We have this to deal with."

"Yes, Sir. Of course. That's why I'm here." Fortescue looked Harrison in his face, determining whether that had been a note of sarcasm in his voice. He moved closer to Harrison.

"Remember your loyalties, Robert. Don't forget how you got to where you are today."

"Yes, Grand Master," Harrison replied with an appropriate tone of subservience. Fortescue held Harrison's gaze forcing Harrison to break the stare first. Fortescue strode away.

"This way, Robert. Take a look at this." They walked towards the front of the hall where the glass display case held the dagger. Placed on the table beside the case was a white business card with the black inked image of a hare thereon. Harrison looked at the table with one eyebrow raised.

"What do you think, man?" asked Fortescue. Harrison stood with arms behind his back, hands clasped together as his eyes surveyed the area.

"Well, the sword has gone and our burglar has left a calling card."

"I bloody know that," yelled Fortescue. "Who the hell is he?" Harrison stepped back, out of Fortescue's reach, watching his red faced associate attempt to control his anger. "Do you know how long it took us to acquire the sword?"

he continued, "The lengths that we had to go to to bring it here? And now some jumped-up snivelling shit has stolen it from under our noses. I want him found, tortured, punished," he screamed. "Now, who is he?" continued Fortescue quietly, his anger abating following his outburst.

"I don't know, Sir," Fortescue grimaced at Harrison, "but I'll find out."

"Damn right you will," he snapped. "Have you seen that before?" Fortescue pointed at the card.

"Over the years it's been seen a number of times. Probably a couple of times in the last three or four months."

"And?"

"We don't know who he is. We know he's good. That he only commits high value burglaries and that he never leaves any forensic clues."

"I want him caught. I want you to put a team on this and I want my sword back."

"Your sword?"

"Our sword. What are you going to do?"

"Well, it would help if you officially reported the burglary to the police."

"That's not going to happen."

"It would help me to allocate resources."

"Tough. You'll have to work that one out for yourself. Who have we got that you can put on this?" Harrison could tell that Fortescue would not be moved on this.

"I can put a small task force together to review all the previous jobs. Float it as a developmental opportunity for Detective Inspector Ali Smith. He's one of ours."

"Which one's he?"

"Dark hair, thinning on top. Plays golf with Fitzroy."

"Ah yes! Good, good."

"They'll have to be overseen by a regular though. She's a bit of a stickler but I think that I'll be able to convince her."

"Don't think, Robert. Do."

"Yes, Sir."

"Another couple of ours on the team would help."

"I'll see if I can squeeze a couple of low rankers in."

"Right, brilliant. I want them up and running today," Harrison looked like he was about to object. "No excuses, Robert." Harrison's shoulders slumped in defeat. Fortescue started walking towards the exit doors of the hall, he halted and turned. "Robert, when we find out who he is then the guild will be dealing with him, not the police. Do I make myself clear?"

"Yes, Grand Master." Fortescue spun round and walked from the hall leaving Harrison to deal with the mess.

Chapter 2

Jane walked away from the bank and headed back towards Cannon Street Station. She had finished work an hour early and strolled out into bright sunshine and warm air. Following her call this morning, Jane had found it hard to concentrate at work, with feelings of both excitement and trepidation circulating in her body. She had a prearranged meeting near Covent Garden and didn't wish to be late. Jane knew of Terry through family conversations but had never met him. The Lomaxes were a large extended family and though primarily law-abiding citizens, certain members were happy to turn a blind eye to anyone who could make a profit. Tommy's exploits in crime were well known amongst all, and some of the family had benefited from them. He was accepted as being a bit of a rogue and, although not a black sheep, definitely veered on the side of grey rather than white. Jane was interested to see what Terry was like, and though today she had received the call she had been waiting for, this was her first foray into the criminal world. Jane wasn't scared but she was cautious. She had been prepared for this but now it felt like reality was starting to bite. Joining the crowds, she entered the station and headed towards the platform. No repair work was being completed at Cannon Street today and the trip to Embankment would only take about six minutes. Plenty of time for her to scout the area out and be ready to meet Terry at the designated spot.

* * *

Terry was standing watching the market entrance to Covent Garden waiting for Jane to arrive. His father had provided him with a photograph of her and a description of the clothing that she was wearing today. He was confident that he would recognise her. The Market was still busy with people going about their daily business. Jane had been given instructions to walk there and to wait in a specific area. Terry had ensured that he was early so that he could scan the crowds and judge the safety for the meeting. He was comfortable with the busy surroundings and had found a cafe nearby where he could take Jane and, right on cue, *There you are*, he thought as he watched her slowly walk towards the meeting place. She looked uncomfortable, with her eyes darting around nervously. *You'll need to calm down, love, if you're gonna be working with me.* Terry checked the area as Jane stopped outside the Gardens. Nothing looked untoward. There was no reason why anything should be, but Terry just liked to be sure of himself. Caution never harmed anyone. He walked towards Jane, retrieving a cigarette from his pack of Benson & Hedges and, lifting it to his mouth, approached her.

"You haven't got a light have you, love?" Jane jumped at the sound of his voice and, although recognising the words, squinted at him in confusion. "A light, love. For my cigarette?" Terry watched the penny drop as realisation dawned on Jane's face with recognition of the agreed codewords.

"I'm sorry, no. I gave up a year ago." She waited for his confirmation.

"No problem. I'll use m'own then." He produced a Zippo from his pocket and lit his cigarette. "Nice to meet you, Jane, I'm Terry." She smiled now, noticing his resemblance to Tommy.

"And you. What do we do now?" Jane looked around, shoulders hunched, still anxious. Terry smiled and took her arm to guide her through the crowds.

"We straighten up, walk tall and have a stroll along to a little cafe that I've found for us." He could feel Jane relax slightly and spoke quietly to her. "Remember, we have done nothing wrong. We are just family who haven't seen each other for years, and we're just meeting for a coffee. Relax, Jane. Everything's OK." Jane followed Terry's lead as they walked towards a local cafe, seated themselves and ordered.

"I could do with something stronger really," Jane giggled nervously.

"All in good time. Now, how's your day been?" Jane started telling Terry about her day, her position in the bank, and, when prompted, a little bit about her background. Terry reciprocated with a redacted version of his life. It was clear to them both that they gelled and that working with each other would not be a problem. Once coffee was finished, Terry paid the bill and they left the cafe, heading for something stiffer to drink.

Five minutes later, and now ensconced within a boutique of a local bar, a pint of lager and a white wine were their chosen beverages.

"What's the plan then?" asked Jane, taking a sip and leaning forward conspiratorially.

"Not to be discussed here," advised Terry. "That can be sorted at a safer venue." Jane nodded, absorbing his words.

"When will that be?"

"Soon I hope. I'm still recruiting the team."

"How many of us? What do we need?"

"My, you are keen." Terry laughed. "Clearly the Lomax blood runs thick through your veins." Jane frowned at him. "Take it as a compliment. Much can be achieved with enthusiasm and a calming hand steering the boat. The main problem for you to start thinking about is how to defeat the security."

"Oh!" Jane took a swig from her now half-empty glass, "That's easy."

"Easy! How's it easy?"

"We've got Ronnie,"

"Who the hell is Ronnie?"

"Ronnie. Everyone needs a Ronnie, they just don't know it," replied Jane with a smug look on her face.

"Go on."

"Ronnie the Phish, aka Veronica Pilcher, aka my aunt."

"Ronnie the Fish!!!"

"No Phish. P H I S H," Jane spelled it out. Terry looked confused. "She's an expert, T. Yes, T for Terry." Jane giggled.

"Are you pissed on one glass of wine?" Jane looked at her empty glass.

"No, but I am excited about all of this." She gestured with her hands, referring to the plotting and scheming.

"An expert with what?"

"With computers, T. She is bloody brilliant. Can hack anything. She's the best you will ever have worked with." Terry leaned forward.

"Tell me more."

* * *

Veronica stirred a tea bag around in her mother's yellow pottery teapot and watched the diffusion of the leaves swirl into the boiled water. A packet of chocolate digestives lay unopened upon the worktop, calling to her, and Veronica knew that the temptation would prove too much. She placed the pot lid on and took a mug, plus a China teacup and saucer, from the cupboard above the kettle.

"Is my tea ready yet, dear?" spoke an elderly voice from the living room.

"Nearly, mum. It'll be with you in a minute."

Veronica Pilcher stared out of the kitchen window, looking at their small yard, with its square postage stamp sized area of grass, and contemplated her lot. At forty-five years old, Veronica still lived with her mother, and though she was happy, she had always wondered what her life could have been like had she met someone and taken a different route. Veronica's choice of clothes were jeans and a T-shirt, with today's shirt showing an image of a Minecraft 'Creeper' on the front. Her look was completed with dark hair, styled in the Quatro 'shag', and unusual green eyes which hinted at a high intellect. Veronica was very comfortable with herself but had always felt held back by her agoraphobia. She'd never overcome it, never mixed with her peers, and therefore felt socially inept. She shrugged her thoughts away, knowing that her skills lay in other areas. Veronica poured the tea and, having taken her mother her cup, grabbed her own mug and entered her office.

In front of Veronica were an array of screens and computers. With the curtains being closed, up-lighters illuminated the room. Veronica physically relaxed as she sat down at the desk. Placing her cup, and the now opened pack of biscuits, next to her keyboard she scanned the screens, noting different activities on each. This room was where Veronica felt comfortable. The World Wide Web was displayed before her and responsive to the touch of her fingertips with none of the awkwardness of physical interactions. Veronica, aka Ronnie, had spent years honing her skills on computers. There was no task that she couldn't complete and no challenges that she wouldn't take on. If some of them veered into the world of crime then so be it. Everyone had to pay their household bills and Ronnie's skills were in demand. Satisfied that her mother would be settled watching daytime television for the next hour or so, Ronnie placed on some Skull Candy headphones, cranked up some rock music and, munching on biscuits, started work.

In the midst of testing an algorithm, Ronnie's phone indicated that she had received a text. She halted her work, took her phone from her pocket and read the message.

Can we meet? Ronnie hadn't heard from Jane for a few months.
Yes, of course. Call around sometime.
I'll be there in thirty minutes. Ronnie raised an eyebrow. *Must be important,* she thought.
Cool, I'll stick the kettle on. Bring some cakes.
X, the reply.

* * *

Robert Harrison had thought long and hard about how he would approach his colleague, Serena Gillespie, about forming a small team to investigate the burglaries. The request would be seen as unusual and would sit outside of the normal tasking priorities. Despite that, he knew that he had a responsibility to the lodge, and for him, that took precedence. He'd been a member for many years, and in this broken world of law and justice, he had convinced himself that the network of freemasons worked for the good of the country, unconstrained by the ministerial red tape that the police were forced to deal with. The Police and Criminal Complaints Department may think differently but Robert felt that he was now so entrenched within the police service, at an appropriate rank, that they could never touch him. He walked along a small corridor and knocked on Serena's office door.

"Come in," spoke a clear, confident voice. Robert pushed against the door and entered. Serena Gillespie was standing next to her desk wearing a crisp white shirt and black suit. With short, greying hair, a slim figure and standing at 5'10" she looked every part of the strong woman she was. Robert internally admired her look but maintained his professional countenance, not allowing his mind to drift from the task at hand.

"Robert, what brings you here?"

"Serena. How was the tasking meeting?"

"Same as usual. Believe me, you didn't miss anything."

"Any new jobs on the horizon?" asked Robert. Serena ignored his question and gestured towards some soft chairs and a coffee table, which were positioned in one corner of the large office. Robert took a seat as Serena poured them both a coffee from a percolator. She handed a cup to Robert and placed a small milk jug on the table.

"Thank you." He placed his cup on the table, slightly raising his bottom from the chair in a half stance of politeness, as Serena sat down. She smiled in recognition of his manners.

"So, to what do I owe this pleasure?" *Direct and to the point as ever*, thought Robert.

"I have a proposal for you, Serena."

"A proposal indeed. You're so forward, Robert. I thought you were married." He chuckled, keenly aware that Serena was extremely capable of controlling the conversation for her own means. He held up his hand showing his wedding ring.

"Yes, twenty happy years. You never fancied it yourself?" He pointed to her empty ring finger.

"I've never found anyone that will take me on." They both laughed. *There's no one out there strong enough*, thought Robert.

"It's never too late," he joked, "but no, a different type of proposal. I'd like to give one of my DI's a little development opportunity."

"Who?"

"Ali Smith,"

"He's a good man. What are you looking at?"

"Well, he's been researching some historical burglaries and may have some ideas about how to identify the "Hare" burglar. You know, the unknown who leaves his calling card."

"Why don't you put it through the tasking process?"

"Well, I've missed this meeting or I would have. The next one isn't due for a month. It probably won't take him that long to review everything. If it looks like it's got some legs then I can submit it to the next meeting." Serena sipped from her cup, looking thoughtfully at Robert.

"What's in it for me?"

"Kudos, Serena." She raised an eyebrow. "This man has never been identified. All his jobs have been high value or high profile. I'll provide Smith and a couple of other officers for free. Bloody hell, I'll even chuck in an analyst. It will cost you nothing." She smiled with the predatory focus of a basking shark.

"And you, Robert. What's in it for you?"

"If we capture him then you get to claim the investigation as your idea. I get to stand shoulder to shoulder with you as your right-hand man. Both our careers benefit."

"I get to oversee the investigation."

"Yes." She held his eyes and reached out her hand.

"Deal. Smith has three weeks to show progress. You sort out the team." They both stood up and shook hands. Robert turned and walked towards the door.

"And Robert," he turned to look at Serena. "If this backfires on me then look forward to a career in admin." He smiled and walked from the office. *There's just something about her. I love a strong woman.* Robert walked briskly down the corridor, eager to inform Simeon of his success and looked forward to a pleasant evening with his mistress.

* * *

"Alright, son." Terry greeted the counter attendant as he walked into a small pawn shop owned by Keith the Quiff. "Is he out back, mate?"

"He was two minutes ago." Terry walked through the small store, behind the counter towards a storage area in the back.

"You in here, Keith?" called Terry, now standing confronted by miscellaneous wardrobes, drawers, standard lamps and such like.

"Up here," yelled a voice from the upper floor. Terry climbed some creaking wooden stairs which led to a dimly lit room. Keith was sitting behind an old wooden desk, peering through a jeweller's loupe at a piece of silverware in his hand. He looked up at Terry and smiled.

"Take a seat," Terry sat down in a worn leather Chesterfield and looked warily at a stuffed boar's head hanging from one of the roof joists.

"Nice place," he stated. Keith laughed, appreciating Terry's scepticism.

"Fancy a nip?"

"A small one." Keith produced a hip flask and drinking measures from his desk drawer and poured a small port for each of them.

"Cheers," he announced as they both necked their cups and he refilled. "How's things going?"

"Good, mate. I've got a job on."

"Have you now? Anything in it for me?"

"Yes. Gold. I'll need you to move some gold. A lot of gold."

"How much?"

"I have no idea yet but a lot."

"I'll need some time to put things in place."

"You've got loads of time. I'm still in the planning stages. I need a burglar. You know anyone who's up for some work? Someone good though, I don't want just anyone. I want the best."

"I know of one bloke but he'll cost."

"Money ain't a problem. The job pays for itself." Keith's interest was piqued.

"Spill the beans then?" Terry told Keith the details of the job so far and of his plans to date. Their cups of port sat untouched on the desk as Terry explained and Keith listened. Keith reached for his port, whistled out loud and took a sip. "That's ballsy, Terry."

"That's why I need the best."

"There's only one bloke that I know who is good enough and may be up for it. He'll want to meet you first though."

"What's his name?"

"Jack."

"Jack who?"

"Just Jack. You want me to arrange an introduction?"

"Yes."

"Leave it with me. Now take a look at this." Keith held forward the silver-backed hairbrush that he had been examining and both males discussed the current value in the stolen silverware market.

* * *

Terry drove towards the Boundary Estate, E17, Walthamstow where he had a planned meeting with Jack. He had borrowed a friend's crappy little Corsa, as the estate was nowhere where anyone would want to take a decent motor. Standing on various corners were the usual young lads wearing hoodies, sweatpants and sliders, some of who would be working as lookouts or delivery boys for local drug gangs. Terry slowed and parked his vehicle, keeping the engine idling. He lowered his window and was greeted by the palpable sweet aroma of cannabis in the air. He watched as a young lad jumped on a BMX and cycled lazily over to an old Fiesta whose headlights had just flashed. The boy approached the driver's side, reached into his pocket, retrieved something which he handed to the driver and received cash in exchange. Dealing openly in broad daylight, gangs on the street, discarded roach ends and small silver canisters 'whippets' littering the ground, the estate was a mess.

"This place is a shit hole," said Terry to himself, taking out a cigarette and lighting up. The young lad on the BMX came cycling towards the Corsa, eyeballing Terry and stopping next to him.

"What you after?"

"Nothing to do with you, son." The boy didn't move but sat cockily looking at Terry.

"Are you the filth?"

"Piss off," Terry started opening his car door, climbing out ready to cuff the little brat.

"Get lost, Jonny," stated a rough-looking man who had approached the car. The kid looked at him and cycled back towards his designated corner. The man looked to be in his mid-twenties and wore the obligatory pants and hoodie. Unshaven, with shadows under his dark eyes and a skinny body, he looked tired.

"Back in your car, Terry. Let's get away from here." Terry looked at the male in confusion.

"Jack?" The male nodded as he walked around to the passenger side.

"Yep." He climbed into the car and sat waiting for Terry to join him. Terry bent over, looking into the car, unsure of what to do.

"Get in, Terry. I haven't got long." Obeying the instruction, Terry climbed in. "Let's just move away from here. Too many eyes." Terry started driving.

"Jack? Friend of Keith's?"

"That's me. Good to meet you." Jack pointed towards a small car park which Terry drove into and parked the vehicle.

"You're not what I expected."

"Clearly." Jack felt no inclination to expand and continued. "Down to business. When's the job?"

"Within the next three months."

"How big is the team?"

"Maximum of ten."

"How much is my cut?"

"All shared equally. If anyone gets caught their share is kept safely for them until they're released." Jack turned his head and looked directly at Terry.

"You done anything like this before?"

"Plenty of jobs but nothing this big. Do I get to ask any questions?"

"No. Keith's given me the details. Can I trust you?" Terry laughed.

"Course not, I'm a crook." Jack opened his door and stepped out. He took one look at Terry, closed the door and walked away. Terry sat wondering what had just happened. He glanced around looking for anything suspicious. "Is this a fuckin' set up?" Stepping out of the car, he looked around. No one was to be seen, not even Jack. *You havin' a laugh, Keith. A bloody high-level burglar my arse.* Climbing back in, Terry manoeuvred his car out of the car park and away from the estate. "You and I are going to have some serious words, Keith the bloody Quiff." Terry's mobile phone rang displaying Keith's number. He pressed accept.

"Just the bloody man. Are you out of your ..."

"He'll take the job," Keith interrupted.

"What?"

"He's on board. He'll take the job."

"Take the job! I don't bloody think so. Have you seen the state of him? Looks like he couldn't even rob your Granny."

"Just as well she's dead then, isn't it? I'm telling you, he's our man and we're lucky to have him."

"You sure?" Terry questioned in a calmer voice.

"Positive, Terry. That little beggar has just broken into the Freemason's Hall in Soho and stolen a priceless antique."

"How do you know?"

"Cos I fenced it for him. He's good, Terry. Very good." Keith ended the call leaving Terry wondering who had recruited whom during the past half hour.

* * *

Keith was standing within one of his many warehouses, checking that everything had been prepared as requested. Refreshments were on hand in the form of orange juice and water, and to the side, a kettle and an assortment of mugs. One projector screen and laptop with associated leads, a selection of armchairs and dining chairs, including an old wooden commode (chamber pot removed and wooden seat in its place) to accommodate his guests. People were due to arrive shortly and he felt a building sense of excitement.

The warehouse was well positioned; out of the city, accessible by road and was a building that his criminal colleagues and the police knew nothing about. Keith stored his most valued criminal acquisitions here and knew the location was safe from prying eyes. Today was the first meeting of the team that had been gathered so far and it was sure to be interesting. Keith loved the excitement of planning a job, of bringing the most skilled operatives together to defeat a problem, and thwart the inevitable police investigation that followed. Walking to his desk he checked the camera screens which displayed the exterior of the warehouse. He had installed covert cameras at various locations to give him the best views of the building's exterior. Housed in an industrial estate, the building lay naturally camouflaged within its environment. He watched as a small blue Corsa appeared at the side of the building, and recognised Terry as he climbed out. Terry squinted through the smoke of his burning cigarette as he scanned the area before heading towards an open side door.

"Good to see you," said Keith walking towards Terry and shaking his hand. Dressed in white jeans, thick-soled shoes, and a bright blue jacket with a quiff newly dyed, Keith never failed to amuse Terry.

"Keith." They both walked towards the furniture. "Everything sorted?"

"Of course. Even managed to bag some KitKats and Wotsits." Terry looked at the back of one of the crisp packets and threw it back down. "Out of date, mate. How long you had these?"

"Just acquired them last week. They'll taste fine."

"Suppose the Kit Kats fell off the back of a lorry too."

"Maybe, but beggars can't be choosers, can they?"

"Not at all and not complaining. We can all go fine dining once the job's complete." Terry checked the CCTV screens. "Here's Jane." A red Fiat 500 pulled up outside the building and parked next to the Corsa. Jane climbed out of the Fiat, dressed in a pair of jeans and a black T-shirt. They watched as she placed a bag over her shoulder and walked to the open door. Terry walked across to greet her.

"Jane," he gave her a brief hug and then turned to Keith. "Jane, Keith. Keith, Jane." They shook hands. "Let's leave full introductions until we're all together shall we," suggested Keith, hearing the roar of a motorbike entering the yard.

"That'll be Jack," stated Keith, "He said that he'd be arriving on two wheels." The sound of the engine died outside and all turned to the sound of footsteps approaching the door.

Jack walked into the building. Blue jeans, Adidas trainers, a white shirt and a black biker jacket to match. He looked like a modern-day James Dean. Clean-shaven with short hair, tanned complexion and a lithe figure, he smiled at the others.

"Morning, all." He placed his bike helmet down on a tabletop. "Keith," Jack nodded to Keith. "Terry, we meet again. Good to see you." He shook Terry's hand. Terry reciprocated, not quite believing that this was the same Jack that he met at Walthamstow. "And this is?" He faced Jane.

"Jane," she replied with an enthusiastic smile on her face, holding her right hand out to him.

"Lovely to meet you, Jane." Jack firmly shook her hand and returned her smile. Terry, now having gathered himself, moved towards the tables and chairs.

"Come on then. Grab a drink and a seat. We've still got one missing. Where's Ronnie, Jane?"

"Oh! She'll be with us shortly, T." Keith chuckled, which was noted by Terry. He had previously explained to Keith about Jane's habit of calling him T. If Terry was honest he quite liked it, feeling that it gave him both an air of mystery and anonymity. However, it appeared that Keith did not quite agree. Terry checked his watch. He wanted to get started. He looked to Jane, who pointed towards the projector screen. As if by magic, a fuzziness appeared on the screen and a woman's voice could be heard.

"Just give me a second," the voice spoke as the screen cleared, showing a management page for Zoom. A cursor moved swiftly around the screen as a meeting was accepted and an image came into view.

"Hi there," said Veronica.

"Everyone, meet Ronnie," said Jane addressing the room. The men raised their hands in greeting, bewilderment on each face.

"Zoom?" asked Terry of Jane, "A bloody Zoom meeting for the crime of the century!"

"Eh, hello. Over here," Ronnie sat waving at the camera. Terry turned to look at her. "That's better. Mr T is it? My idea Mr T. I have a medical condition that prevents me from leaving the house," Jack sat back hiding the smile on his face with his hand, "so I thought that I'd just hijack a Zoom. It's perfectly safe and secure. There's a back door to the system so the software doesn't recognise us as being on the platform." She smiled, pushing her hair back from her face.

"Does this mean that we've only got forty minutes for the meeting?" Terry asked, flummoxed by Veronica's virtual attendance.

"Don't be stupid," replied Ronnie taking a loud slurp of coke from a can. "I'm not an idiot. Here for as long as you need me." She winked at the camera and sat back waiting for Terry to begin.

"Everyone OK with this?" he asked. Responses of assent were provided. "OK, then let's get started. Keith if you can start with Tommy." Keith moved towards the laptop.

"Allow me," said Ronnie. Keith watched as the cursor moved around the screen. "Is it this one?"

"You've hijacked my laptop!" exclaimed Keith.

"Borrowed it. Just trying to help."

"How have you done that?" he asked.

"Too complicated to explain. Let's just accept that I am good. Here we go." Ronnie's screen image compressed to one corner. The main image on the projector screen changed to that of Tommy with a view of the ocean and Italian coastline behind him.

"It's a recording from yesterday, guys. He can't see us but he's aware of who you all are. Pin your ears back for two minutes and let him indulge himself. Team, this is Tommy Lomax, my father and, for our purposes, our benefactor." He nodded towards Ronnie's small image and the video played.

"Am I on, am I on?" Tommy squinted at someone behind the screen and having been given a signal sat back within a seat. "Hi everyone, great that you've all made it here today. I'm assuming that because you are all present, the job's on or, let's face it, you wouldn't be listening to me now," his expression of slight confusion cleared as he realised that he was rambling. "I'm not used to this modern-day technology, in case you hadn't noticed. Anyway, back to the start." Tommy took a sip of tea, relaxed and started again.

"Hi everyone, for those who don't know me I'm Tommy Lomax. About a month ago I sat down with Terry and we spoke about this job. My days of pulling a stunt like this are over but you're all professionals and I know that you are capable of it. You'll get to know each other over the next couple of days, weeks and months and realise that Terry has picked his team well. You need to trust each other, trust in each other's abilities, and know that the benefits of success far outweigh the risks. Take it from a man who knows," Tommy spread his arms wide showing off his location and wealth. "I wish you luck in this venture and look forward to personally meeting you all on the other side. Remember, to be a winner, you must plan to win, prepare to win, and expect to win." Tommy raised his hand in farewell and again leaned towards the camera. "Always liked that one," he said to himself. "Are we done yet? Come on, man, switch it off." Tommy's hand obscured his face and dominated the screen as he reached to switch the camera off. The projector image now changed to that of Ronnie, who appeared to be stuffing the remains of a biscuit quickly into her mouth.

"Right, everyone," commenced Terry. "It's clear that Tommy is not going to make a living in the film industry." Smiles and a chortle from Keith were the response. "Time for us to discuss why we're here. The target is the Bank of England. Specifically, the gold vault." He turned to the screen where Ronnie had now displayed an image of the building and a separate image of Her Majesty the Queen visiting the vault. "Thank you, Ronnie. First off, introductions. I'm Terry, you all know me. To my left," he indicated with his arm, "Keith the Quiff, for obvious reasons. We grew up together and he's our fence. He'll launder the gold once we get it all. Also, should you need any specialist equipment, go to him first. If he hasn't got it, he'll be able to source it." Keith looked at the rest of the team with a smile on his face.

"Next, Jane. Our inside person. She works there, has got herself a management position and can provide us with all of the information that we need. She's family."

"Hi," Jane raised a hand in greeting. Jack looked quietly impressed.

"On the screen we have Ronnie," the image of the bank changed to that of Ronnie. "A computer specialist. There's nothing she can't get into. She's here to defeat any technical issues that we come across. She's family."

"Good to see you guys," she responded.

"Lastly, there's Jack. He comes highly recommended. Jack, tell everyone what you do?" Jack sat forward and smiled.

"I'm your burglar. I can get us in, and out, of anywhere, and make sure that we leave with the goods we went in for."

"A bold statement, Jack," stated Jane. He looked at her.

"Indeed, but I'm good, Jane. Very good." He smiled at her. Jane looked away with a slight flush to her face as Jack sat back. Terry looked contemplatively towards him.

"Well, Jack. You're part of our family now. I'm glad we've got you." The team understood that Jack now had Terry's seal of approval. "Let's get down to business."

Chapter 3

The front doorbell rang. Simeon looked expectantly over the top of his newspaper at his wife, who was taking a sip of sherry. He waited patiently as the bell rang once more.

"Oh! Sorry, dear, I'll get that." In a fluster, Mrs Fortescue placed her glass down and walked towards the dining room door.

"Are you expecting someone?" she asked.

"Yes," he replied, folding up his newspaper and placing it next to his empty plate. "I'll be in my study, if you can show him in there please." He gave her a tight-lipped smile and left the room via a door behind him.

The study was Simeon's private haven. A room where his wife would never enter and where he could seek the solitude that he often craved. A large oak desk dominated one side of the room, bookshelves lined one wall and, opposite the desk, a seating area with two dark green leather chairs. A small cards table and carved oak side table, with various bottles of alcohol and glasses thereon, finished the room. Lighting was subtle and the walls were unadorned except for a small original sketch ascribed to Degas, holding its esteemed position above the sideboard. Smaller than a square foot in size and sketched with pencils, inks, washes and charcoal Fortescue was proud of the item which he had acquired some time ago. He walked to the sideboard and placed two glasses side by side, a small knock on the room door disturbed his pouring of brandy.

"Yes," he spoke aloud.

"A Mr Digby for you, Simeon," stated his wife from the other side of the door.

"Come in, Digby." The door opened and a man wearing a grey dishevelled suit strode into the room. The door closed gently behind him as Mrs Fortescue left the men to their meeting.

"Brandy?"

"That's very kind of you, Simeon," replied the male in a thick Cockney accent. Fortescue disliked the familiarity that this man treated him with but tolerated it. For the time being, Digby was useful.

John Digby was an ex-Metropolitan Police Officer. Having served for several years in the force and uncomfortable with the 'modernisation' of the service he had elected to resign before completing his full service, in order to pursue other career opportunities. This was the tale that he had spun to Fortescue when they first became acquainted. Fortescue suspected it to be a lie and thought it more likely that Digby jumped before he was pushed. Digby did appear to be somewhat archaic in his methods of investigation but he got results and that is what Fortescue required. He handed Digby a glass.

"Take a seat, John." Digby settled himself down, took a nip of the drink and then nursed the rest of the brandy, cupping the glass with his hands to warm it.

"John," Fortescue sat down opposite Digby. "I've got a new job for you," Digby remained sitting quietly studying Fortescue's face as he did so. "It's a slightly delicate matter. I'm sure it goes without saying that it needs to be done on the hush-hush." Silence. "Last night there was a burglary committed at the Lodge. An item of significant value was stolen."

"Have you reported it to the police?"

"Not exactly, but I'll come on to that. It appears that the thief left his calling card." Fortescue placed the card on the table between both men. Digby leaned forward to take a look, making no move to pick it up. "This card was positioned in place of the stolen item." Digby sat back. "My enquiries so far reveal that this same card has been left behind at several high-value burglaries that have been committed." Digby took another look.

"What was stolen last night?"

"A sword."

"A sword!"

"Yes, a valuable sword."

"Didn't take you to be the swashbuckling sort," stated Digby. Fortescue continued, ignoring Digby's comment.

"The sword is an extremely valuable item which we," he paused, "let us say, acquired, some years ago."

"Nicked it, you mean."

"Acquired, at great expense to the lodge, I might add."

"So that's why you haven't reported it to the Met."

"Not officially. One of our members works within the service and has set up a small enquiry team to try to establish who the burglar is."

"What do you need me for then?" asked Digby, placing his now empty glass on the table.

"The head of the team will be reporting directly to me and is under strict instruction that the lodge will be dealing directly with the perpetrator ourselves. Your job will be to work on our side, using all of the information that they obtain, catch the burglar first and bring him to me."

"Him? How do you know that it's a man?"

"I don't." Fortescue's tolerance was wavering. "Here's a list of suspected crimes in the UK." He handed a file over. "Enquiries have been sent to Interpol in case they have come across any similar modus operandi."

"I'll need details of the item, possible suspects etc."

"It's all in the file."

"I'll do my best, Simeon. Usual fee?"

"Yes, of course," he snapped, "John, just do what you do best. The police will get tied up with all their red tape and forms. You will not. Just find him, or her, first." The meeting was finished. Digby stood and moved towards the door as Fortescue looked at the Degas. John opened the door.

"And, John," Digby paused, looking back at Fortescue, "Not too messy when you get him. I will be having a few words with the bastard and I want my sword back."

John walked into the hallway and, with no sight of Mrs Fortescue, let himself out of the house and descended the steps towards the pathway. He walked away from the row of Victorian and Georgian housing towards his Fiesta and climbed in. Well aware of the cash flowing in this district, and wishing to get to more comfortable surroundings, he drove away with the file on the passenger street. Half an hour later he sat in his car, scanning the paperwork.

There looked to have been five jobs recorded that the Met. believed may have been committed by 'The Hare' burglar. Only two in London, two further South and one in York. At three locations, high-value jewellery had been stolen, and irreplaceable antiques at the remaining two. The guild hall made it six, in total, that the police knew about. John noted that at all locations, no forensic evidence had been recovered. The files gave him little, except to say that each job had been investigated to varying standards and that, until now, no one had put any effort into linking them as a crime series. Three things stood out to John though. He took out a small notebook from his glove box and noted them down.

1. Cocky/Confident – why the calling card? Want to get caught or show off?
2. Stealing to order – specific high-value items. Who's fencing them?
3. A climber – four out of five offences involved entry via rooftop/upper floor.

He closed the file and placed it in a plain brown envelope. Climbing out of the car, he walked to the building block where his flat was and, opening the main door, posted the file into his postal box. *I'll grab that later. I need a drink.* John retraced his steps then walked beyond his car in the direction of the local pub. *At least I have the Met working for me this time,* he thought, reflecting on Simeon's comments on providing him with all the information that he could. John was used to doing all the leg work himself, relying on friends who were still in the job and on his informants to help him. At least on this one, someone else could do the hard work. *If Simeon wants to play Dungeons and Dragons and pay me for catching his thief then I'm not complaining.* Taking a cigarette from his packet, he stopped to light it, thinking about how to progress with the information that he had so far. *Who handles your stolen goods Mr Hare? Who sells them for you? That's my starting point.*

* * *

The screen before the team displayed an image of the front aspect of the Bank of England. They had spent the morning getting to know each other and now Keith and Terry had gone outside, leaving Jane and Jack sitting together. Ronnie had disappeared for a toilet break.

"How'd you get wrapped up in all of this then, Jane?"

"Runs in the family, I suppose."

"You're not a crook though. You don't look like one, and I'd be surprised if you've ever committed any sort of crime?"

"Looks can be deceiving. Stole a Mars bar from Tesco's once." She smiled. Jack smiled back.

"That's what I mean. Stealing gold from the B of E seems way out of your league."

"You don't look like a hardened criminal yourself."

"A look that I have to distract, confuse, and even charm. Underneath it, I'm as hard as nails." Jane laughed, leaned in, and replied conspiratorially,

"I hardly think so."

"Looks can deceive."

"Exactly my point! I've been waiting for this moment for most of my adult life. I've worked hard to get where I've got. We all planned to do something like this. The fat cats in the bank, government and top businessmen are creaming money from us all. I want a bit of it. My fair share."

"Fair enough,"

"Why are you doing it?"

"The challenge and the excitement. Yeah, I enjoy stealing from the rich and evening the scales but it's the thrill of it all that grips me." Jane could see that Jack's eyes had come to life with an infectious sparkle.

"Sounds great," interjected the dulcet tones of Ronnie. "You be careful with my niece, young man," she warned in jest. "This makes great television from here though," she smiled on screen. "Where're the other two?"

"Just here," piped up Terry walking back towards the seating area, with Keith in tow. Back to work then. Keith," he gestured to a smartboard. Keith chose a pen and was standing, poised to write. "Brainstorming session. We all know the job," Keith drew a pound sign in the middle of the board and circled it. The sketch changed to that of a solid gold bar. Keith looked at his pen in amazement.

"Bloody great bit of kit this," He drew a flower on the board which swiftly changed into van Gogh's 'Sunflowers'. He laughed.

"It's me, Keith," piped up Ronnie. "Just dragging you into the modern age of technology."

"Oh!" He looked slightly crestfallen.

"Keep it up. Ronnie, make sure it's all deleted when we are done."

"Will do, boss." *Boss! I like that,* thought Terry. Terry continued.

"What do we need to get it done? Everyone yell out. We'll note it down." The team called out their ideas.

"Cars."

"Drivers."

"A lorry."

"Uniforms,"

"Communications."

"A decoy." Keith continued noting them all down as Terry watched the list grow longer.

"And a bloody miracle," Terry mumbled under his breath. He held his hands up and halted the team's voices. "As you can see we have a lot to do. We need to divide up the work evenly or we'll never get through it all." He looked over to Ronnie. "Veronica, you got all that?" He pointed to the screen.

"Yes."

"Then clear it. Blank screen, please." The writing and images disappeared from the screen leaving Terry with a blank canvas. "Keith and I have had a chat outside and so here are your responsibilities. I've lined it up best with your skill sets. First, I'm on cars and transportation." He looked around the team, receiving no complaints. "Ronnie, you are dealing with all the technology. First priority, get us some secure phones. Second, start working out how to defeat the bank's systems."

"On it," she replied.

"Keith, you are on decoy, equipment, fencing the gold and any other crap that comes up." Keith nodded.

"Jane, plans of the bank, security systems, details of the gold, weak points in the bank. Anything to help us get in and out safely."

"Yes, T."

"Jack, you are gonna get us in, out and away. You'll have to work closely with Jane and Ronnie."

"Got it," he replied, smiling at Jane.

"Good. This is where it gets serious. From the outset, to make it clear, going into the bank are Jack, myself and Jane. No one else, unless I decide it's needed." His audience nodded. He continued. "No one. I mean no one is told about this job unless I have approved it." He looked at each person directly ensuring that they understood. "Anyone who spills, including to family and friends, will be dealt with severely should they open their gobs." The air in the room was suddenly tense. "Lastly, I want to know your plans for solving your tasks in three days."

"Three days!" exclaimed Keith, Ronnie and Jane.

"Three days," repeated Terry. "This is the serious end of the business, folks. No pissing about." He looked at them all, lifted his wrist and looked towards it. "The clock's ticking. Get to work." With that, he strode towards the exit door happy in himself that he had left an impression.

* * *

Barry parked his car and retrieved the package from underneath the passenger seat. He'd had the call an hour ago and had been to a housing estate to collect it. Only a small amount of cash on this occasion, five grand in total but each delivery was still risky. Life as an Uber taxi driver didn't pay all the bills, so Barry often took on some more illicit type of work to support his income. He was known to be reliable and so the transportation of cash around the city was entrusted to him. The Uber gave him a legitimate reason to travel all over London and during the past five years he had gradually learnt all the fastest routes from A to B, shortcuts that could help in the navigation of the city.

Today's delivery was on behalf of the family. The Lomaxes were known in the city for their legitimate enterprises which actually camouflaged their underlying criminal activities. Barry was only a minor member in the family, but hoped that if he remained reliable, then he could move up through the ranks to hold a senior position. Every man has to dream. At twenty-two years old, he was still young and had time to get there. Today, he'd collected from one of the Boroughs, having received a last-minute call that one of the Lomaxes required a cash top-up. He'd arrived to collect promptly and, as usual, took a circuitous route to get to his end destination, using anti-surveillance techniques that he'd read about online.

Today, not knowing why, he just felt on edge. Although confident that he hadn't been followed, he was feeling paranoid. His eyes sweeping the street, Barry walked casually along, looking for the bizzies. They were almost impossible to spot but on some occasions they gave themselves away, such as wearing clothing that didn't suit the environment, lips moving as if talking with no phone or person near them, or maybe a couple walking together who just didn't look right. Barry halted on the street, observing a coffee bar where a man was sitting on his own, looking directly towards him. *Shit!* He checked the package in his pocket and scanned left and right. He returned to the man as a young woman approached him. The man stood up, greeted the woman and pecked her on both cheeks, then held up his hand for a waiter.

"For Christ's sake, Barry. Get a grip," Barry said quietly. *What I would do for some weed now.* Barry continued walking and crossed the road towards an Italian restaurant, his target location in sight. His eyes swept the area again. *No stationary vehicles on the street, and no one watching opposite the place. Just a grubby tramp two doors up raking through a dustbin. It looks clear.* He took out his mobile and rang.

"Ciao, Luciano's Restaurant. How can I help you?" said an Italian-accented voice on the other end of the phone.

"Delivery for Franco."

"Sure, whenever you wish." Codewords supplied and agreed, Barry terminated the call and moved towards the restaurant. He pushed open the door, hearing the chime of the entry bell as he did so.

"POLICE, DON'T MOVE," screamed a voice as Barry was shoved violently from behind and propelled into a table. "STRIKE, STRIKE, STRIKE," shouted a voice as officers piled in through the front door. A bar person stood mouth open in shock. No customers were present.

The owner ran towards the serving door, colliding with it as it was thrown open. He screamed, holding his face, falling back with blood streaming from his nose. Fighting and screaming sounded in the kitchen. Feet pounded on the stairs, moving upwards. Barry took it all in as he regained his balance and turned. Hands grabbed his shoulders. Spun him around. He was forced prone over a table. His hands were grabbed and forced behind his back, his face mashed into the table. An officer screamed something in his ear. *Fuck! How did they know?* Barry thought, oblivious to the words spoken as his hands were cuffed. He was pulled into a standing position and saw a carnage of tables pushed to the sides, officers everywhere, and blood congealing near the staff door from the boss' head injury. *Bastards!*

"Not so clever now, son, are we?" spoke a tall, stubbled male in his ear.

"Nice one, Gaffer," said a young plainclothes copper walking past. "The power of phones, eh."

"Shut it, Smith." The tall male turned to a uniformed officer nearby. "Take him away." The officer took hold of Barry. Glancing right, Barry saw his delivery package poking from underneath a restaurant table. *It must have flown out when they hit me. Lucky.* He knew he'd been careful handling it and that his prints wouldn't be on it. It would take a lot to pin that package on him. As he was led to a van, the officer's comment replayed in his mind, "The power of phones". He clicked. *They were listening. That's how they knew. They were listening to the phone calls. The sneaky bastards.* Placed into the rear of the van, Barry tolerated the officer searching him in silence. *You're getting nowt from me, pigs.*

* * *

"Interview concluded." The officer pressed the stop button on the recording device. Barry sat there, silently staring straight ahead of him.

"Thanks for that, officers. Now, if you'd like to leave the room, I'd like to have a private talk with my client." Barry's solicitor, Frank Roper, stood up, expecting the officers to follow his actions. The officers slowly packed their paperwork away, taking their time before they both stood in unison. Neither were here to be bossed about by Roper. Roper was well known on the circuit for representing dubious clients and was always brought in by the Lomaxes when one of their own was arrested.

As expected, Barry had given a 'No reply' interview, despite the officers informing him that a large cash sum had been recovered. Roper walked towards the interview room door and opened it.

"Officers," he gestured with his free arm encouraging them to leave. Both turned, and with disgusted looks, left the room. Roper closed the door behind them.

"Well done, Barry."

"What do you think will happen?"

"Oh, undoubtedly you'll get out on bail. You're happy that your prints won't be on the packaging?"

"No, I was careful."

"Good lad, then you have nothing to worry about."

"What about the phones? They must have been listening."

"Maybe they are, maybe they're not. Doesn't matter."

"They've got my phone."

"Was it clean?"

"Yeah, a burner. I only just got it. That was the only call on it."

"Nothing to worry about there then." Barry frowned at Roper. "Trust me, son. I've got this covered." He smiled at Barry. "Right, I'll go to the desk and confirm your release. I'll wait for you outside. I'm guessing you need a lift somewhere?"

"Yeah, to my car."

"I'll drive you there. I've got a new burner in the car for you too."

"What about the family?"

"Leave that with me. I'll give them a bell and let them know what's happening. Now sit tight." Roper collected his briefcase and walked towards the door.

"Frank," Roper turned to the sound of Barry's voice. "Thanks. It's appreciated."

"No problem, Barry. That's what I'm here for." He left the room, closing the door behind him.

Twenty minutes later the door reopened. Barry looked up, expecting to see Roper, but was confronted by a long-haired, tattooed middle-aged bloke wearing a lanyard.

"Who are you?" asked Barry.

"I'm Mitch and this is Helen." A tall young female wearing jeans and a T-shirt entered behind Mitch and smiled at Barry.

"Punching a bit above your weight aren't you, mate" joked Barry. Mitch looked at Helen and smiled.

"Maybe so, Barry. Maybe so." Mitch smiled at Helen and took a seat opposite Barry. Helen took the free chair, the scent of her perfume drifting across the table towards Barry. *Smells lovely*, he thought, *and looks lovely too.*

"Maybe you are too," stated Mitch, his voice dragging Barry's attention away from Helen.

"What do you mean? Who are you?" Barry asked. Mitch held up his lanyard. Barry noted that Helen wore one too.

"The social, Barry." The lanyard held an identification card. Barry leant forward looking at the photograph on it.

"Bit younger there aren't you, mate," stated Barry with a laugh. "What about you?" Barry turned to Helen.

"Same," she replied, turning her card around. Barry leant towards the card which lay resting against her chest. *I could sit here all day.*

"How's the Uber business?" asked Mitch. Barry sat back.

"It's OK. What's it to do with you?"

"Paying well?"

"Covers the bills."

"Bollocks, it's probably just covering your fuel bills." Barry wriggled in his seat.

"How's the family?"

"I'm single."

"There you go, Helen. Told you he was." She smiled.

"Surely not," she replied, looking Barry up and down.

"Between girlfriends," stated Barry.

"Mmm," replied Helen, sitting back and appraising him. Barry anxiously rubbed the back of his neck.

"What do you want?" repeated Barry.

"Listen, mate. The Met has this new initiative. We come and visit everyone once they are getting bail. Check they are all fine, see if we can help them, give them a point of contact if they are struggling mentally, financially, etc."

"So why do I need you?"

"I don't know. You just may. It's these donuts trying to show that they're trying to support criminals. You know, direct them away from reoffending."

"I've done nowt?"

"Neither has anyone else in the cells here, Barry."

"I don't need anything."

"What, nothing? How much cash you got on you?"

"None, and they've taken my phone!"

"Helen," Mitch nodded towards Helen who stood up. Her hand moved to her jeans pocket, her hips now at Barry's eye level. Barry watched intently. She pulled a small purse from her pocket and slowly sat down.

"Here you go, son. There's a score." Helen held out a twenty-pound note.

"I don't want your money,"

"It's not mine. It's the social's. Take it. It's hard enough to get money from the social when they owe it to you! Put it towards a taxi or a new phone. Buy a bloody McDonald's with it."

"What's the catch?"

"There isn't one, mate. Like I said. New initiative." Barry reached forward and took hold of the note, taking it from Helen. *Did she keep hold of the note longer than she needed to or was it just my imagination*? He looked at her face. She looked back, lips slightly parted, smiled and sat back.

"Good lad. May as well be in your pocket." Mitch stood up to leave along with Helen. "You'll be released in five, Barry." He placed a business card on the table." If you need anything, my number's on there."

"What about yours?" Barry asked Helen.

"Maybe next time." She winked at Barry and left the room with Mitch. An officer entered through the closing door.

"Right, Barry. Let's get you bailed." Barry stood, carefully slipping the note and card into his jeans pocket, and followed the officer.

* * *

Mitch and Helen left the custody suite, entering an internal corridor of the police station. Mitch reached inside his shirt and retrieved a digital voice recorder.

"You get it all?" asked Helen.

"Yes."

"What do you think?"

"I think he bloody loves you. Well played, Helen."

"Only time will tell," she replied. They both removed their lanyards and continued along the corridor.

"Well, it's a good start. He's taken the Queen's shilling which is great. Now for the hard work of reeling him in." Both officers headed towards their offices within the Covert Human Intelligence Source Unit.

* * *

"Can you repeat that, please?" Robert Harrison walked into the small office that was attached to his own. He had just finished a phone call when he heard the analyst next door mention something about Interpol. Hazel the analyst was sitting behind a desk in the corner of the room with two monitors dominating the desktop. The investigation team had been gathered and Robert had decided to keep them close to hand. The room was small but he had managed to squeeze six desks in. Four desks were currently occupied by the analyst, an intelligence officer, a detective constable and Ali Smith.

"Hazel's just received her enquiry back from Interpol, Sir," stated Smith.

"Remind me."

"The MO of our unknown burglar." Harrison looked confused. "The calling card," explained Smith.

"Ah, yes. Of course." Harrison looked expectantly at Hazel. She looked at her screen as her fingers pressed the keyboard. The room waited.

"Here it is," she squinted through her spectacles at the screen. "It appears that our person has been active abroad. Linked to jobs in Germany, France and ..." she continued reading the document, ".... Belgium."

"Well, well," Harrison smiled. "It appears that we are investigating an international thief." He knew that this piece of intelligence may get him more resources. On a personal note, he could already smell the aromas of the continent wafting his way. *I'm sure to get a paid trip abroad on this one.*

"Let's keep this tight, team. No loose mouths," he looked directly at Ali Smith who discreetly nodded back. "Let's get some more details on the crimes, Hazel, if we can. Anything standing out on your document?"

"They haven't identified our suspect but the jobs are all high-value burglaries."

"Good job, team. Keep digging." Harrison walked back to his office rubbing his hands together.

"I must get Mrs Harrison to dig out my passport," he mumbled to himself.

Chapter 4

Jack stepped out of the lift onto his landing and walked towards his flat door. The hallway was quiet, with only the slight murmur of a television coming from behind one of his neighbour's doors. Overhead motion lights triggered as he walked along the corridor. He'd checked the view of the hallway on his Android phone before entering the building. The image projected from a pinhole camera he'd installed reassured him that it was safe to enter. He approached his door, activated the digital lock and walked in, securing the door behind him. He placed his bike helmet on a sideboard as he moved towards the main open-plan living room.

Jack resided in a comfortable rental flat within the city. Living a transient lifestyle which was dependent on where his work took him, he held little in the way of personal possessions. The installation of the pinhole camera was for his safety and peace of mind, and once he moved on, he'd remove the equipment and take it with him. The current arrangement allowed him to pay full cash upfront for the rent. The extent of human greed never surprised him and even in modern times, people would gratefully receive real money rather than go through the rigmarole of security checks and measures usually used to secure tenants. A large cash deposit or bond bought many people's silence. Jack flicked on the television where the news reported yet another politician lying to the public. He walked to the fridge, took out a bottle of Bud and unscrewed the cap, before taking a large swig from the bottle. *Busy day*, he thought. *Lots to think about.* He walked over to the windows, looked out over the skyline and looked down to see headlights of cars buzzing along the roads as they serviced the needs of their queen, the City of London. His burner phone vibrated in his pocket, the team's temporary means of communication at the moment, and saw that Jane had texted him with arrangements for their meeting tomorrow. *A nice woman*, he thought, picturing her smiling in his mind. *Keep your mind on work, Jack*, he told himself.

Stripping off his shirt, Jack walked to his bedroom and headed towards the ensuite, tossing his shirt on the luxurious double king-size as he passed. Having switched on the shower he returned, catching his reflection in the full-length mirror. He worked hard at his fitness, which was reflected in the toned muscles of his pectorals and abdomen. Slight of build, he had a wiry strength which allowed him to perform the feats of gymnastics required of a rooftop burglar. A couple of old scars marked his chest, and on his back, the healed mark of a long rooftop descent that had gone wrong. This wasn't a game for soft men but with the scars of battle came the greatness of rewards. Jack still got a thrill when reflecting on some of the jobs he'd pulled off. He'd hit the in-house gym tomorrow morning, but in the meantime, he took a shower.

Now wrapped in a bathrobe, Jack walked to the wardrobe that held the small amount of clothing that he possessed. He took the hangers from the rail, placing both clothing and hangers on the bed. Reaching back in, he removed the central clothes pole and pulled on a small piece of string stuffed into one end. Jack always stashed his goods in a permanent structure. Shoe boxes, clothing, and food boxes could all be stolen but the chances of a thief stealing something within a fixed structure was small. He held the pole over the bed and watched the item drop out. *There you are.* He unwrapped the stone and admired its beauty. *What are you though? Why did they want you?* Now held in his hand Jack gazed upon the magnificence of what looked to be a yellow diamond.

Recovered from within the same casement as the sword, Jack could only assume that it was valuable. The stone had a yellow tint to it and looked to have equilateral facets. Now having dried, he dressed quickly in a vest and shorts and carried the stone to the dining table where his laptop was. Jack switched on the device and watched as it went through a security and encryption process. *Ronnie isn't the only one with skills*, he thought. Now happy that his IP location was hidden he entered 'yellow diamond' into the search engine. The results were a fairly standard response of necklaces and engagement rings. Searching again he entered 'large yellow diamond' and was presented with an image of the Tiffany Yellow Diamond.

He checked the image against the stone on the table. "Similar but wrong shape," he murmured to himself, sitting back and thinking. "Why did the Grand Lodge have you?" Jack adjusted his search and entered an addition of 'missing'. The search engine pinged, the first hit being Wikipedia stating boldly 'The Florentine Diamond'. Scrolling further down the site showed a black-and-white image of a large diamond. "Too hard to tell." He typed into the keyboard and sat back as multiple images of a large yellow diamond were displayed.

"Bloody hell!" he exclaimed looking at the exact image of the stone that was sitting on his dining room table. "It can't be!" Jack read on. The origin of the stone was in dispute but it appeared clear that historians believed that the stone was still in circulation. Whether originally from India or Burgundy, a rhinestone copy had been made and was now kept at the Natural History Museum in Vienna. *How the hell did the Masonic guild get hold of it? First the sword, now this. What else are the guilds hiding from us?* Jack's fingers flew across the keyboard as he checked out flight prices to Vienna.

* * *

Terry was sitting within a cafe, watching the rain pouring down outside. The atmosphere had been humid this morning and, although sunny, large clouds crowded the silhouette of the skyline. A thunderstorm had been predicted and was now delivering its quenching drops to the thirsty streets. The pavements outside were still busy, with pedestrians bustling along, protected under their mixed colours of taught umbrellas. The city was unsociable at the best of times but now people could hide under their protective shells whilst negotiating their way to work and meetings. *Poor bastards*, thought Terry, contemplating the nine-to-five existence of much of the population whose lives were dominated by adhering to the norm.

The cafe door opened as a young male entered in his designer suit and turned, shaking the raindrops from his umbrella before closing it. A cool draft had entered with the man and the smell of the rain on the warm tarmac drifted in with it. Terry smiled at the him as he walked past his table but only received a brief look of confusion from the male in response. *Shocked that he's even been acknowledged. The city is making robots out of us.* Terry enjoyed not being the norm. He made his own rules up, baulked against enforced ones and enjoyed the life he lived. The rain was starting to abate outside and he watched as the young man sat down as far away as possible from him. The male then produced his laptop and opened it creating yet another barrier, another piece of armour, to distance himself from any human interaction.

Terry looked away, coming out of his reverie. He had his own problems to solve. Transport for the job. After leaving the meeting with the team yesterday his mind had worked nonstop developing plans about how to get the gold away from the bank. None of his team were getaway drivers, not that he knew of. Jack rode a motorbike so wasn't adverse to speed but it didn't mean that he could drive. Terry knew that he wasn't good enough himself and thought that Keith would crap himself if he went over fifty mph. Jane was young but she was driving around in a little red Fiat 500. He doubted that she'd be doing more than forty mph in the city when driving it. However, his mind kept flicking back to that little red car as if he were trying to tell himself something.

He pushed the thought away and took out a piece of paper on which he had scribbled some rough calculations describing the dimensions of the payload. Width, length and height were fine. It was the weight of the gold bars that was the issue. He'd need a vehicle that was capable of taking the weight and of being driven at speed away from the heist. *I'll need a van, a short wheelbase with a decent motor in it. Harden its suspension.* The image of Jane's Fiat again encroached into his thoughts. *Or we could split the load, split the weight, and meet up after.* He looked at the calculations, and taking a bookie's pen from his pocket, divided the overall weight. *Possible. Maybe both,* he thought.

Looking out, the sun had now broken through the clouds and umbrellas were being lowered. Terry finished his coffee, placed a tip by his cup and stepped out to the cleansed air. He made a call.

"Hi, Ronnie."

"Mr T., What can I do for you?"

"Two things. When are the encrypted handsets arriving?"

"Today. Jane's collecting them and she'll hand them out to everyone as soon as possible."

"Great. Secondly, can you find me the nearest car dealership to where I am now?"

"Buying a new car?"

"Maybe. Just need to take a look at some."

"Give me a minute. I'll ring you back." Terry moved away from the cafe and lit a cigarette as he watched a small Citroen C1 pass him by on the roadway. *Maybe a sign.* He laughed then coughed as the smoke hit the back of his throat. His phone rang.

"About twenty minutes away. I've sent you directions," stated Ronnie. "What about a Classic? Old school. There's always cheap do ups on Club sites." She giggled.

"You enjoying this?" asked Terry.

"You bet," she replied. "I'm stuck in this house and haven't had as much fun in years. It's so exciting." Terry laughed in return.

"We're gonna do great, Ronnie. Trust me. I'd better get going," he continued.

"Right you are, Boss. Speak later."

"Ronnie?"

"Yes, I'm still here."

"If you get a minute, just take a look at some owner's club. See if there are any about."

"Will do." Terry terminated the call, checked his phone for directions and headed towards the tube, his brain ticking over with ideas.

* * *

The unmistakable tones of Bill Haley filled the air as Keith perfected his quiff in the bathroom mirror. Dressed in drain pipes, a white-collared shirt with a thin black tie, and dark purple thick-soled shoes, Keith just had his black velvet collared blazer to put on to complete his look. Keith was currently single and lived in a small one-bedroomed bedsit above one of his antique shops in the city. He'd left the meeting yesterday feeling pretty chipper with himself. Business was OK but there was nothing like a challenge to stimulate the senses, especially as he grew older. He was happy with the tasks allocated to him by Tommy. Finding the correct equipment to aid the team would provide him with no problem at all. However, creating a distraction. Now that was another matter. He'd thought long and hard about it and also had a couple of discussions with Terry. Something big enough to keep police resources busy, away from the Threadneedle Street area, that wasn't going to harm or hurt anybody. None of the team wanted anybody hurt as a result of their actions either directly or indirectly. With all of that in mind, he had a planned meeting today that could provide him with his decoy.

Keith put his jacket on and walked across to the turntable where he gently lifted the stylus from the LP, silencing the music.

"Sorry, Bill. Things to do." He carefully cleaned the record with an anti-static cloth, placed it gently back into its sleeve, and returned it to its place in his collection. The downstairs shop was closed today, so he took the back entrance out and descended the emergency fire steps to street level. He checked the time on his Breitling and headed towards the back of the shop, where he collected his Brompton and, placing his foot on one pedal, propelled himself forward, before mounting the bicycle and joining the flow of traffic.

One hour later, Keith exited Abbey Wood Station, having secured his bike there, and took a slow walk towards the Abbey Arms for a meeting. The pub had longevity and the building had stood at the boundary between London and Kent as long as anyone could remember. It had always been popular for its later closing times. The pub was now modernised but Keith felt comfortable in its welcoming atmosphere. He ordered a glass of Malbec and took a seat at a table with a view of the door.

The pub was fairly quiet but would likely get busier over the lunchtime period. He checked his watch and sure enough, on time as usual, Patrick walked in. Patrick was a large male, stockily built with powerful shoulders, weathered face, with short cropped hair and a nose displaced to the right. He wore a short-sleeved collared shirt, smart trousers and walked with an air of confidence. His eyes scanned the room, noting Keith at his table, as he approached the bar.

"Hi there, Pat." said the barman.

"I'll take a Malbec, please," stated Patrick, he looked over to Keith's half-empty glass. "Make that two." Keith was always amused by the image that Pat portrayed to the public, compared to the reality of his life on the Thistlebrook Estate.

A member of the travelling fraternity, Pat had never learnt to read or write – his parents had never believed in it. He had never let that hold him back though. Why should it? He was intelligent, streetwise, hard as nails and a man to be reckoned with. Best of all, in Keith's eyes, he was a gent. A criminal, of course, but a gent nonetheless, and that was to be respected.

Pat drew a roll of banknotes from his pocket, paid the barman and lifted the two glasses, dwarfing them in his bearlike paws. As he approached the table, Keith noticed the grazes across Pat's knuckles.

"Keith," Pat placed a glass before him.

"Thank you, Pat."

"My pleasure." Pat sat down on a chair which creaked under the weight of him.

"You're looking well." Keith glanced at Pat's hands.

"I'm good Keith, I'm good." He rubbed his knuckles. "Just one of the young ones thinking that he could better me." He said, showing Keith his hands. "Needed putting in his place."

"Is he OK?"

"Yes, a couple of bruises here and there. He was alright and apologised afterwards."

"Good, and the family?"

"All good. Bri's at university now. Studying economics. Who would have thought, eh?"

"A bright lad, Pat. Great to hear he's doing well."

"You?"

"Still on my own. Too old to change you see but I'm happy with it," said Keith.

"Good, good." Pat took a sip of his wine. "Pleasantries over then, mate. What have you got?"

"I need a favour." Pat looked at Keith but said nothing. "I've got a job in planning, a team set up, but I need a decoy. Something to keep the coppers busy. Keep them away from us." Pat nodded his head. *A good sign*, Keith thought, if he wasn't happy to listen Pat would have walked.

"Can you tell me the job?"

"That's the crunch, mate. I'm sworn to secrecy." Pat placed his glass down and leaned towards Keith invading his personal space. Keith held his position.

"Fair enough." Pat smiled and leaned backwards. "Got you there." He chuckled and pointed at Keith who unclenched his hands under the table.

"Bloody right you did," he replied. "I was bricking meself."

"I trust you, Keith. You're a man of your word and I know that. If I don't need to know then I don't need to know. What have you got in mind?"

"The dates are not set yet but when it is I need your lads to create a bit of mayhem."

"What's in it for us?"

"Money. A lot of money."

"How much?"

"A monkey per man before the job and a monkey after. Also, your teams get to keep all the readies from the job. One night's work." Pat looked thoughtful, the interest obvious on his face.

"Risky then?"

"A little bit. What's life without a bit of risk?"

"True, true."

"No one's to be hurt though. None of yours and none of the public."

"What's the job?"

"Cash points. Hole in the walls. ATM's"

"An ATM!"

"No, Pat. Five ATMs, all at the same time, on the same night and in the city."

"You have got to be joking?"

"No. That's why I'm here. I couldn't think of anyone better to ask." Keith looked towards Pat's drink. "Let me get you another one of those." He winked at Pat and stood up to go to the bar.

"I think I'll be needing something stronger," replied Pat as he sat back, his mind already working out whether Keith's 'favour' could be achieved.

* * *

The front doorbell chimed, causing Ronnie to look up from a book she was studying towards her computer screen. Displayed on the screen was an image of Jane squinting at the front door.

"I'll get it, dear," spoke the shaky voice of Veronica's mother.

"Don't worry, I've got it," shouted Ronnie. She walked to the front door and saw Mrs Pilcher walking towards the kitchen door and the back of the house.

"It's the front door anyway, Mum." She gently took hold of Mrs Pilcher's shoulders and guided her back to her armchair.

"You take a seat there." She settled her mother into her favourite armchair.

"OK, dear." Mrs Pilcher sat looking at the television which remained constantly on. The doorbell rang again. Ronnie looked around the room with its dated wallpaper and furniture. It needed an overhaul but with her mother suffering from early dementia, it felt more appropriate to keep the room in the style of her choosing, a style that she was comfortable with. Ronnie sighed and gently closed the room door as she went to fetch Jane.

Jane watched as the door opened slowly and she heard the dulcet tones of Ronnie.

"Come in, love." Jane knew that Ronnie would be standing behind the door, unable to expose herself to the outside world.

"We must try to get you out sometime," said Jane, turning to Ronnie as the door closed behind her.

"Not for a million quid."

"Well, you'll be getting more than that soon. So don't rule out the possibility." Jane giggled at her own joke as Ronnie led her to the dining room of the house. An oval dining table with six Ercol chairs held the centre of the room, with a dark wooden sideboard positioned on one wall and a glass cabinet holding Lladro figurines, the only other furniture. Velour curtains, half drawn, cast the room into shade until Ronnie switched on the central light of the room. Upon the table sat five cardboard boxes. Veronica gestured towards them.

"Encrypted mobile phones. One for each of us."

"Brilliant," Jane replied, reaching out, "which one is mine?"

"Take the box with the number two written on it. I've sorted all the SIM cards, data and all that. You can take the rest for the others if that's OK. I'll tell you whose is whose."

"All safe for us to talk on, you know, about the job?"

"Yes, can't be detected. They're not cheap so we need to look after them."

"How did you afford them?"

"Mr T sorted me out with a cash advance."

"Cool. So what do you need from me?"

"A couple of hours of your time. I need to empty your brain of all the information you know about the bank that can help me break into their security systems."

"Can I open these curtains?" Jane gestured towards the window.

"Yes, just put the phones away in your rucksack before you do. Also, I've got a small device that I need you to plug in temporarily at the bank," continued Ronnie.

"Won't they know that something's amiss?"

"Don't worry, I'll look after that."

"How?" Ronnie chuckled.

"If I had to explain to you how I manage to do all of my computer wizardry then we would be here for days, frazzling our brains with caffeine, instead of hours. You just need to trust me. I'll be online hiding anything you do."

"Where do I plug it in?"

"The main server would be good. If not, then a work terminal, preferably not your own."

"When?"

"We'll discuss that. I have to write some software first. Probably within the next week or so."

"Anything else?"

"I think I'll need to speak with Jack. I'll need to know how he plans to get in and out."

"That's fine. I can sort that out."

"I'll bet you can!" Ronnie laughed.

"What?" stated Jane, a smile on her face.

"Well… He's a bit fit isn't he?"

"I don't know what you mean?" Both ladies were now giggling.

"You must be tempted," replied Ronnie. "I mean, I'm tempted and I'm twice his age!"

"Veronica Pilcher! You little minx."

Their laughter drifted through to Mrs Pilcher who smiled. It had been a long time since she had heard Veronica laughing. It was lovely to hear her enjoying herself.

"I'll put the kettle on," said Mrs Pilcher to herself. Standing up from her chair she left the living room, entered the hall and opened the front door with a look of confusion on her face.

"Hey Mum, where are you going?" said Veronica who had quietly entered the hallway, after hearing the front door open. Mrs Pilcher turned around with a frown on her face.

"I was looking for the kitchen. I've gone the wrong way again. Oh, Veronica, I'm useless."

"No, you're not mum. You just got confused. Don't worry about it." Veronica gently guided her mum away from the door and closed it behind her. "Let's go and make a cup of tea together." Mrs Pilcher allowed herself to be guided towards the kitchen. Jane had watched the scene play out in front of her, empathising with both parties. Mrs Pilcher, an elderly lady who was trying to cope with the vagaries of ageing, and Ronnie, a young lady trapped by her own vulnerabilities and the wish to care for her mother. *Strong support for each other though,* she thought. *Many people just have to cope with their lives on their own.* Ten minutes later, Ronnie returned with a cup of tea for them both.

"Is she OK?" asked Jane.

"Oh, yes. She's fine. She gets upset but we talk it through and set her back on track. She gets frustrated with herself."

"You're so good with her."

"She always has been with me, Jane. Still is. It's the least I can do." Jane smiled.

"Anyway, she's settled in the living room. Let's crack on. You had any thoughts about moving the gold?" continued Ronnie.

"A couple of thoughts. Physically moving it out of the vault shouldn't be too hard?"

"Why's that?"

"There are hoists on wheels within the vault, designed to move the gold if needed. The hoists are in there permanently. We can use them to take the gold to the extraction point."

"Extraction point? Aren't you sounding professional." joked Ronnie. Jane blushed.

"It was something that Jack said," she clarified. "You know, move it to the place where we're going to load it onto a vehicle."

"Have we identified that place yet?"

"Not yet. I need to discuss that with Jack and get back to you. It may depend on how much control you can get of the security systems."

"Total," stated Ronnie.

"Total?"

"Yes, I will have full control of it all."

"You're very confident."

"Well, you came to the best for a reason," said Ronnie, leaning back and throwing her arms wide. "Any thoughts on what you're going to replace the gold with?"

"Replace it?"

"Yeah! To buy us time to get away. You know, so they don't realise straight away that it's missing."

"Won't the alarms let them know that there's been a job?"

"Not if I can help it they won't. We can be in and out with the gold without them realising it. I'll make sure that no sensors, CCTV etcetera are activated and therefore there will be no alarm. You need to let Jack know that." Jane nodded, taking it all in.

"You done a lot of bank robberies, have you?" asked Jane.

"This is the first but I have messed around in a lot of security systems and watched a lot of films." Ronnie had a big grin on her face. "Which takes us back to replacing the gold. Making the room look as if nothing has gone."

"I'll discuss it with Jack. I think we should all meet up."

"Soap," stated Ronnie.

"Soap?" replied Jane.

"Soap bars. I've been thinking about soap bars."

"That's well and good, Ronnie. Do you need me to go out and buy you some?"

"No, you idiot. Pay attention and listen."

* * *

Barry walked out of the police station and spotted Roper sitting at a table outside of a coffee shop, reading a newspaper. Roper looked up, folded his newspaper and, having placed something on the table, waited for Barry to join him. As Barry approached, he noted a ten-pound note poking out from underneath an empty coffee cup.

"Smoke?" asked Roper, holding out an opened pack towards him. Barry took the offered cigarette and leaned forward, cupping his hands around the proffered lighter.

"Cheers, Frank."

"That's OK, son. Bailed with no problems?"

"Yeah, just like you said. You're a lifesaver." Barry drew deeply on the cigarette, his craving for nicotine abating.

"Anyone else speak to you in there?"

"Just some do-gooders trying to offer me counseling?"

"And?"

"Told them to fuck off. Bloody idiots." Barry had already decided to keep the conversation and cash to himself. Frank didn't need to know everything. Frank raised an eyebrow, unnoticed by Barry.

"Do-gooders about what?"

"You know, the usual crap. Getting out of crime, drug prevention, even quitting smoking." *Unusual*, thought Frank, noting a nervousness to Barry's laugh. *You lying to me?*

"They should know better than to speak to you," Frank laughed and, placing a hand on Barry's shoulder, guided him. "This way to the car."

"Everything OK with the family?" asked Barry.

"All good, mate. No worries there. There's always a risk in what we are doing and they know that." Both males climbed into Roper's BMW. He revved the engine and pulled away from his parking place, entering into the stream of traffic.

"I'll drive you to the closest tube station, Barry. You got any money on you?"

"None."

"Just open the glove box. There's fifty in there. Should keep you going." Barry opened the catch and took five crisp ten-pound notes from the compartment. *Flash bastard, in a flash car, with money to hand*, he thought, envious of Roper's wealth.

"You do alright, don't you?" said Barry.

"I've worked hard to get where I am, Barry. It takes a lot of training and experience to be where I am and that doesn't come cheap."

"Suppose it helps that you have my family backing you as well." *Clever sod*, thought Barry.

"Well, you all need me, mate. We all get the benefit." They continued in silence and five minutes later approached a station. Roper indicated, pulled to the side of the road and stopped the vehicle.

"Here we are, Barry. This'll do you. I have another appointment." Barry opened the door, climbed out and leant back in.

"Cheers, Frank."

"No problem, mate. Careful with the door." Barry turned, shut the car door heavily and walked towards the station. *We're going to have to keep an eye on you, Barry. There's something not quite right*, thought Roper. *I'll have to give Angelo a call and arrange a meeting.* Roper pulled back into the traffic, heading for his favourite restaurant. As usual, following the arrest of one of the workers, Roper would arrange a meeting this evening with Angelo Lomax to provide him with the details of the arrest, interview and likely outcome. Angelo would need to know that Frank had some concerns.

Chapter 5

"John! Hello, John! Are you there?"

"Yes, Simeon. How can I help?"

"Well, by answering the phone correctly first of all. It's not hard. Just say hello and state your name."

"Force of habit, Simeon. I always let the caller speak first."

"Be that as it may. I've got some information for you."

"Go on."

"The Hare has done a job in America. The enquiry team have just received the information about it. I'll get hold of the details. There will be a file ready to collect tonight."

"Thank you."

"Well, you could sound more enthusiastic about it."

"I am, Simeon, but patience will catch this man. The information will provide me with more … shall we say, opportunities."

"What do you mean?"

"Nothing that you need to worry about. It will allow me to broaden my investigation."

"Well, see that it does." The phone line went dead. Digby checked his watch. Ricco should be up and about. He dialled a number and held the phone to his ear.

"John, it's been a while," said an Italian male voice on the other end of the line.

"Ricco, how's things?"

"All good. What can I do for you?"

"I need a hand with a job. You and the team free?"

"We are. You wanna meet up?"

"Yes, how about lunch at Frankie's?"

"Sounds good. See you there about one."

"Great." John terminated the call.

* * *

John Digby had met Ricco Giutini during his former career within the police service. They had both worked on a joint murder enquiry which crossed international borders between the UK and Italy. Upon meeting they had immediately gelled and now that Ricco had retired from his policing career, each would call upon the other's skills and resources when required. Ricco ran a small team of operatives who specialised in covert capture missions (CCMs). The team worked in the UK and John was certain that Ricco would like some involvement in this job, given it now had international appeal.

John walked towards Frankie's, the chosen meeting place for both men. Set within the back streets of the suburbs, Frankie's Fish 'n' Chip shop gave diners the ability to take away or sit within their restaurant. The establishment offered anonymity for both males. They'd been using the place for about six months now but this would be their last meeting here, both knowing that a change of venue was needed. They moved their meeting places every three to six months, never returning to the same one again, maintaining a fluidity in their working relationship.

John entered, and walked towards the back of the restaurant, where he saw the unmistakable bald head of Ricco, who was already sitting at a table. He took a seat, feeling slightly uncomfortable with his back facing the door. Ricco squinted down his thin nose and smiled.

"Don't worry, my friend," he said, in stilted English, "I can see around and I've got one of mine near the door too." John knew better than to turn and look. "One is watching the road also."

"A bit heavy," replied John.

"Can never be too careful, John. Means we can relax. I've ordered, by the way." A young lady walked towards the table carrying a tray holding silver teapots and a side plate of buttered bread. She placed them on the table. Ricco looked the waitress up and down.

"Food will be with you soon, luv," she said.

"Thank you, young lady." Ricco smiled at the waitress who walked away to clear another table. Though in his early fifties, Ricco looked a commanding figure. At six foot two, with a lythe wiry frame, he obviously kept himself fit. Bald and tanned with bleached white teeth, Ricco picked up the teapot and poured. Both watched the pots' compulsory drip of tea onto the yellow formica table top.

"I love this little plate of buttered bread that you Brits insist on. Makes me smile every time."

"Tradition, my friend. British tradition." Two plates of fish and chips were delivered to the table by the same waitress.

"Thanks," said John.

"No problem. Do you need anything else?"

"No, that's fine."

"Enjoy your meal, gentlemen." She walked away from the table. Ricco watched the waitress leave, admiring her figure as he did so. He turned to face John.

"So, what havva we got?" asked Ricco as he soaked his food with a liberal amount of vinegar.

"Rooftop burglar, identity unknown. Targets high value goods or cash only and is working internationally."

"Interesting," replied Ricco, dipping his fish into some tartare sauce.

"He has really pissed off my boss. I need to identify him and track him down. That's where you come in." Ricco nodded his head as he continued eating. John started his meal as he explained what he had so far.

* * *

Jane entered St James' Park from The Mall and walked towards the Artillery Memorial. Dressed only in a light summer dress, she still felt warm in the early evening heat. She had arranged to meet Jack here, who had said he would find her on the path which led towards Blue Bridge. Turning right, Jane took a gentle stroll, watching other members of the public enjoying the greenery within central London. A mixture of couples, families and local groups of tourists were being led by guides around the park. Other people sat upon the grass or on rented deck chairs, as they enjoyed soaking up the atmosphere of the park. In contrast to the streets of the city, the park was a sociable area. Couples talked, families played without the insidious infiltration of mobile phones and tablets. Laughter and short clips of conversation drifted to Jane's ears as the park exuded an air of comfort and happiness. Jane reached in her bag, retrieved her Ray Bans and placed them on.

"Hi there," said Jack quietly in her ear. Jane jumped, nearly dropping her bag.

"Where'd you come from?" she fumbled her handbag closed and straightened her sunglasses.

"I was just behind you entering the park. Didn't want to shout in case I shocked you. Clearly I judged that wrong." He chuckled. Jane smiled.

"Indeed." She turned. "Shall we?"

"Yes, of course." They both continued walking along the path, towards the bandstand. Jane could smell the aroma of Eau Sauvage wafting to her from Jack. Dressed in a white linen shirt and chinos, he looked casual, and complimented her outfit. *He's lovely,* she thought, thinking of her previous conversation with Ronnie.

"So, how are things going your end?" asked Jack, bringing Jane out from her reverie.

"Good," she replied, "I've got your new phone with me." She reached towards her bag.

"Not here. I'll get it later." His hand reached gently to stall her, his fingers innocently brushing her forearm as he took his hand away, causing a flutter in her chest and a blush to her face.

"Sorry. I should be more careful."

"Don't worry. You'll get the hang of it all. You meet with Ronnie?"

"Yes, she's got a couple of things to talk with you about."

"Cool. We'll all have to meet up soon."

"Next couple of days if that's OK?"

"Fine by me. Fancy a coffee? There's a temporary shack up by Marlborough Gate."

"Yes, please." Reaching the the gate, Jack strode towards the hut to get their drinks. *He walks with grace*, thought Jane, *light footed. Not cocky, but sure in himself.* She admired his physique from behind her sunglasses as he returned.

"Shall we?" he gestured to an area of grass for them to sit upon. Jane walked towards it and lowered herself, stretching her legs out and trapping her skirt between her knees. She glimpsed Jack checking out her legs.

"Any great revelations from our technical wonder woman?" asked Jack.

"She's been thinking about soap."

"Soap?"

"That's what I said," she smiled, "Well, soap amongst other things. She's come up with an idea and wants us to give it some thought." Jack sipped from his coffee admiring the quiet confidence which he saw emanating from Jane.

"Well, give it some thought we shall. Tell me what she's thinking."

* * *

"Good to see you. I trust that you've all been busy over the last three days," said Terry, addressing the rest of the team. He was standing in the warehouse, where the team had last met, with a cigarette in one hand and a mug of coffee in the other. Keith, Jane and Jack all were sitting opposite Terry and a live stream image of Ronnie, seated within her den, was smiling back at them all. They all looked at Terry in anticipation of his next words.

"This is the last time that we will meet here. Keith will sort out the next meeting location and let you know. You all got your new phones?" Responses came in the affirmative with a couple of phones held up. "All communications between us are to be made on these phones only from now on." He didn't wait for a response knowing that they all understood the importance of this. "Right. Keith, do you wanna start off?"

"Yes," Keith said, rising from his chair.

"We're not at school now, mate. No need to stand. Make yourself comfortable." Terry took a seat completing the circle of five.

"Cheers, Tel." Keith shuffled on his seat. "I've been working on the decoy. I discussed this with Tel before the approach so I've been off to see an old mate of mine over at Thistlebrook. He's a traveller, a man I can trust, and a man that I've worked with before. No need for you to know his name. Less names we know the better, eh?" Mumbled assents agreed to this. "He's solid. That's what matters." Terry nodded to Keith encouraging him to continue.

"So," explained Keith, "on the night that we do our job there's gonna be a number of things that will keep the Old Bill busy. The travellers are gonna do an ATM job in the city."

"What do you mean?" asked Jane.

"Rob a cashpoint," clarified Jack. "One won't be enough," he said.

"You're right," Keith pointed at Jack, smiling. "Not one ATM. They're gonna nick five of them, all on the same night, all simultaneously and all whilst we are making our withdrawal from the B of E."

"Phew!" Jack sat back. "That's a big ask."

"I know but they're up for it and Keith's mate says it's achievable," said Terry.

"It'll drive the police switchboard mad," said Ronnie, clapping her hands and laughing.

"Exactly," said Terry. "There'll be cops flying around everywhere." He looked around.

"Everywhere apart from near the B of E. Keith's planning the locations with his man. Effectively we'll be sitting in the calm within the eye of the storm."

"How much are we paying them?" asked Jack. *Straight to the point and incisive*, thought Terry. *You're definitely growing on me.*

"A decent amount and they get to keep whatever they nick."

"Fair enough," Jack sat back in his seat. "It could work."

"Early planning stages yet, but my man's confident," said Keith.

"Where are you with your planning, Jack?" asked Terry.

"Also in its early stages. I've done an initial recce of the bank."

"Have you?" asked Jane.

"Yes. I've had a good look at the outside, and visited the inside. Just to get a good feeling for the building."

"The inside? When?" said Jane in surprise. Jack laughed.

"Don't panic. I've not broken in yet. Just some preliminary work. No sensors triggered or anything like that."

"You need any support with your recces?" asked Terry.

"Not at the moment. I will though," he conceded. "I've met with Jane and will be meeting Ronnie in the next couple of days." Ronnie gave a thumbs up in confirmation.

"Any ideas of how we are going to take the gold?"

"I'm thinking of subterfuge with technical support from Ronnie. We don't need to overcomplicate this. The gold has to be taken into the building through an entrance, so let's use that entrance to take it out. Getting it out is the easy bit. Getting it safely away could be harder. That's me so far." Keith nodded and turned to Jane.

"Jane?"

"I've met with both Jack and Veronica. We'll all be meeting again tomorrow. I've sorted the phones and given Jack a detailed description of the vault. Ronnie and I have spent some hours discussing the security systems. A bit more to do there. Ronnie has come up with an idea. You want to tell us?" she asked Ronnie.

"You explain it," replied Ronnie. Jane looked at Terry.

"So, we can defeat alarms, move the gold and get it out of the bank, but that doesn't necessarily buy us a lot of time to get it out of the city. We need to create that time to help us. We..." she gestured to Ronnie and Jack, "think that if we replace the gold we steal with something else, you know, something similar in appearance, then the bank won't realise that it has gone. At least, not straight away."

"What do we replace it with?" asked Terry.

"We replace the gold bars with soap bars disguised as gold bars."

"Where do we get them?" asked Terry dubiously.

"We make them. The family makes them. Cousin Jo has her own business. She makes them at home, sells them online. We get her on with working it out and making them."

"What do we think?" asked Terry, addressing Keith, understanding that the others had already discussed it. Keith pondered the question.

"Get her to make a prototype. She doesn't need to know why. Just a present for someone." Jane and Ronnie looked hopeful.

"We're still developing the idea," piped in Ronnie enthusiastically. Terry looked at Jack, Jane and Ronnie.

"Develop the prototype and let me have a look." Jane smiled, Ronnie clenched her fists in triumph and Jack remained calm as ever.

"What about you, Terry? How have you got on?" Terry reached into his jacket pocket, retrieved a toy model of a white long based van, and placed it upon the table within the centre of the group. He held a hand up and silently reached into a further pocket.

"It's like watching Paul Daniels," joked Keith.

"Damn right it is," replied Terry, producing three small model motor cars from his pocket. Jane squinted at the cars now placed upon the table.

"Are they old Citreons?" asked Jane, pointing to one of the cars.

"Indeed they are," replied Keith, "Citreon 2 CVs and our getaway vehicles."

"And the van?" asked Jack.

"For the initial movement of the gold."

"Are they big enough?" asked Jane.

"They'll have to be."

"Never mind that. Are they fast enough?" asked Jack.

"Oh, they will be. Once they're modified they certainly will be."

"Who is going to drive them?" asked Keith.

"Family," replied Terry, "we need to expand the team," he continued. "We need three drivers. I've got the men in mind. They drive for a living and know the city streets like the back of their hands. Ted, Will and Barry. Let me explain it to you." Keith went through his plans for the vehicles and drivers.

After a short comfort break following Terry's explanation the team reconvened their meeting.

"We're making good progress," said Terry. "We're all focussing in the right areas and moving things forward. Anyone foreseen any problems so far?"

"Money," stated Jack.

"Go on."

"For a start we need to buy a van, three 2 CVs. We then have to get the engines tuned up. Ronnie is going to need some equipment. None of it's cheap. Where's the money to do the job coming from?"

"Thought you'd never ask," replied Terry with a grin on his face. Everyone looked at him expectantly.

"Come on, then," interjected Keith, "spill the beans."

"We're gonna do a quick job. In and out. A house break."

"We?" asked Jack.

"Well, when I say we, I sort of mean you, with our back up of course."

"Am I really," replied Jack. "When, where, how long have I got to plan?" Jack sat with an amused look on his face. "Maybe you could have asked me or at least consulted me?"

"That's what we are doing now," replied Terry, raising a hand before Jack could interject. "It's all planned. I've got all the information that you need. Tommy, our lovely benefactor, has been working hard on this one and I think that you'll be happy with it." Jack's curiosity was now piqued.

"When and where?"

"Next week. Italy." Jack laughed.

"You've got some balls, Terry. I'll give you that."

"I have my friend and so have you. I know that you'll enjoy doing this one."

"What about the rest of us?" asked Jane.

"Don't panic. We're all doing this one. Ronnie, I'll need you running the technical side."

"Roger dodger, Mr T," she replied. Terry frowned at her then carried on.

"Keith, I'll need you here, ready to fence some goods."

"What like?"

"Gold, diamonds, jewellery. I'll give you the details."

"No problem."

"Jack and Jane, pack your cases. We are off to Italy in two days to meet up with Tommy." Jane smiled, excited at the prospect of the adventure. She beamed at Jack.

"And Jane,"

"Yes," she turned to Terry.

"Can you pack a nice dress? You'll be going to a private party."

"I certainly can," she replied. *This is incredible,* she thought. *I need to pack a case. What about getting some Euros? How do I get time off work?* Her head was spinning.

* * *

"He's been a busy lad this morning," said Mitch looking at the data set on his laptop. "All over the city." Mitch was examining the information supplied to him from the device which one of his team had deployed on Barry's car. The analyst had already tracked all of his movements, none of which appeared abnormal. On the face of it, Barry was a legitimate Uber driver who was working hard for a living. Underneath the facade the police knew him to be working as a runner for the Lomax family. His status in the family was probably at a low level but with no current informants able to infiltrate the criminal gang, Barry was looking to be a good bet to recruit for the police. Barry was vulnerable, on bail and had taken money from the police, albeit he didn't know that ... yet! Now, Mitch's job was to reel him in and land him. He had played his hand following Barry's arrest and now it was time to move into the next stage. Helen was his key player in this recruitment. It was clear that Barry had liked her, possibly even fancied her, and Mitch intended to use that to his advantage.

"How are you feeling?" he turned and asked Helen.

"I'm fine, mate. He's just another punter." Helen was dressed casually in a T-shirt and denim shorts. She had chosen her outfit deliberately for the warm weather, not provocative but hopefully enough to draw Barry's attention. The van in which she and Mitch were sitting was warm and she felt her back dampen with the heat and the adrenaline which was building within her.

"That's right, let's keep this nice and simple. We're just after getting a quick chat with him today. I'm going to switch to live tracking." Normally, Mitch would have held off moving on Barry so quickly but he'd received a clear message from the top that they wanted someone quickly into the Lomaxes. Rumour had it, the police service being the largest information sieve in existence, that the force was chasing a high level burglar and that they believed that the burglar must be running with the Lomaxes.

Barry's vehicle tracking had shown during the past two days that the vehicle stopped around about one p.m. in the same location. A local chuck wagon was nearby so they had taken the guess that this was his regular lunch haunt.

"Vehicle's moving slowly in the traffic, Helen. Time to go." Helen moved to the side door of the van, gently opened it, took a quick look and, seeing it was all clear, stepped out.

"Helen with a comms check," transmitted in the earphones that Mitch was wearing.

"Nice and clear, Helen," replied Mitch. There were five team members deployed today. Mitch, Helen, their driver and two operatives on the street. One was deployed at the coffee wagon and the other with a view of the whole area.

"Sighting of our target vehicle. Our man's the driver. No passengers," transmitted a female's voice over the radio airwaves. "The vehicle is pulling into the parking area and it's stopped."

"Helen is moving forward," said Helen.

"Pete is supporting you," a male operative's voice said.

* * *

Barry pulled into his usual parking spot, near the takeout van. He'd had a busy morning ferrying customers around the city and traffic was busy. He was gagging for a coffee and luckily there was only one bloke at the wagon who was being served. He climbed out of the car, closed the door and looked left, where a woman in shorts and a T-shirt was walking on the footpath in his direction. *You are looking hot,* he thought, staring at her bare legs and admiring them. He moved from her legs, running his eyes up her body, making no pretence at hiding the fact that he was enjoying the view. His eyes halted on her face. *Do I know you?* The woman walked closer to him, clearly intending to pass him by. She looked towards him and flashed him a wide smile. His mind kept working. *I've met you before. Where did we meet?* The cogs halted.

"Helen?" he said aloud. The woman halted and looked at him. "Helen, is that you?" She squinted her eyes and raised a hand to her brow to shade from the sunshine.

"Barry?"

"Yes," he smiled and walked towards her. "It's me. We met the other day. Not in the best of circumstances." He sniggered. "I thought I recognised you. What are you doing here?"

"It's my day off. I'm heading for a nail appointment," she held her left hand forward, showing Barry a broken nail. *No ring on her finger,* thought Barry.

"I could have given you a lift," he replied. "I'm an Uber."

"Oh, it's not far."

"Well, if you need a lift in the future, then ring me."

"I haven't got your number." He handed her his business card.

"Not everyone gets that," he replied.

"Only young ladies wearing shorts?" she asked, brushing her hair away from her face.

"Maybe," he replied flirtatiously.

"Really," she joined in the joke. "You're a bad boy, Barry." He laughed.

"I can be." Helen blushed and checked her watch. "I've got to go. I'll be late. See you around."

"Make sure you do. Call me," he shouted to her.

"Will do," she replied speedily walking away to her fictitious appointment. *Could be in there,* thought Barry watching Helen walk away.

* * *

"Still watching you," received Helen in her covert earpiece.

"Take your next right, Helen. Ahead and waiting for you," said Mitch in her ear.

"Will do." Helen walked towards the next junction, where the van was parked, and turned right.

"Got you in my wing mirrors, Helen," said the van driver, "all clear." Helen approached the side door and climbed in as the van pulled away.

"Mitch to the team, that's a rap." The deployed members acknowledged knowing that they could now leave the area and regroup back at the office. Mitch turned to Helen.

"Nice one. You OK?"

"All good. It seemed to go smoothly."

"Indeed it did," he replied. The team had successfully made their first approach to their potential informant. Now they could plan the next stages and when they pounced, little Barry would not know what hit him.

* * *

Robert Harrison walked along St James, towards the five-storey Victorian building that was White's Gentleman's Club. Climbing the front steps, he reached a hand out to press for entry as the door was opened. A man wearing a dark suit and tie had opened the door before Harrison could press the bell.

"Can I help you, Sir?"

"I have an appointment." The male looked Robinson up and down, noting his dark suit and well polished shoes.

"Who may that be with, Sir?"

"Simeon Fortescue."

"Ah, of course. Mr Fortescue told me to expect your arrival."

"Has he been waiting long?"

"This way if you please." The male gestured into the hallway. Harrison stepped forward as the door was closed behind him. "Follow me, please." The male walked towards a central staircase, ignoring Harrison's question. Harrison followed him through the building. He walked down a small corridor and entered a room with a small bar area situated in one corner. The light plum-coloured carpet cushioned his footsteps and ornately carved wooden panelled walls absorbed the quiet murmur of male voices. The room spoke of decadence with its high coffered ceilings and leather oxblood furnishings. At the far end of the room sat Simeon, reading a newspaper. He looked up and smiled at Harrison, folding his paper and standing as Harrison approached.

"Your guest, Sir."

"Thank you. Shall we?" Simeon gestured to a door situated behind his chair and both males entered a private meeting room. Simeon closed the door behind him. "Have you got it?" Harrison held out a file which he handed to Simeon.

"All there, Sir. As requested."

"Thank you, Robert." Simeon placed the file upon a small green baize cards table without examining it. "Have a seat. How are things going?"

"I'm very good, thank you, Simeon. Can't complain. Looking forward to a holiday soon."

"That's all very well," Simeon frowned, "but I meant with the investigation. How's it going?"

"Oh, sorry! Well, I've pulled the team together, got support from my colleagues and we're drawing things together."

"Who is he?" snapped Simeon.

"It's not quite that simple, Simeon. These types of investigations are slow moving. We've got all the jobs that we know of and we're analysing the data to look for patterns. Clues, if you like."

"Do you know who he is yet?"

"No."

"Well, you need to try harder."

"Yes, Sir."

"Any leads at all?"

"We're progressing with a possible informant. Someone who we believe may lead us somewhere."

"Who?"

"Well, that's restricted information, Simeon. Let's just say that we have a hunch that your burglar may be linked to the Lomax family. They're a large crime family based in the city."

"Restricted information, Harrison! Restricted bloody information! From me!" Fortescue's face was reddening, his clipped words barely holding his temper. "His name?"

"Barry Lomax. Sorry, Sir," stated Harrison.

"That's better," Simeon's face and demeanour calmed. "Know your place, Harrison. Now tell me what you know about Barry." Simeon reached for the file, opened the front cover and wrote Barry's name on the inside sleeve.

* * *

Digby had attended Fortescue's house where Mrs Fortescue had handed him a large buff envelope, advising him that Simeon was otherwise occupied. Now back in his hotel room, following a tube ride across the city, he threw the envelope onto his bed. He placed his jacket on a chair and poured himself a glass of whisky from a half drunk bottle of grouse upon the dresser top. *I'm drinking too much*, he thought, as he reached for the envelope and sat down in the only comfortable chair in the room. He removed a green file from the envelope, took his cigarettes from his shirt pocket and selected one. He looked to the mirror where a stick on sign stated NO SMOKING, sighed and placed the cigarette behind his ear. Digby lifted the file and opened it, noting the name Barry Lomax and other details written on the inside cover. He scanned the handwritten information. *I'll come back to that*, he thought.

One hour later, cigarette unsmoked and drink untouched, Digby sat back, having absorbed the information held within the file. He couldn't help but admire the clear professionalism of 'The Hare'. Top quality criminal burglaries, no clues and no one had any idea who he was. However, this seemed to be the first time that anyone had pulled all the jobs together. The first time that anyone had even realised that the burglaries may be linked. *He must have made a mistake somewhere.* He looked at the front sleeve of the file again. *Barry Lomax, Barry Lomax. A tenuous link at best but maybe someone to start with. I need to get the car and phone data to Ricco.* Placing the file back in its envelope, then placing it on the top of his wardrobe, he left his room desperate for a cigarette. Now standing outside of the hotel in the balmy night air he rang Ricco.

"It's me," he stated.

"What ya got?"

"A name. Not much. He's not our man but his family is connected."

"Who are they?"

"The Lomaxes."

"Ah! Send me what you've got."

"Will do."

"I'll ring tomorrow." Ricco terminated the call. Digby lit another cigarette before returning to his room. Fortescue had provided him with an encrypted USB. He opened it and, using his secure server, sent the information to Ricco.

Chapter 6

"I'd imagine he'll be here soon," stated Tommy after checking his wristwatch. Terry and Jane were sitting at a dining table with him, waiting at a small restaurant in Catania, Italy. Jane took a sip of her wine as Terry enjoyed his chilled Birra Messina. They had both flown into Catania Fontanarossa airport early this morning and had, at Jack's request, travelled separately from him.

"He bloomin' better be," stated Terry, singling out an arancino and popping it in his mouth.

"He'll be here," promised Jane. She sat back, enjoying the warm afternoon sun and the quiet music being played in the background. Tommy sat opposite, in a white linen shirt, wafting himself with his Fedora. Terry sat next to her, looking slightly uncomfortable in the heat, wearing a black shirt with sweat marks already showing at his armpits.

"It's getting bloody warmer," said Terry, emptying his glass and indicating to the waiter for another.

"Well you won't be here long enough to acclimatise," said Tommy, looking over his shoulder. "Ah! Here he is." Jane checked behind her and saw Jack approaching. Dressed in a light-tailored suit and white shirt, he looked good. Slightly tanned, with his shirt open at the neck, he looked comfortable with the warmth. She placed her sunglasses on and smiled at him which was reciprocated. Something that did not go unnoticed by Tommy. Tommy stood up.

"Welcome, my lad. Great to meet you in the flesh." He reached out and took Jack's hand. Bringing him into an embrace, he kissed the air gently to either side of his cheeks. Jack fell naturally into the greeting and then nodded to Terry. He took Jane's proffered hand.

"Signora." She smiled.

"Jack, you made it," said Jane.

"Of course." Tommy clapped a hand on his shoulder.

"A drink, Jack?"

"Yes, please." Tommy signalled to the waiter, who approached the table.

"Un bicchiere di vino bianco." The waiter nodded and returned with a glass of wine for Jack and a second beer for Terry. Jack sat down with the group at the table.

"Very impressive," stated Jane to Tommy.

"When in Rome …" he replied. "Right, we're all here. Terry, are you happy that everyone is fully briefed?"

"Yeah. Ronnie is just waiting for a call this evening, then she'll be up and running. Jack, you got booked into a hotel?"

"Yes. Booked in last night." Terry looked at him in confusion.

"Why so late today?"

"I've been up to have a look at the house. Plans of the building are all well and good but there's nothing like physically seeing the structure in real life." Tommy sat back, smiling at Jack. *A consummate professional. You'll do son*, he thought.

"Any issues?" continued Terry.

"I think I'll be fine. It's busy there this morning. There's a lot of catering and cleaning staff going in and out. Preparing for the party. It's a beautiful building, very impressive."

"It'll be a hell of a party," interjected Tommy. "Marco only started renting it out a couple of months ago. He'll be wanting it to look good tonight."

"It looks like they're going to hold most of the gathering out on the back terraces facing the grounds. Tables are being set up there and a marquee of some sort."

"How do you know?" asked Jane.

"I walked in to have a look this morning."

"You walked in?" stated Terry, nearly choking on his beer. Tommy sat watching, hands together with pyramided fingers resting against his smiling lips.

"Yes, I walked in with some caterers this morning. Had a quick look around whilst I had the chance."

"Were you seen?" asked Terry.

"Oh, undoubtedly," replied Jack, "but there's being seen and being seen."

"Explain."

"I walked in with the catering team, carrying their goods. In all appearances, I was one of them so yes, I was seen. Did anyone pay me any attention? No. All they saw was one of their own walking into the building."

"Oh!"

"No obvious security cameras by the way."

"He probably hasn't had time to get any installed yet," said Tommy. "We can assume that the safe will be well protected though."

"Yes, indeed. Ronnie will deal with that. There were also a couple of likely-looking lads patrolling the first-floor landing. It was marked private. The men were dressed in dark suits."

"Carrying?" asked Terry.

"Carrying? What do you mean?", asked Jane, "Carrying what?"

"Guns," clarified Terry. Jane's eyes widened.

"Not sure," replied Jack, "though we'll have to assume that they are due to the pedigree of our host this evening." The team continued talking, completing their final plans for this evening's burglary.

* * *

Jane checked her appearance in her hotel mirror. Dressed in a black evening dress, complemented by diamond earrings and necklace, with hair loosely tied up, she felt that she looked presentable for the party. A gentle knock sounded at her door as she slipped on some black high heels. Another quick check of her makeup and she walked to the door and opened it to be greeted by Tommy, dressed in a chic black suit, white shirt and black bowtie.

"May I come in?" he asked.

"Of course." Jane stepped back holding the door open allowing him to enter. Tommy carried a black slim briefcase which he placed on the bed.

"You feeling OK?" he asked.

"A bit nervous, if I'm honest."

"You'll be fine. I won't leave your side." He stepped back and looked at Jane. "If you don't mind me saying, you look stunning." Jane blushed.

"I scrub up OK then?"

"You really look the part. I'll have to keep the young men away from you." Jane laughed, feeling some of her tension ease. Tommy had always had a relaxing air about him and Jane knew that he would look after her. "As discussed earlier, we are family and I'm just treating you to the highlights of Sicily." Jane nodded. Tommy opened his briefcase. "I've brought your bag," He produced a small black handbag with a shoulder strap and handed it to Jane, "compliments of Ronnie, and here's your earpiece." He handed Jane a small black pouch. She looked inside and saw a small flesh-coloured hearing aid. Ronnie had gone through the equipment with the team before they left England and, after a few practices, everyone was confident in using it. Jane checked inside the handbag where a small radio was secreted in a back zipper pocket.

"New batteries in all of it," stated Tommy. Jane placed the hearing aid in her ear and switched on the radio. Pressing her thumb to a specific area on the bag strap she heard a familiar click for transmission.

"Jane, with a comms check." She spoke out loud.

"Receiving you loud and clear," boomed the jovial voice of Ronnie in her left ear. Jane adjusted the volume on her radio. "That's all of you checked in and we're ready to roll." Ronnie had stayed at home working within her own developed nerve centre to support the team.

"Good luck, everyone," stated Terry over the airwaves with the sound of a car engine in the background. Jane knew that Terry would be driving to pick up Jack to transport him to the house.

"Time to go," stated Tommy, closing his briefcase. "Do I look OK?" he asked.

"Very dapper," replied Jane.

"Let's go then." He walked to the room door and opened it, allowing Jane to walk through, closing it behind himself as they headed towards the hotel reception.

* * *

Jack was sitting in the rear seat of a battered old Fiat Panda with Terry driving. Dressed in dark clothing with a dark-coloured backpack next to him, Jack was ready for work. Terry had completed his final radio checks, wished the team good luck and now it was game on. Both men had discussed their plans and Jack had made Terry repeat drop off, pick up and backup plans, should things go wrong, until he was confident that they were ingrained in his memory. Flights had already been booked by the team for their extraction so whatever happened this evening the team would be leaving the country in the early hours.

"Approaching drop off," said Terry with no hint of nervousness in his voice. The estate driveway loomed in front of them with trees silhouetted in the fading sunlight.

"All set," replied Jack. He took hold of his bag and prepared to leave the vehicle. Tommy turned left, mirroring the wall of the estate grounds. The road was quiet. No pedestrians were in view.

"Three, two, one..." Terry stalled the car and veered towards the verge coming to a halt. Jack slipped out of the rear door as Terry turned the key to the vehicle. The car engine sputtered. *No one around,* thought Jack as he checked his surroundings. Taking ten steps beyond the car, he checked his bag straps and turned to face it. Terry looked directly at him and nodded. Jack tensed, and with a burst of speed, ran at the car. He launched, left leg hitting the bonnet. Sprang to his right foot and pushed, his arms in the air. Jack's hands grabbed the top of the wall, twisting his feet up he landed briefly and then pushed, his body rolling as it descended into the estate grounds of the Piazza Agostino Pennisi, Acireale.

* * *

"Jack's in," Jane heard Terry's transmission quietly in her right ear. She felt her heartbeat flutter and her skin dampen with the excitement and tension of the situation. Tommy squeezed her hand and smiled. *Cool as a cucumber*, she thought. She returned the smile as their taxi entered the grounds and drove along the palm-studded drive towards what Jane could only describe as a castle. The building, illuminated by ground-based lighting, presented an imposing demeanour the likes of which Jane had only seen in films.

"Impressive, isn't it?" said Tommy, noting Jane's countenance.

"I'll say," replied Jane.

"Welcome to the home of Marco Ragusa," said Tommy. The car pulled towards the front of the building. Women wearing fine dresses and men in black tie and suits were departing vehicles and walking towards the building. Each group of guests were greeted by men wearing dark suits who appeared to be checking them in via registers before allowing them entry. Drivers of vehicles handed their keys to valets who moved the vehicles to a private parking area for them. The taxi stopped and Tommy paid the fare to the driver.

"Grazie," he said, opening the door of the taxi and stepping out. He held the door for Jane, extending his arm out to assist her out of the car. Both stepped away and the car manoeuvred back towards the drive. Tommy straightened his jacket and looked at Jane.

"You look terrific. Let's enjoy the party." She took his arm, holding it tightly as they approached a suited male.

"Relax, dear," whispered Tommy.

"Name, please," said the suited male. He was broad and tall, squeezed into his suit, and spoke with a European accent.

"Thomas Lomax and guest," replied Tommy looking at the list of names on the iPad which the man held and scrolled through.

"There," Tommy pointed at his name on the screen. "Busy evening for you," Tommy smiled. The male looked at him blankly.

"Yes," he replied in monotone.

"Thank you, young man," Tommy brushed past him, noting the strap of a shoulder holster as he did so. "Come on, Jane. Let's get a drink." Jane followed Tommy towards the front entrance of the building, where they were directed through to the rear terraces. She heard the now familiar click in her ear.

"Tommy and Jane are in. Armed guards," stated the voice of Tommy.

"Received," replied the whisper of Jack.

Tommy and Jane walked out onto one of the large terraces where waiters and waitresses carried silver trays containing champagne flutes and canapes which they were offering to flushed-faced guests. The party had started two hours previously and the guests were enjoying the extravagance of free food and alcohol. Quiet music played over an external sound system and a line of braziers led from the terraces into the grounds. There, an open marquee covered a further entertainment area, with a free bar and dance floor which was being monopolised by the younger portion of partygoers.

"There he is," said Tommy, turning Jane gently by the elbow towards the dance floor. From the terrace, she looked down and saw a tall dark male with long wavy hair wearing a white tuxedo and open-necked shirt. Around him, a group of individuals courted his attention. Younger than Jane thought, she guessed him to be around fifty and, to be fair to him, he looked to be in his prime. Tommy looked around, noting several dark-suited males on the periphery of all the partygoers. *Plenty of protection,* he thought to himself. He watched Ragusa moving towards the DJ as one of his henchmen removed a microphone from its stand.

"He's going to make a speech," transmitted Tommy over the airwaves.

* * *

"You get that, Ronnie?"

"Yes, Jack." Jack acknowledged Tommy's transmission on the radio. "You ready?"

"Yes, let's go."

"Right on. Good luck."

Jack had negotiated his way through the shrubbery along the driveway and was now positioned in cover to the right of the mansion. He had studied his route and waited for the right information from his colleagues to begin his approach. Now was the time, with Ragusa speaking to a captive audience and his guards watching them closely for any threat. Jack moved.

Feet crunching quietly on the stoned drive, he crept towards the exterior light uplifter, dropping a leafy branch over it as he passed, then headed towards the building line. The leaves' shadows now dappled the side of the building, causing areas of shade and light which would assist in camouflaging him. He stood silently, with his back to the building, and pulled down the roll of the beanie hat he was wearing, a balaclava now secreting his face. He checked his watch, pressed its stopwatch, turned, and started to climb. Not requiring the luxury of gloves on his climb, which would protect his fingers, his bare hands and climbing shoe-embraced feet found crevices to aid his assent to the crenellated battlements.

Halfway, he rested on a protruding buttress line and peered through a slim arched window into a dimly lit room. The room was furnished but empty. A shadow passed the doorway. *Guards on the landings*, he thought. He smiled to himself, thriving in the danger of the experience. *Up,* he thought. Jack negotiated the window side and used its arch to push himself higher. Hearing something, he stopped. The crunch of gravel below. This side of the building. He looked down.

A man wearing a dark suit lit a cigarette and inhaled deeply. *Guard,* thought Jack. The male moved towards the light uplifter and casually kicked away the branch. The building side lit up. Jack hung there exposed, clinging to the wall. His heart was thumping, his breathing increased. *Calm, Jack. Calm.* He slowed his breathing and held tightly. *Don't look up, mate.* A phone rang from below. The man moved, took a mobile from his pocket and returned to the building. Jack moved. Pulled his body higher. Now near the overhang of the top wall, he stretched out his left leg, his body almost horizontal to the ground. His foot slipped. Legs and hips moving down. No time to think he went with the momentum. Braced his arms. Swung right. Hit his apex and drove his body left like a pendulum. Again at apex, he drove right and clenching his body on his upward swing released his arms and reached upwards, his abdomen forcing a body extension. Arms out he felt the top wall and pulled. His body rose, legs hooked over and tumbled onto the roof breathing heavily. *Close one*, he thought.

"On the roof," he transmitted. Gathering himself, he stood and walked carefully to the rear aspect of the building where a voice was speaking out loud. People below were all turned to face Ragusa who was addressing them. *Time check, five minutes.* He moved to the other side of the building towards a roof window and checked it thoroughly.

"Roof window clear, Ronnie."

"Received." Jack removed a small pick and dealt with the latch. An old building which no one would believe could be assaulted from the roof. Jack's luck held. He carefully opened the window and produced a small mirror to check if the landing was clear. It was. Jack climbed in. He slowly lowered himself then hanging from one arm pulled the window shut behind him as he dropped silently to the floor. He moved along the landing hearing the murmur of voices downstairs. He would hear footsteps on the marble stairs should anyone ascend. Jack crouched low and listened for footsteps. Silence. Keeping low he moved towards his target door.

"Approaching the room," he whispered.

"Received," Ronnie's quiet reply.

Jack looked at the door before approaching it. No sensors were obvious. He stopped dead when he heard the sound of a footstep! Backing away he checked the stairs. A single guard ascended. The hallway below the guard was clear. Jack looked around. *Nowhere to hid*e. Jack felt the flutter of panic.

The man was nearing the top of the stairs. *Turn left, turn left*, pleaded Jack. His luck held. The guard turned left. Jack had spotted one area where the guard would disappear before coming around the corner towards him. He waited. The guard walked on, checking door handles as he passed. He disappeared from view. Jack swiftly stepped over the balcony balustrade and lowered himself slowly.

He moved towards the guard, shimmying along the handrail. *Still quiet below.* His one option was an upright marbled pillar, reaching from the lower floor to the ceiling. His body tense, he trusted instinct and moved just as the guard came into view. Jack's synthetic-soled shoes gripped as he embraced the pillar. The guard passed. Jacked moved beyond and gripped a further bannister. The guard halted. Jack pulled his body in tight. The guard moved towards the door as Jack pulled himself back over the rail, away from view. Jack heard a door handle turn, but no door opened.

"All clear," stated a European voice out loud. His footsteps moved away as Jack watched him continue on his circuit of the landing before walking back towards the marble stairs. Jack pulled himself back over the rail, the guard descended, and approached the door with lock picks in hand. Placing on thin leather gloves he checked the handle, confirming it locked, then swiftly used his tools to enter, quietly closing the door behind him.

He was confronted by a plainly furnished, marble-floored bedroom. A king-size bed dominated the room with a large red rug laid before it. A full-length mirror held one wall, and an old iron radiator provided the room's winter warmth. Voile curtains covered the arched windows and an inbuilt wardrobe stood within one wall.

"Ronnie, I'm in." Jack checked behind the mirror. *Nothing there.* "Sparsely furnished. Either a floor safe or in the wardrobe."

"Floor safe unlikely," came her quiet reply. "Try the wardrobe." Jack moved silently towards the arched windows. He checked the latch on one window, released it, opened it slightly, then moved to the wardrobe. Selecting the largest door he opened it, pulled clothes hangers aside and was confronted by a large electronic safe.

"Bingo!" he exclaimed. Taking out his team phone he photographed it and sent the image to Ronnie. Thirty seconds later she replied.

"Got it, Jack. Give me a minute." Jack knew that back in her room Ronnie would be working hard to identify the safe and its security features. He stood patiently waiting, listening for any sounds of compromise.

"He's just finishing off," said Tommy on the radio.

"Get out the key, Jack," said Ronnie. Jack retrieved a gadget from his bag and held it in readiness. "Right, when I say, reach under the digital key lock that you can see. You got that?"

"Yes, the black box."

"Yes. Take the connector from your pack. Reach behind the lock. Detach theirs and plug me in. Just like we discussed."

"Got it."

"Three, two, one. Now!" Jack followed the instructions, holding the device in his hand. *Come on, Ronnie.* The room was silent, the air thick. Jack shrugged his shoulders, easing his tense muscles.

"He's finished," said Tommy. Jack stood silently, listening to the quiet mechanics of the safe locks manoeuvring.

"We're in," said Ronnie, excitement apparent in her voice. Jack reached forward, pulled on the safe handle and watched the door swing silently towards him. He placed his device down silently and positioned his bag in front of the safe. The safe held cash, and lots of it. He methodically began placing it in his backpack with a big smile on his face. The radio airwaves were silent and he knew that everyone would be waiting in anticipation. Cash acquired, he opened a bottom drawer within the safe which revealed jewellery and a selection of watches. He retrieved them carefully and dropped them into the bag. Lastly, he removed his balaclava and a thin layered outer shirt, placing them within the same bag.

"Safe is now empty," he said over the radio.

"Complete the procedure in reverse," said Ronnie. Jack retrieved his calling card from his shirt pocket and placed it in the drawer. He closed the drawer and the safe door.

"Ready, Ronnie." Ronnie worked her magic and Jack removed his device, reattached the safe leads and closed the wardrobe door. Placing his device in the bag, Jack fastened it and moved to the window. He opened it slowly and, now hearing loud music being played, checked below was clear before he dropped the heavy bag into some undergrowth. Jack closed and secured the window. Reaching to a hanger on the wardrobe he picked up Ragusa's black tuxedo, slipped it on and moved to the door. Silently opening it and checking the landing, which was clear, he left the room and closed the door which locked automatically behind him. Jack brushed a hand through his hair, straightening it and walked confidently down the staircase where a group of guests were chatting on various steps. A guard stood at the bottom facing the front doors. Amongst the guests were standing Tommy and Jane. Jack slipped into the group and took a glass of champagne from a passing waiter's tray. He looked at Jane and smiled, tipping his glass in salute.

"Time we should be going, dear," said Tommy to Jane. "If you could excuse us," he said to the group of guests. Unbeknown to them he had also transmitted this over the radio to the rest of the team. Jane and Tommy moved towards the front doors where outside a group of taxis waited to take guests home. On leaving the building they approached the two security guards present and engaged them in conversation. Jack seized the moment and slipped around the building to retrieve his pack and return to Terry.

* * *

Terry sat, waiting for his signal to collect Jack. He had just watched Tommy's taxi drive past which would be heading towards Jane's hotel where she would be dropped. He checked his watch.

"Come on, man," he spoke aloud.

"Ready when you are, Terry," transmitted Jack's voice. Terry retraced the route from the drop off and sure enough as he passed the main gates Jack walked out from the treeline carrying his pack. Terry slowed and stopped. Jack jumped in, placing the bag next to him.

"Let's go," said Jack. Terry slowly accelerated, keeping a watchful eye in his rearview mirror as he did so.

"How'd it go?" he asked.

"Sweet, Terry. A good haul. Cash and jewellery, just as we expected."

"Any issues?"

"None at all. They haven't a clue that I've been there."

"Cool. Let's get out of here. Where do you want to be dropped off?"

"Where you collected me."

"Right. Your flight booked?"

"Yes, all sorted."

"Straight home?"

"Not quite. I have other plans but I'll be back in a couple of days."

"Your business, mate, but keep safe."

"Will do." Jack took the clothing out of his bag and replaced it with his radio equipment. He then removed the tuxedo as they drove along. "You can ditch the jacket," he said.

"Where'd you get it?"

"Borrowed from Ragusa," he smiled.

"You cheeky bastard," laughed Terry as they headed back into town.

* * *

Jane walked into the hotel lobby and collected her keys from reception. Still feeling tense from the evenings activities, she knew that they weren't in the clear yet. She had a flight booked in three hours and needed to get changed and then head out to the airport. Tommy had set off to meet up with Terry. Both were to travel from Acireale to Messina, where Tommy had arranged for his yacht to be anchored. The stolen cash and goods would be taken by yacht from Sicily, where Tommy was to arrange distribution of the wealth. Cash would be handled by him and placed within a secure offshore account where Ronnie could easily access it. Jewellery was to be handled by Terry with the able assistance of Keith.

Jane's job was to get back to the UK, as was Jack's. A flight to mainland Italy first and then on to the UK. She entered her hotel room, stripped off her dress and pulled on some trousers and a T-shirt.

"Right, Jane," she spoke aloud to herself, a habit which she had acquired especially when nervous. "Everything packed," She scanned around the room. "Passport, purse, phone." She checked her back pocket for the phone just as it quietly vibrated. Jane checked the screen. It was Jack.

"Jack, are you OK?"

"Fine, fine. It all went well."

"I was really scared," she giggled nervously.

"Well, you did well. You ready for your flight?"

"Yes, just about to leave."

"Cool. I'll meet you when we land. Wait until we get out of the airport."

"You sure? I thought you didn't want to mix with us."

"Not here. If you see me at Catania just ignore me. We'll be fine when we get to the mainland."

"That would be great. It'll calm my nerves. I don't think I'll feel safe until we get home."

"Just keep it together. I'll look after you. See you in a few hours."

"Can't wait," replied Jane, smiling to herself.

* * *

Jane walked out of the arrivals gates at Rome-Fiumicino, desperate for the loo and in need of a coffee. Though still early morning people were waiting for the arrival of friends and family, their faces raised in anticipation every time the arrival doors opened. The atmosphere in the airport was palpable with a positive vibe in the air, with smiling faces of people meeting, or witnessing the embraces of loved ones as they arrived in Rome. Jane checked the crowds and wasn't disappointed when she spotted Jack moving towards her with a wide beam on his face. She moved to him and welcomed his warm embrace as he greeted her.

"I can't believe you did it?" she exclaimed.

"Not so loud." He laughed. "We're not out of the woods yet." Jane looked worried. "Don't panic. We will be soon. Let's get going."

"I need the loo," said Jane, "I must look a mess."

"You look great," he replied. She smiled.

"Nevertheless, my bladder is about to pop."

"This way," Jack guided her towards a sign indicating female toilets.

"Two minutes," Jane entered the toilets as he waited. She used the loo and checked her countenance in the mirror. Combed her hair, washed her face and pinched her cheeks. "Looking tired, girl but not too bad." An elderly lady standing next to her smiled at her.

"Molto bella," said the woman.

"You too," replied Jane, not understanding a word that the woman had spoken. The old lady giggled as Jane left the room. Jack stood patiently waiting.

"That's better," said Jane.

"Good. Slight change of plan if that's OK?"

"What do you mean?"

"I've just got a quick job to do before we go back. I could do with your help."

"Oh! Right. What about my flight?"

"Don't worry about that. I'll sort us another one. Do you want a coffee?"

"I'd love one," replied Jane as Jack gently guided her through the airport.

"Great! We'll grab one before we set off."

"Set off! Set off where?"

"I've hired us a car."

"A car!" Jane stopped walking, halting Jack's progress. "Jack, what's going on?"

"Nothing to worry about. I'll explain over our coffee. You'll love it. A bit of fun. We're off to Austria." He smiled widely at her, took her hand and walked to the exit doors of the airport.

* * *

Helen was standing waiting for her lift. She'd texted Barry thirty minutes ago asking for his Uber powers so that she could get to a meeting with a friend. He'd responded straight away as she had hoped. Mitch had briefed the team this morning and they were all prepared. She knew that a couple were sitting in the coffee shop opposite with a clear view of her and that a car would shadow Barry's car's movements. Mitch was back at the office, in the control room, where he could have an overview of the meeting.

Dressed casually Helen felt comfortable with her task. She had checked her covert equipment and knew that Mitch would be listening in to everything.

Vehicle approaching, was texted to her mobile.

She placed the phone in her handbag and switched on a covert listening device secreted within the bag. Today she had no covert communications, to limit any compromise but the device in her bag would record everything and also transmit it 'live' to Mitch. The Uber pulled up with a slight squeal of the tyres as it braked. Barry smiled up at Helen.

"Hi lovely, thought you'd never call."

"Always planned to," she replied, reaching towards the back door.

"Jump in the front, Helen. More comfortable up here." She smiled and walked around the front of the car, ensuring that Barry got a good look at her, then climbed in the vehicle.

"Meeting a friend?" he asked, pulling away from the kerb.

"Yes, just for a bit of lunch."

"Very nice. You could maybe have tubed it quicker?"

"Then that wouldn't have given me an excuse to call you, would it?"

"You need an excuse?"

"Not really, but early days."

"I'll get there in a jiffy anyway," claimed Barry, "I know a few shortcuts."

"I bet you do." They both laughed.

"How'd you get by on an Uber wage?" she asked.

"I do OK," he replied. "That stuff the other day was just messed up. They got the wrong guy. I'm innocent."

"A Lomax though. One of the family." He frowned and glanced at her.

"But still a nobody, love. Just carry the name."

"That's a shame," she replied, "I like a bit of danger in my life." He smiled.

"Do you now?" Barry turned swiftly right into a no-entry, blasted down the short road and exited at the other side. Helen squealed. "Shortcut," he clarified.

"Naughty," Helen replied.

"Naughty indeed. If it's naughty you want then I'm your man."

"Sounds intriguing."

"Yeah, I'm going places. Won't always drive an Uber. Blood's thicker, if you know what I mean." Barry said with a cockiness in his voice. "Could do with this bail thing disappearing though."

"I'll bet."

"I was lucky there though. Don't think they'll pin anything on me." Barry appeared to be talking to himself.

"Let's hope not," said Helen.

"Can you help?"

"I just offer a way out," she clarified. "The police do their thing and I do mine." Barry started to slow the car.

"And does your job allow you to have a drink with a client?" He stopped the car.

"Well, technically you're not a client. You refused, remember?" She looked out of the window. "We're here." She opened the door and turned to go.

"Drink?" asked Barry. Helen turned back and looked at him studying his face.

"Why not? When?"

"Tonight?"

"Boy, you're keen," she paused, "Ok, you're on. I'll text you."

"Great." Helen stepped out of the car, knowing that Barry would be checking out her figure as she did so. She leant down, looking through the door.

"Tonight then," Helen closed the door and entered the pub they had stopped outside. She passed the bar and walked out of the rear door straight into the unmarked police car waiting for her.

Chapter 7

"He's an Uber driver."

"Yes, I know that Ricco. So what?"

"Fairly straightforward for us. We book a ride, take him to where we want to go and he's yours from there."

"When?"

"Next couple days. We don't use Uber. Any name that I can book it in?" Digby thought about it.

"Use the name Fortescue. He's used them before." *A little bit of insurance for me* thought John. *If the Lomax's link things together then Simeon can deal with it.*

"Will do. I'll plan it today. Be ready for a call."

"Where will you take him?"

"There's an old run-down gas station on the East side. I'll take him there. I'll send you the location."

"Great. I'll be ready."

* * *

Barry walked away from his flat and headed into the city. Dressed in smart trousers and shirt, he'd spruced himself up for his date with Helen. He couldn't believe his luck. Helen was a good-looking woman with a great figure on her and she fancied him. He'd trimmed his stubble and sprayed liberally with Lynx body spray and aftershave. He wanted to impress and had even had a haircut this afternoon. He was feeling lucky and if Helen played her cards right she might just snatch up one of the city's eligible bachelors. Barry walked with a bounce in his step, unaware of a male who had just snapped his photograph whilst being driven past him.

Thirty minutes later he was approaching the Cross Keys where he would meet Helen.

* * *

"All set," said Helen to Mitch. Both were sitting within a small flat, rented covertly by the Metropolitan Police, near to the Cross Keys.

"Good. Checked all of your kit?"

"Yes."

"Happy with your cover story?"

"Yes."

"Keep to the rules. You're there to get information, nothing else. Just enough to snare him."

"Understood."

"Safety sign?"

"Spill my drink. Go to the loo."

"Good. The team is deployed there already. Ignore them unless you have no choice. I'll be here listening. Encourage him to talk. Don't put the words in his mouth."

"OK." Mitch halted listening to a transmission in his earpiece. "He's just entered the pub," Mitch paused. "He's at the bar and bought a pint. Looking around and waiting. Time for you to go." Helen checked her bag and walked to the door.

"Helen," She turned.

"Yes?"

"Good luck. Remember you're good at this." She smiled and walked out of the flat, the healthy nervousness making her body tingle with the energy she felt when being deployed undercover.

Five minutes later, Helen walked into the Cross Keys, stopped, and looked around for Barry. He raised a hand from his position at the bar and beckoned her over. She noticed that he'd made an effort.

"Thought you'd stood me up. I was about to ring you."

"Sorry, Barry. I've never been here before. Lady's prerogative to be late though."

"Of course it is." Barry leant in kissing Helen clumsily on both cheeks and stepped back. "You are looking beautiful if you don't mind me saying."

"I don't. You don't look too bad yourself."

"Can I get you a drink?" Helen noted from the glasses on the bar that Barry had nearly finished his second pint.

"I'll have a small house white, please," she said to the bar lady.

"Another lager for me, and a vodka shot," said Barry. "You want a shot. Calm the nerves?"

"No, I'm fine, thanks. You go for it." The drinks arrived at the bar. Barry necked the shot and took both glasses.

"Shall we sit down?" he asked, gesturing to an empty table.

"Yes, that would be great." Helen led the way to a high table and seated herself in a chair which offered her a view of the main entrance and the toilets.

She placed her handbag on the table, took her drink and tasted the wine. "Very nice." She smiled. There was a pregnant pause.

"So..." stated both together. Then nervously laughed.

"You first," said Barry, taking a large mouthful from his beer glass.

"Do you go on many blind dates?" asked Helen.

"Nope. Don't have the time. Driving all the time you see."

"You must pick up some lovely fares though."

"Oh yes, plenty. No time for me though. Busy city life. All working hard. They just want a quick A to B. They don't care who does it."

"A bit sad though. Isn't it?"

"It's just life. There's more important things in life than work."

"I agree," said Helen, "Friends," she gestured to Barry, "partners, family." Barry took a long drink from his pint. "Slow down, cowboy," said Helen laughing.

"I'm fine," Barry laughed. "You want another?" Helen covered the top of her glass with her hand. "I'm fine."

"One more," he said. *You keep going*, thought Helen. She watched as he returned to the bar, finished his pint and ordered another and a shot. He returned to the table with the pint, only having drunk the shot.

"Where were we?"

"Talking about the importance of family."

"What about yours?"

"Only child, parents live Northside. Bit of a loner."

"Why me?" he asked.

"Why not?" she replied. "A good-looking lad, works hard, a bit rough around the edges but attractive." He smiled. "Anyway, enough about me. What about you, Barry Lomax? Uber driver but destined for better, I think you said."

"I certainly am," he slurred slightly.

"Go on. What then? What makes you so sure of success? What makes you a bad boy?" she teased.

During the next two hours, Barry drank and Helen coaxed details from him about his family and the small part that he played in their criminal activity. All of it was recorded on the device in her bag. Back at the flat Mitch smiled.

"Got you, you little shit." He picked up his phone to make a call.

* * *

The pounding of his head slowly drew Barry to consciousness. He reached a hand to his temple holding it in an attempt to alleviate the throbbing pain. His mouth dry and an aching throat, combined with eyes that resisted opening, told him that he was hungover. With his other hand he felt down his body realising that he was still dressed. A groan escaped his lips as he turned onto his side making preparations to sit up. *One, two, three,* he thought, rising to one elbow and checking his bedside clock.

"Eight O'Clock," he groaned. Now in a sitting position, he looked around the flat. He must have knocked a side table over coming in but apart from that, everything looked pretty OK.

"A good night," he smiled to himself. Slight panic set in when he wondered what Helen might think of him. *She'll be fine, she had a good night.* He walked towards his front door, to ensure that he'd managed to close it, reached into the back pocket of his jeans for his key and pulled out a piece of paper.

See you at 9. Can't wait. Helen

"Shit!" *I'd forgotten.* Barry looked down at his clothes. *Can't go like this. Wore these last night.* He walked carefully to his small kitchen and flicked the kettle on, grabbed a mug from the drying rack and some milk from the fridge. He checked the date and, unsure, opened the lid and sniffed. *Mistake,* he thought, with bile rising in his throat. He threw the milk into the sink and ran as chunks of solid milk and thin clear liquid escaped the plastic bottle. He reached the toilet and reciprocated as vomit unloaded into the toilet escaping through his mouth and nose, the acid burning its vindictive trail through his body. His eyes watered, barely focussing on the bowl, as once again he heaved, reaching for the toilet roll to wipe his mouth. Barry stood up, tears streaming down his cheeks and seeing the reflection of his spattered shirt in the mirror, realised that he'd have to change anyway. He switched the shower on and stripped off his shirt.

"Black coffee it is then." Barry walked back towards the kitchen, turning the kitchen sink tap on as he reached for the Nescafe, "and paracetamol," he croaked.

Thirty minutes later, Barry emerged onto the pavement outside his block, freshened up, changed and sporting a pair of sunglasses. Despite brushing his teeth, he could still taste the acidity of his stomach contents but knew he had a tub of Extra in the car which would mask the alcoholic fumes. Making a dubious decision to drive, he headed towards his car and his arranged meeting with Helen.

Helen had told him early in the evening that she had booked a room at a local Premier Inn to stay in but despite his suggestion last night, she had failed to succumb to his drunken advances. However, she had agreed to let him take her to breakfast the next day. Barry didn't feel that he could stomach breakfast but he might try one, feeling remarkably better following his vomiting episode. He pulled up in the car park and texted Helen.

Outside in the carpark. He received a swift reply.
Come on up. Not quite ready. Room 23

Barry smiled, popped in some gum and checked his face in the rearview mirror. *Maybe my luck's in this morning,* he thought, feeling a tremor of excitement in his body. He walked towards the hotel, entered and headed for Room 23. Checking the doors as he walked along the corridor he found it, straightened his clothes and knocked. The door opened, and Barry walked through peering around the door as it shut behind him. He was confronted with the face of Mitch.

"Sit down, Barry. We need to talk." Mitch gestured to two chairs and a coffee table.

"What's this? I haven't done anything."

"I said sit down!" Automatically, Barry moved to the chairs. "You're not in trouble."

"I'll go then," Barry turned towards the door, his anger building. Mitch held up one hand to halt him and in the other produced a small device. He pressed a button and Barry heard his own voice speaking to him.

"So I run a bit of the drug money around for the fam and I'll be getting involved in the full distribution soon." His voice repeated to him in the drunken tones of last night. His stomach rumbled, his guts churned and he farted.

"Oh, shit!" His hands went to his face. "Oh, shit!" Mitch halted the recording.

"Calm down, son. All's gonna be fine. Take a seat and meet DS Field from the police informants' unit." Barry turned to see a bald, stocky male with a goatee beard leaning against one of the chairs.

"Morning, mate," DS Field chirped up. "Busy morning for you, I'm afraid."

Oh, Helen. What have you done, thought Barry.

* * *

Barry walked away from the hotel reception, climbed into his car, started the engine and drove away. All of his actions were automatic, his brain numbed by the last two hours with his meeting with the Metropolitan Police Covert Human Intelligence Unit. They wanted him to grass on his family. The recording that they had played to him clearly demonstrated to anyone that he already had. He'd told Helen about his involvement in cash deliveries, that the family were involved in illegal drug supply and intimated that they were involved in a lot more.

"I'm fucked," he said aloud. Barry couldn't deny what had been captured on audio. He hadn't told the cops anything else at the meeting. They had done most of the talking. They acted like his friends, his saviours. They could not make his recent arrest disappear but would there be anything they could prosecute him with? Only Barry knew that.

They were unclear, but he could help himself by working with them. He now knew that he'd been set up by Mitch and Helen and that he'd allowed his hormones to control his brain.

"Bloody idiot," he said, thumping the steering wheel. He drove aimlessly then parked up, lighting up a cigarette in his car before realising what he'd done and stepping out. *How can I get out of this? Can't go to my family, they'll kill me. I need some time to think.* His phone pinged in the car. A request for an Uber lift. He confirmed his attendance. *Just keep going Barry, until you can work things out.*

Ten minutes later, Barry rolled up to collect his fare. A couple were waiting for collection.

"Morning, guys, I'm Barry. Jump in." He sat waiting whilst the male opened the door for his partner and they settled into the back seat. Barry set off. The couple were quiet in the back and he was in no mood to talk so that suited him. Twenty minutes later, he pulled onto a disused garage forecourt which the customers had directed him to, which they were apparently looking to convert into a flat. Barry set the handbrake.

"Here we are." He turned his head and was backhanded across the face. His head whipped sideways, hands grabbed his shoulders, pulling him back, a hood was pulled over his head and all he could see was darkness as a cord tightened around his throat. His driver's door opened, and he started to scream, which was halted as a fist was rammed into his stomach. He buckled, restrained by the noose. Hands grabbed him. The noose relaxed as he was dragged out of the car.

"Get the car inside," said a male voice. Barry hit the ground chest first, winded as he collided with concrete. Hands pulled behind him, his wrists and ankles were quickly tied. He felt his whole body lifted from the ground as he was moved. The slam of a car door and an engine approaching became louder and echoed off walls. *I'm inside a building.* Barry heard the rattle of a chain and a weight descend around his neck and the rasp of links as it tightened.

"Stand up," said a man's voice.

"I can't," he croaked.

"Take your weight or I'll hang you." Barry felt the chain around his neck lifting him. He straightened his tied legs, trying to balance on his toes. Suddenly, the ties around his ankles loosened. He steadied himself.

"Don't kill me," he pleaded.

"SHUT UP," a voice screamed in his ear. A fist drove into his side. Barry yelled. Another fist and a blow to his chest. "I SAID SHUT UP!" Barry whimpered.

"Shall I call him?"

"Yes," replied the same male. "Tell him we've got him." Barry heard footsteps approaching him.

"So you're Barry," spoke a male with a European accent. Footsteps walked around him, he could smell the scent of a strong aftershave, as the steps circled and retreated. Barry was terrified. Scared into silence, retracted within himself. *What now?* The chain tightened and SMASH! as the sound of metal on metal assaulted his ears. He jumped, startled, his feet slipping as he dangled by his neck. He righted himself, toes touching the ground, supporting his weight.

"Now we wait," stated the original male. Someone walked away. Barry heard a door close. He felt alone. Heart pounding, his breathing rapid, Barry tried to calm himself. *I'm still alive.* He waited. His calves cramped, body aching as fear invaded his being. A door opened. Footsteps entered the room.

"Ok, lower him and take the hood off," said a male. *Different though*, thought Barry, *a Londoner*. He heard the scrape of a chair. Pressure behind his knees. The chain loosened and his legs gave way, his backside hitting the chair. Arms steadied him. The leash around his neck loosened and the hood was ripped away. Daylight caused him to squint as his eyes adjusted.

"Water, please," he croaked, his neck aching with the effort. SLAP! Barry's head careened to the side and a hand grabbed his hair pulling his head back.

"Speak only when you're spoken to, son."

"Not his face," said the Londoner. "Get him a drink." The hand released, pushing his head away, the weight of chains remained collared on his neck and shoulders. Barry looked through his tears, his cheek burning. He was inside the garage. Disused equipment lying around with a car lift standing in front of him. He looked up and followed the chain from his neck up to a block in the ceiling. A woman walked towards him with a bottle of water and raised it to his lips, pouring it slowly. He drank from the bottle, feeling the caress of warm water soothing his throat. A loud clap of hands and he jumped.

"EYES FORWARD!" Then quietly, "We're going to have a chat." Barry braced himself. This wasn't going too well and he couldn't see it getting better. *I'm gonna die*, was all he could think. Fingers clicked in front of his face. "Snap out of it, Barry, or you will." The male knew what he was thinking. "Let's start with your family."

* * *

Barry limped into his flat. He studied himself in a mirror. Just a slight cut to his lip. He peeled off his sweat-soaked shirt, observing the reddened marks and bruising that was beginning to appear on his torso. It hurt to inhale, the red marks on his neck and wrists were prominent but would fade. He turned the shower on and limped to the kitchen, where he ran cold water into a glass. His whole body screamed but he was alive. *You're still alive.* Returning to the bathroom, Barry stripped naked as the steam from the shower clouded the air. His mobile phone sounded and on checking the screen he read the message and dropped the phone onto the floor. He walked into the shower, sat down, and curled his knees to his chest, holding them tightly with his arms. The family wanted to see him tomorrow. '*Ten a.m. sharp. Don't be late*'. Barry began to sob, the fear of his predicament overwhelming him.

* * *

Jane and Jack turned left from the subway station onto Bellariastrasse, Vienna, heading towards the crossroads ahead of them. Jack's demeanour displayed none of the tension that Jane was feeling within. The drive from Naples had given them plenty of time to get to know each other. Jack had arranged everything and advised her where they were going but had not explained the exact nature of why they were there. She'd decided to just go along for the ride and see where it took her, knowing that she was in safe hands.

"Left at the crossroads," said Jack as they approached the junction. Jane was again dressed in her smart black dress and Jack had purchased a light cardigan for her and a large shoulder bag for any shopping that they may do. He was dressed smartly in a shirt and trousers but had purchased a Fedora on the way to Austria. He was now also using a stick to aid his walking. He'd surprised Jane when he'd produced it from the boot of the car earlier in the day, causing her to question his health. Jack had advised her that it was a prop and teasingly told her that all would become clear in time. Frustrating though he was, Jane couldn't help but enjoy the cocky sureness of Jack and the thrill and excitement that he made her feel.

The journey had allowed them to discuss the job in Italy and, if Jane was honest, criminals though they were, she felt in awe of his abilities and of his sheer audacity in his chosen profession of burglary. Later today they would fly back to the UK, but first a trip to the National History Museum. Now at the junction, they turned left and took a leisurely walk down Museum-Platz and turned left once again onto Museum-Theresien-Platz. Jane halted.

"Absolutely beautiful," she said in awe of the architecture and gardens. Confronted on either side by two identical buildings facing each other, with gardens in front of both, which again reflected each other. People leisurely strolled through the walkways, admiring both buildings, or were sitting in areas admiring the gardens, enjoying coffee or just taking in the majesty of the area.

"We're going left," said Jack. "The Natural History Museum. The other building is the Museum of Fine Arts. I take it that you're impressed."

"Who wouldn't be," she replied, looking towards the left-hand building. "You're just showing off," she shoved his shoulder playfully.

"Not quite," he guided her to an empty bench where they sat down. "We have a job to do here."

"Not steal something? Surely not!"

"Quietly, Jane." He coughed and smiled at an elderly couple who walked passed. "More like, making a delivery." Jack had positioned his walking cane across his lap, the rounded handle pointing towards Jane. "I have an item which I believe may belong to them and I'd like them to take a look." Jane smiled.

"Right, an artefact. Do we have an appointment?"

"Not quite. It's not quite that simple." Jane looked confused. Jack leant forward and whispered.

"I stole it from somewhere else when on another job. I think it's been missing for a while." Jane continued looking at him awaiting further explanation. "To keep it simple, Jane. They have a copy of it in there." He discreetly pointed towards the museum. "We are going to go in, you are going to cause a distraction, and I'm going to place the jewel I have next to the copy. Then we're going to leave."

"Cause a distraction," she nodded, sitting back as if taking it in her stride. She grabbed his arm. "Are you bloody mad?!" she whispered.

"Probably, but don't worry. You are going to be terrific." He smiled at her. Jack explained his plan.

* * *

Twenty minutes later, the couple walked up to the formidable double-winged building and walked through the visitors' entrance. They headed to the payment desk where Jack paid their entry fees. Jane placed her handbag on a desk where it was quickly checked and both walked through a metal detector causing no alarms.

"Not sure if they usually go to these extremes," Jack whispered, "but we're through so all's good." Jane took his arm as he scanned the area, knowing that both overt and covert security officers would be in the building. CCTV would cover most areas, hence the hat he wore to hide his features. "We need to head to the Mineralogy and Petrography section," he stopped to check the map on the leaflet he held, though Jane knew he had already memorised the layout of the building.

"This way, love," he spoke aloud and took them on a winding route to the halls before approaching hall four. "I'll just nip to the loo, dear. Do go on ahead." He gently guided her towards the room as he headed to the gents. Jane entered to see cabinets full of stones, gemstones and such like. Her job was to identify any security guard within the hall and to stay close.

Jack entered the gents and walked immediately to a cubicle, securing the door behind him. He placed his stick in one corner and removed his jacket and hat, hanging the coat on the back of the door. Looking at the hat, he held it firmly in two hands and pushed it, reversing it inside to out. The light-coloured hat now looked grey. With a similar procedure with his jacket, turning it inside out, he now had a dark jacket. His appearance now changed, to the casual observer, for a short period. Jack took hold of the stick, placing the ferrule on the toilet lid and examined the round wooden handle. Turning the handle clockwise he slowly removed it from the shaft and, locating the clasp, flicked it and, with a click, the handle halved, revealing the Florentine Diamond within. He looked admiringly at it. *Time for a new home*, he thought.

Jack flushed the toilet, picked up the cane and wiped it with an alcohol wipe that he had brought with him. Now having closed the handle, he placed that carefully in his right jacket pocket and the diamond in his left, he exited the cubicle and headed to hall four. Halting before the hall, he spotted an old fashioned coat stand acting as a sentry, its base holding umbrellas for the use of discerning customers who had anticipated inclement weather. He placed the cane in the holder, leaving no forensic trace as he pocketed the alcoholic wipe and entered the hall quickly.

CCTV covering the room. Security guard to the right. Jane's with him. It's busy. Jack walked slowly, navigating towards the cabinet that held the rhinestone copy of the stone. Jane would know that he was approaching.

"Hello there." He heard her raised English voice. "I wonder if you could help me?" He moved to the cabinet, seeing the copy sitting majestically on a white clothed background. "A man is acting suspiciously out by the ladies toilets."

Jack glanced towards the security guard who started transmitting a message on his radio. He sensed quick movement to his right and saw a plain-clothed male moving swiftly to the hall and exit. *Security*, he thought. Jane followed the guards. "Just out there," she raised her arm swiftly and pointed, mistakenly backhanding a young male across the face. "Oh, I'm so sorry," she said and moved to the male, knocking him further off balance into the coat stand, which toppled over. Jack moved, the audience watching the altercation.

Reaching in his pockets, Jack pulled out the wooden handle and the diamond. With backs turned to him, he released sudden focussed violence, smashing the metal screw on the base of the cane handle against the Florentine cabinet. The cabinet moved. The screw bent. He placed the diamond on top of the casing and walked away. An audible alarm sounded. Heads turned.

The plain-clothed guard ran back in, hand to his ear, listening. He pushed past people towards the Florentine. Jack walked casually to the exit and towards Jane. She was ready and took his arm as they walked into the corridor, joining a stream of people exiting the halls and being ushered out by staff members. They all headed down the stairs, towards the exit and out of the building into the gardens. On leaving the building, Jack casually removed his hat and jacket as Jane took off her cardigan. All were placed in Jane's shopping bag. They headed on a return route to Bellariastrasse and their final destination, the airport.

* * *

The security guards had swiftly cleared hall four and were awaiting the arrival of their supervisor and the director of the museum. Well-practised protocols had been followed and the security team were confident that they had protected the assets within the museum. However, on this occasion they had an anomaly. It appeared that someone had left them an item.

The head of security and the director walked over to the cabinet in question. Within sat the untouched rhinestone copy of the Florentine. Sitting upon the case was what appeared to be a replica, slightly yellower in colour. The director moved forward with gloved hands and gently lifted the stone. He looked at it closely.

"Surely not!" he exclaimed, turning to the room, a large smile lighting his face. Behind him, placed on top of the cabinet and ignored, for the moment, sat a business card with the image of a hare thereon.

* * *

"That hits the mark," said Jane sipping on a glass of white wine at the airport. Jack was sitting opposite, nursing a glass of red wine. They had both melted into the crowds at the airport. Their discarded clothing items were now placed in a public waste bin en route to the subway station. Jack had remained calm throughout their 'escape' from the museum and had managed to keep Jane's excitability in check. He looked at her face, enjoying the slight flush in her cheeks and the delicate manner in which she sipped her wine. She caught him watching her.

"What are you looking at?" she chuckled.

"A master criminal's accomplice."

"I know! What have I got myself into?"

"What indeed? You look to be enjoying it though."

"I'm loving it. I know it's wrong. I know I shouldn't but it feels right." Her diction increased with her enthusiasm. Jack laughed.

"It's addictive," he replied.

"It is. I've moved on from being a boring security adviser."

"You still are," he interjected. Jane sat back with feigned shock, "I don't mean boring," he quickly interjected, "I mean you still work at the B of E." She smiled.

"Yes, but I feel so much more than that now. I feel alive."

"What about your morals?" Jack laughed. "This is my life. I made my decision years ago. What about you?"

"I've thought a lot about things. We've only really stolen from bad people, criminals if you like."

"What about the bank?"

"A mere drop in the ocean for them. It won't affect anything. They'll be too scared to report it 'officially'. It will be like it's never happened. And," she paused, taking a further sip of wine, "we may do some good with the money. Let's face it, we've just given something back to the museum."

She pointed towards a large television screen in the bar where Sky News was broadcasting an image of Vienna's Natural History Museum. The picture changed to that of the Florentine Diamond sitting beside the rhinestone copy. Jack could see the corner of his calling card poking out from under the stone. A caption underneath read.

The Florentine Diamond mysteriously surfaces in Vienna following years of speculation.

Jane watched Jack as he read the caption, enjoying the smile that it brought to his face. He checked his watch.

"Come on. They'll be calling us for our flight in five." He returned their glasses to the bar and both headed to catch their plane to London.

Chapter 8

Simeon Fortescue was enjoying a cup of tea which had dutifully been brought to him by his wife following a light dinner. He glanced over at her, sitting in an armchair, sipping daintily from her china tea cup. He did love her but for him, she offered no excitement. She never had really but he knew that he was partly to blame for that. Simeon had lived the life that he had chosen, done the things that he had wanted to, and over the years had worn Mrs Fortescue down, adapting her into the woman that he wanted. A woman who was there at his beck and call, who was servile to him and who would tolerate his ways. In this modern world he would be seen as a dinosaur, cruel and uncaring. However, in his own eyes he was happy that he provided his wife with a good standard of living, and if she needed to tolerate his behaviour to have that lifestyle, then so be it. He smiled at her.

"Let's put the news on, dear." He made no move to reach for the television remote control, allowing her to stand up and fetch it back to her chair. She switched the television on and navigated the channels until she located Sky News which showed the image of a large ornate building in Austria. She smiled, admiring the beautiful architecture as a newsreader was filmed in the gardens outside. The picture changed to an inside shot and two large diamonds sitting next to each other within a display case, a white business card with a black image sitting between them. The bottom of the screen displayed the words *Florentine Diamond reappears after years missing.*

"Oooh, they look stunning," she said. Simeon sprayed tea over his shirt and dropped his cup and saucer on the floor. Mrs Fortescue jumped in fright, "Are you OK?"

"Turn up the sound, woman," he replied, ignoring the fallen crockery.

"... suddenly turned up yesterday afternoon, following an alarm activation within the building. The diamond is believed to be authentic and was found placed on top of the cabinet. Staff remain confused as to how it arrived there and who their mysterious benefactor could be?"

Simeon stood up and strode towards the doorway to his study.

"I'll be in my study." He left the room, leaving his wife to clean up the mess he had created. Simeon went directly to his study, removed his shirt and placed on a light dressing gown. He was fuming. *The cocky little bastard.* He picked up the landline. He needed to make some calls. *There's no way he's going to get away with this.*

* * *

"Thank you very much, young lady," said Keith as Jane handed him the wristwatch which she had been wearing. He gave it a quick look over. "Very nice too. That's them all," he said to Terry. Five watches sat on a green baize cloth before him, all stolen in the burglary, and now placed next to a small array of stolen platinum, gold and diamond jewellery.

"You gonna be able to shift them OK?" asked Terry.

"Oh, yes. No problem at all. I have a man who deals in watches and a lady who deals in jewellery. They've seen some images and are keen. I'll get good money for them and they'll sell them at a good profit. Possibly into mainland Europe. Who knows, maybe our Sicilian friend will eventually be able to buy them back." He laughed, wrapping up the bundle and placing it in his briefcase.

The team had all gathered in the back room of a disused shop on the outskirts of London. Keith had provided them with a large flask of coffee and a packet of Hobnobs. Ronnie's image watched them all from an iPad which had been placed upon a small table.

"Not the most salubrious of surroundings," stated Terry, gesturing around them, "but needs must. Where's the money, Ronnie?"

"Tommy syphoned it into a few offshore accounts. I have all the details and can access any of them at any time. It's all secure."

"Good stuff." He addressed the rest of the team. "Ronnie's controlling the money. Anything you need to buy or do for your part of the job then go through her. Anything too extravagant she'll contact me. Let's try and keep it sensible though. We had a good tickle in Italy but she's not holding Hermione's handbag. Right?" Murmured assent was his reply. "And, Jack."

"Yes, Terry."

"No more Austria, please. Very noble but we need to keep our heads down."

"Of course," he replied, looking at Jane who smiled at him. Terry saw but ignored the look.

"Right, told you it wouldn't take long. You all know your jobs. I'll be in contact with the details of our next meeting. We need to make some progress now, set a date and focus. Keep safe out there." The team dispersed aiming for the front and back doors, timing their departures to leave discreetly.

* * *

Robert Harrison walked into the enquiry office bristling, the team immediately feeling his tension, as he strode through the room.

"Detective Inspector, my office," he stated, slamming his office door behind him. Ali Smith rose from his chair.

"Any update from the Austrian job?"

"Nothing, Ali," replied Hazel. "We're still awaiting any intelligence. You know how it is with all the red tape."

"Somehow, I don't think that's going to help me," he replied, putting on his suit jacket and heading to Harrison's office.

"Good luck," said Hazel. He knocked and entered. Harrison was standing behind his desk, glaring at the door, his anger palpable within the room.

"Shut the door." Ali did so.

"Sit down." Ali took a seat at the desk. Harrison remained standing and paced.

"Now listen carefully, Ali. I have had my backside chewed by the Grand Master who is not happy with the progress that I, and that means you, are making." DI Smith started to speak. "Don't even think of interrupting," spat Harrison. "We, that means you," he pointed at Ali, "have a moral responsibility, an obligation, to look after the best interests of the Lodge."

"And also the public," interjected Ali. Harrison spun round slamming both hands on his desk and loomed over Ali.

"Don't be smart with me, Inspector. I put you here to help you. I can just as easily take it away. Mr Fortescue is not happy. Not happy with me, not happy with you. I'm not happy with you!"

"But I'm trying. He covers his tracks, leaving no clues."

"You're a bloody Detective, Smith. Find some!" Harrison's voice now simmered in quietened anger. "I will not be dragged down either in the Lodge, or the service, due to your incompetence. Pull your finger out and find him." He turned his back on Ali.

"Sir." Harrison heard the scrape of the chair and Smith's footsteps retreat as he exited the room. *Right, Covert Human Intelligence Unit next. They're in need of a good bollocking too.* He picked up his phone and texted Simeon informing him that things were progressing.

"I bloody hope that they are by the end of the day," he said aloud.

* * *

Dressed in a hoodie and jogging pants, Jack strolled within Boundary Estate, E17, Walthamstow heading towards his sister's place. As a rule, he didn't go on the estate too often, just enough to maintain a presence and to check on the welfare of his sister and her kid. He entered the bottom of one of the blocks, headed up the stairwell to his sister's flat, knocked on the door and entered. The sound of Call of Duty assaulted his ears from the wide-screen television that dominated the room. Jack grabbed the television remote from the tired sofa arm and reduced the sound.

"Oi," yelled his nephew, spinning around, "Uncle Jack!" He threw down his Playstation remote control and ran to Jack, wrapping his arms around his Uncle's waist.

"Howdy, Champ. You winning?" Jack crouched down to cuddle the young seven-year-old Christopher, who hugged him briefly, then stood back and looked at Jack, Christopher's head leaning to one side.

"Of course I am," he replied.

"You sure? Looked like you were getting your butt kicked there."

"Was not." Chris punched Jack on the shoulder.

"Where's your mum?"

"Kitchen," Christopher returned to his game.

Jack looked around the room. One small two-seat sofa and a threadbare armchair. The television was large and looked new. *Probably bought off the back of a lorry,* thought Jack. The floor was poorly laid laminate with various toys strewn about it and the walls needed a lick of paint. *I need to get you out of here.*

"Hi, sis," he said walking into the kitchen where his scrawny younger sister was standing washing the dishes. "I told you that you need to keep that front door locked. Anyone could walk in."

"Hi, Jack. I forgot. Sorry." Jack's sister was petite and skinny, and though younger than him, looked tired and older. The strain of living in a one-bedroom flat was telling on her. Sharing a bed with Christopher and just trying to earn some money to pay her way wasn't working out for her. Tania had mixed with the wrong crowd as a youth and her subsequent choice of partners had been dubious. She loved Christopher but his father was nowhere to be seen and hadn't been for eighteen months now. She had been adamant that she wanted no help from Jack and he had not interfered except to keep an eye on her. Jack looked around the kitchen which was clean and smelled fresh.

"How are you coping? Haven't seen you for a while," he asked.

"We're doing OK. Can't complain."

"Found a job yet?"

"Only bits here and there. It's hard to find something just to cover school hours. Chris is doing well at school though," she smiled up at him, handing him a mug of coffee.

"How about you? You're looking well."

"You know how it is. Been busy working outside a lot." Tania never asked him what he did for a living. She was just happy that he was well and seemed to be getting by. "Just so you know I'm gonna be off the scene for a while."

"You're not in trouble are you?"

"No, course not. Just working away. Thought I'd call and drop Chris some pocket money." He took a small roll of cash from his pocket, taking out twenty pounds and handing it to her.

"You don't need to," said Tania.

"I like to. I may miss your birthday too." He handed Tania fifty more pounds.

"It's not for a couple of months!"

"I know but I could be back after that." He pushed the cash towards her, knowing that she would go along with the pretence that he wasn't helping her out. Tania took the cash, placed it in a pocket and lifted her drink from the sideboard. The volume of the television rose in the living room.

"How do you put up with that?" asked Jack, nudging the door closed.

"You get used to it," she replied, "You should hear him when he's on with his mates. The screaming is terrible. If the neighbours weren't pissed all the time I'm sure they'd be braying on the walls."

"You need to get out of here."

"Yeah and how's that ever gonna happen?" She stared into space, any hope dead in her eyes.

"You never know," said Jack, the light of hope in his eyes in contrast to Tania's, "Anyway, better sacrifice myself and show Chris how to play this game properly."

"Go for it, Rambo," she replied. Jack walked into the living room, grabbed a PS controller and launched himself onto the sofa beside Christopher.

"Who shall I be?" asked Jack.

"Sniper," replied Christopher. Tania watched them, smiling at the family resemblance between them and wondered how she could ever get out of the squalor of her life.

* * *

A flatbed, transit van and Ford Focus entered the Thistlebrook estate driving towards the back of the compound.

"That's the last of them, Granda," said a young twelve-year-old who cycled past on his BMX. Pat raised his hand, acknowledging the message, knowing that his Grandson would move back to the entrance of the estate, keeping an eye out for the muskers. It was unlikely that they'd come onto the estate, at least in a single patrol car. When they did come, they came mob-handed with police cars, transits, dogmen, the lot. Pat wasn't expecting a police raid, he'd have heard if there was to be one, but it was always better to act with caution. He finished supping his mug of tea, placed the cup down and lifted himself from the deckchair which groaned in relief. Pat shrugged his shoulders, loosening his muscles.

"Dat dem all here, Pat?" said a woman from within his caravan. A red-haired female poked her hair out from the caravan door squinting at him. He looked at her and smiled.

"Sure is. We need to get you some specs, pet."

"I'll manage," she replied. "You be gentle with them now."

"Indeed I will."

"But don't take any shit, I tell ya."

"I won't." He walked away with a smile loving his Irish wife's bluntness. He knew she was a good one and wouldn't change her for the world. *Hard as nails like*, he thought.

He strolled through the camp, greeting or nodding to his friends and family as he passed. The men that he'd invited today would be parked near the rear wash house where he'd called a meeting. All would know that the police had an overt CCTV camera on the front of the site so had travelled in cars known by the police.

On site it was different. Although not impossible it was unlikely that the police would have any covert cameras on the site. Pat knew that the washroom was safe as he had it checked weekly, sometimes daily for any secreted devices. He used an RFD wand when searching, which would detect any electronic signal transmission. He'd had it checked first thing this morning and was happy that it was safe. One of his sons was sitting on guard outside the block smoking a reefer, the sweet pungent aroma of cannabis drifting in the air.

"All good, Da."

"Good lad, Alf." Pat walked into the washroom where several males were standing waiting and chatting to each other.

"Morning, lads," boomed Pat, arms wide open in greeting.

"Pat," responded various voices.

"Thanks for coming. Much appreciated. It's cramped but it's safe and we need to talk business." The males quietened waiting for him to continue. "I won't keep you long as I know you want to be out grafting, drinking and shagging." His comment brought some laughs from the group.

"Not Jimmy over there," shouted out a voice, "he won't have taken his Viagra yet today." The men laughed.

"Cheeky bastard," said a middle-aged balding male.

"He's only joking," interjected Pat laughing, "your Mary's told me that's not even working for you!" The balding man frowned at Pat and then burst into laughter along with the others. "Enough, lads. Enough," said Pat, his voice raised, "I've not brought you here to practise me stand-up routine. Down to business." The room quietened. "I've been given a job to do and I need some help," he paused for dramatic effect.

"Go on then," voiced a male.

"Five ATMs, one night. All in the city. We all get paid and we get to keep everything that we nick."

"Get away!" voiced the same male.

"Not joking," clarified Pat.

"How much we getting paid?" asked Jimmy.

"Five hundred before and five hundred after."

"For each ATM?" another voice.

"Per man," he said "For every man on the job," he clarified.

"I'm in," said Jimmy. Pat smiled to himself. Despite the piss-taking, he knew that if he had Jimmy, then they'd all do it. Jimmy was a respected member of the community, an expert in his field and they all knew it.

"We'll need some more specialists," continued Jimmy. "They've got some good guys up north, Manchester way."

"What do we need them for?" asked a male called Casey Jr.

"They know how to blow the ATMs. They've been training up there with the acetylene. Quickest way to do them, then straight out onto a four by four and away. We'll need them if we're doing five."

"What area in the city?" Pat produced a map from his back pocket.

"Old school, eh?" said Casey Jnr.

"Shut up, ya fool," said Jimmy, "ya might just learn something." The males gathered around as Pat spread the map on the floor between them.

* * *

"What do you think?" Keith looked at Terry who walked around the small garage examining the vehicles.

"They look OK, mate. Little things aren't they."

"They are but with a bit of work they'll do what you need."

Keith had taken Terry on a short trip out of the city to a disused garage where he had stashed the cars. Sitting proudly were two Citroen 2 CVs.

"How do they drive?" asked Terry.

"They're OK and will be great when tuned," replied Keith, smiling. "Can't help but smile when you get behind the wheel. When you get them altered they'll be flying machines."

"What about a third car?"

"Still working on it."

"Are the lads ready for them?"

"Yep, expecting delivery of one this morning."

"Which one?"

"Doesn't matter to them. They just need to take a look around one. You tell them exactly what you want and they'll get cracking."

"You got the money?"

"Yes." Keith patted the pocket of his red draped jacket.

"What we waiting for then? Let's take the red one. Matches your coat." Keith threw the keys to Terry and walked towards the garage door, opening it as Terry gently pulled the vehicle out onto some hard standing. The area was a quiet part of the suburbs with run-down manufacturing businesses and disused warehouses dominating the architecture. Keith climbed in.

"Steady out of here, Tel. It's quiet but let's not draw any attention to ourselves. We need to get the other one moved out safely also."

"We on the original plates?"

"Yes. I've got some false ones on order. The cars are legit. Well, apart from no insurance on them."

"Where'd you get them?" Keith looked at Terry with a frown. Terry could feel him looking at him.

"Sorry, mate. Force of habit."

"They won't be traced to us. I haven't nicked them." They moved away from the area and moved into traffic heading towards a small village where the Ball brothers worked.

"How we getting back?" asked Terry.

"There's a car up there already. We'll bring that back. Left here Tel, there's some open road for you. Terry took the turning, slowly accelerating after the junction. "S bend ahead." Terry shuffled in his seat, gently positioned the car on the road, increased his acceleration slightly and prepared for the bend.

"Let's see how she handles." Keith placed one hand on the dashboard. The car moved smoothly into the first corner. Terry maintained his speed, his foot held steadily in position as he felt the car hug the road. A smile broke through the concentration on his face. Holding the wheel gently but firmly, he came out of the first corner, slipping easily into the next bend. Again, with the speed maintained, he looked carefully ahead, watching for the natural break in the corner where the road would start opening up in front of him. *There you are*, he thought as he saw the point. He increased his acceleration. *Let's see what you've got.* The car came shooting out of the chicane at speed with Terry whooping aloud; a large grin on his face and Keith grimacing next to him.

"Terrific!" shouted Terry, "When we get this engine altered it'll fly." He continued accelerating on the straight stretch away from the bend.

* * *

"Left here. It's a little bit bumpy so take it easy." Keith released his hold on the car with both hands having coped with the wantonness of Terry's driving. "There's a hangar down at the end where the lads run their workshop." Terry slowly negotiated the grass-verged lane avoiding a couple of small potholes as he drove. The lane started widening and soon opened into a small yard area with a green metallic hangar to one side. Tarpaulins covered the shape of two vehicles and as Terry had expected a couple of cars awaiting repair stood lined up next to the tarps.

"We can park near the hangar doors, mate. They're expecting us." Terry slowed the vehicle, halted at the front, cut the engine and opened the driver's door. He turned to Keith whose pallid complexion looked back at him.

"You OK, son?"

"I've been better," replied Keith, opening his door.

"What's up with you man? That was great fun."

"Maybe for you," said Keith. "Did you say that you'd passed your driving test?"

"Cheeky bastard," laughed Terry, "We're here in one piece aren't we?"

"I think I've survived. Not sure about my trousers though!" Keith climbed out of the car checking his backside as he did so.

"All clear there, you soft git," clarified Terry after watching Keith extract himself. Terry managed to get his right leg out of the car and peel himself from the vehicle. "Cosy fit though, I must admit." He stretched out his arms unlocking the stiffness in his body following the speedy ride. Keith walked to a small entrance door of the hangar, knocked and entered. Terry strode over and followed him in.

Vehicle parts lay strewn around the outskirts of the main workspace. The shell of a black MG BGT stood with its bonnet open; parts of a disassembled engine spewing from its mouth. towards the back stood a car lift holding an old 2 CV suspended in mid-air. The smell of steel, petrol and engine oil dominated the air whilst the clang of a hammer striking metal assaulted their ears. Terry pointed towards the 2 CV looking at Keith.

"BASTARD!" shouted a male, the hammering swiftly halted. "That fucking hurt!" The grimy face of an elderly male, wearing a flat cap, appeared from behind a workbench, clutching his left hand under his right armpit. "You useless piece of crap!" He kicked out at something unseen, walking away from the bench in disgust, seemingly oblivious to Keith and Terry.

"Now then lads. How are you?" Keith and Terry both jumped at the sound of a man's voice behind them. "Steady now, it's only me." They turned to see another elderly gentleman, balding with a white fringe of hair and thick spectacles, chuckling to himself. He held a dirty rag, which was seemingly depositing more oil on his palms than it was removing, as he tried to wipe them clean. "Don't mind Goose over there, he's just struggling with a seized piston." He stuck his hand out to shake their hands. "I'm Dougal. I take it you are Keith and Terry. Terry opened his mouth to speak as Dougal took his hand. "No, no, don't tell me." He looked at the men thoughtfully. "You are Terry," he released Terry's hand and took Keith's, "which makes you Keith. Am I right?" he asked, standing back.

"Indeed you are, young man," replied Keith. Dougal beamed.

"Always been good at putting names to faces," replied Dougal. "It's a talent." He started walking away, towards the area where Goose was working. Keith and Terry remained now, rubbing their hands as Dougal turned to look at them.

"Come on, lads. Look lively, I'll make us a brew," he turned and continued walking. The men looked at each other. "Nice outfit, Keith. Takes me back." Keith smiled, pleased with the compliment. He nudged Terry and they both followed. Terry leaned in close to Keith.

"They're a couple of pensioners!" he whispered.

"Yep and they also come with a gold star recommendation, Tel. Trust me, they'll sort the cars for us." They walked over to a bench upon which was an old cheap kettle and some stained mugs. Dougal introduced them to his brother, Goose.

"Your hand OK?" asked Terry.

"Bloody hurts but it'll be fine," he replied.

"Tea or coffee?" asked Dougal. Both men selected coffee and watched as Dougal scooped a hefty spoonful of Mellow Birds into two cups, poured in hot water and, after sniffing a carton and frowning, poured some milk into each. He handed them each a mug. "Goose?"

"Coffee, please." Dougal reached under the bench, lifted out an old cloth bait bag and produced a large thermos flask from within, followed by two dark blue Denby mugs. He casually poured himself and his brother a drink and took a sip from his own. "Lovely," he stated aloud. "Now, down to business. What are you after?"

"Conversion of three cars. All Citroen 2 CVs. I need them race-ready but also capable of taking a heavy load if needed." The mechanics knew better than to ask why. They also knew that the financial reward to complete the work was substantial.

"Timescale?" asked Goose.

"Three weeks. Four at a push." Goose whistled. "We'd have to work at full tilt. Also, put some other jobs on hold," he said to Dougal.

"Aye," replied Dougal.

"When can we have the cars?" asked Goose.

"I've brought one with me. The other one later today," Dougal broke from staring into space. "and I'd like that one," finished Terry, gesturing to the 2 CV on the car lift. "Is it for sale?"

"Can be," said Goose, "It'll cost you though."

"That's fine," said Terry.

"So, 2 CVs. Air-cooled engine, front wheel drive, excellent suspension and a four-speed transmission. Quirky little thing."

"It is, but we need it to be better." Dougal looked at Goose, ignoring their customers. "We need to upgrade the engine."

"What you thinking?"

"Rip it out and put a Ducati Panigale V4 in." Goose pondered the suggestion.

"That should raise it to about 200 bhp. It'll need a turbo chip and a new tailpipe." Goose started taking notes. Keith and Terry watched as the men discussed the conversion. Keith sipped on the coffee and nearly spat it out. Both men placed their cups carefully on the bench. Dougal looked at Terry.

"Carrying a passenger?" he asked.

"Yes, driver and passenger." Dougal turned to Goose.

"Take the back seats out, remove the passenger seat, and replace that with a lightweight one." Terry placed the Citroen car keys on the bench as Keith leaned in and whispered.

"Let's leave them to it and get the other car." Terry gave a thumbs up and they walked away listening to the two men working.

"Door cards out," said Goose.

"Headlining and carpets," clarified Dougal.

"Rally fuel tank in,"

"Run flats?"

"Maybe." The men continued planning.

* * *

Ronnie was standing in the kitchen, staring out of the window at their small green square of garden. The neighbour's cat was, yet again, positioning itself to defecate in the back right-hand corner of a small flower bed. She swiftly opened the door, causing the cat to jump onto the fence and bound into another garden.

"A win there, Veronica," she said aloud, halting in the doorway and breathing in the freshness of the morning. She admired cats, although would never choose to own one herself. They were free spirits. Walked where they liked, ate where they liked and flitted between different people as they saw fit. *No one really owns a cat,* she thought. *The cat chooses to do as it pleases and fits in where it wants to.* Veronica wished that she could be so carefree but her mind kept her imprisoned in this house. She loved her mother, the house was OK and it was her comfort zone but seeing the team so active in the UK and now working abroad. Wow!

That was something! Something Veronica knew that she was missing out on. Feeling brave, she stepped out of the door and inhaled deeply.

"Today's the day, Veronica. Carpe diem and all that." She checked her wristwatch. Jane would be arriving within the hour and Veronica needed to get ready. Her mother was already dressed and this morning they were going to take her to a Women's Institute meeting where her friends would look after her. Jane and Veronica had other plans. They were going to visit family, at the gold soap production house, and see how they were getting on. Ronnie could already feel her nervousness building, the butterflies fluttering and an urgent need to run to the toilet. The thought of leaving the house terrified her but Jane was there to support her. Deliberately, she took a further step into the garden knowing that today could be her first step towards freedom.

Jane arrived at nine-thirty rapping excitedly on the door as well as pressing the doorbell.

"I'll get it, Mum. It's Jane," yelled Ronnie from her den. Dressed in jeans and a Black Sabbath t-shirt she walked to the door, opening it slowly and greeted Jane.

"You ready?" asked Jane, smiling at Ronnie.

"Well, I've opened the door, so that's the first step. I'll fetch Mum." She walked towards the living room leaving Jane on the doorstep with the door ajar. "Right, Mum. We're going." Her mother had just switched on the daytime television and was fluffing the cushions in her chair ready to settle in for the morning.

"Going where, dear?"

"That meeting I told you about. The one with your friends. You're meeting up with them for a coffee and a chat. The WI, Mum," Ronnie clarified, raising the pitch of her voice to help her mum hear.

"I'm not deaf, Veronica. Of course, I remember. It just slipped my mind. Now, where's my handbag?" Veronica looked around and spotted it neatly stored in the magazine rack. She recovered it and held it out to her mum. "Ah, there it is. Thank you, dear."

"You won't need a coat, your cardi will do." They both walked towards the front door and Jane.

"Good morning, Mrs Pilcher. How are you?"

"I'm fine, dear."

"Can you take Mum to the car?" asked Ronnie. "I'll lock up." Jane guided Mrs Pilcher down the path to her car and helped her get in the front passenger seat. Ronnie returned to the house.

"Come on, Veronica. You can do this," Ronnie said aloud. Her stomach still churned and she noticed that her hands were shaking. *It's just the adrenalin*, she thought. Grabbing her stuff from her room, she grabbed her front door keys and froze in the hallway. *Get a grip of yourself, woman*, her mind screamed. She heard footsteps on the path and forced herself to move to the door.

Jane had entered the front garden, having settled Mrs Pilcher into the car, and walked up the path to the house. She realised that today was a big step for Ronnie to take but also that it was important to her to do it. The front door remained open as Jane approached and Ronnie appeared from behind it. Jane silenced a laugh. Ronnie stood in the doorway wearing jeans, a green bomber jacket, black bucket hat and sunglasses and was holding tightly to the door.

"I don't know if I can do this."

"You can, Ronnie. You're a strong woman."

"I'm absolutely shitting myself."

"You can still do it. Come on. Your mum's in the car waiting and we don't want her absentmindedly wandering off." The mention of her mother triggered something in Ronnie. *Mum will need me. If she can cope I can.* Ronnie stepped out of the door and pulled it slowly shut behind her. Jane approached her.

"Here," she held out an elbow. "Grab my arm. We'll go together." Ronnie linked her arm in and with effort released the front door handle. They walked tentatively down the path, Ronnie slightly crouched in posture as if the world was a weight upon her shoulders.

"Your mum's still there," said Jane as they approached the Fiat. "You squeeze in behind me." Jane opened the driver's door allowing Ronnie to clamber into the back, then climbed into the driver's seat herself, closing the door. Ronnie felt a tightness in her chest easing with the proximity of the car shell around her.

"Steady drive, please," she said to Jane.

"No problem," replied Jane, "you're doing great by the way." Ronnie smiled. *You're a good 'un*, she thought.

Chapter 9

Fortescue had been fuming when he had telephoned. As a result, and now for the umpteenth time, Digby sat watching a digital recording of the newscast regarding the recovery of the Florentine. The Hare's calling card taunted him as he zoomed in on its image. Austria, indeed the world, had reported the story, and the museum was 'eternally grateful' to the unknown person who had brought the stone home. *They think that he or she is a bloody saint.* The activation of the alarm and terrifying the public at the museum had drifted into the ether and, although the press wished to know who had returned the item, the museum were merely satisfied that the diamond had reappeared. John slammed his computer shut, grabbed a cigarette and headed outside with his mind churning.

Dragging deeply on his cigarette, he inhaled and felt the immediate calm as the nicotine infused into his body. He knew that smoking was bad for him, knew that nicotine didn't physically calm anything and was actually a stimulant, but like many others, he was hooked on it. He looked to his right where a young man in a shirt and tie strolled up and down, talking on his mobile phone whilst vaping from a coloured device. To his left, a down-and-out combed the pavement looking for stub ends and a homeless male sat on folded cardboard, hand-rolling a cigarette. John took his cig from his mouth and looked at the burning end before throwing it away. *The world's fucked,* he thought, walking back into the hotel not seeing the stub collector pouncing on his half-finished cigarette and collecting the prized possession. John walked towards the hotel reception.

"Any messages for me? Room 131."

"Just let me check, Sir." The receptionist quickly flicked through her computer screen holding a forced smile on her face. "A parcel was delivered late last night, Sir. I'll just get it." She turned to a locked cabinet behind her and retrieved a padded envelope from within handing it over. "I see that you are checking out today, Sir. Checkout is by ten, please. Unless you want to extend your stay?"

"No, I'll be leaving thanks."

"Would you like to settle your account now, Sir?"

"I guess so." The woman went through the process of calculating and printing his invoice and John tapped his card against the card reader. She smiled at him.

"Thank you, Sir. I hope you have enjoyed your stay. Is there anything else I can do for you?"

"No thanks, luv." he turned and walked away. The receptionist returned to her other duties. In a fit of energy John took the stairs. He had an hour before leaving and tapping the envelope as he climbed he was keen to look at its contents. A parcel from Simeon. One which he knew contained footage obtained from the Natural History Museum on the day that the diamond was returned.

Now, having returned to his room John opened his laptop, entered his password and left it to work through the login procedure. He lowered himself onto the bed, opened the envelope and retrieved an encrypted USB stick from within. *Let's see what they've got.* He inserted the USB into a port, entered the password and watched the screen open to reveal an image displaying nine separate camera shots of various areas within the museum. He smiled. *You're in here somewhere.*

John checked the time on the screen noting that the recording started at nine am. The incident had been reported later in the day, he used the keyboard keys to fast-forward the footage to the approximate time. *Too late*, he thought as he viewed an image of one of the galleries which had been cleared of the public, security guards were standing guard at the main entrance and also next to a cabinet within the room. Using the mouse he selected one image which changed the computer screen from displaying nine rooms to displaying the selected room only. John noted the time shown at the bottom of the screen on the envelope. He pressed playback and slowly watched the footage in reverse, searching for the time when the diamond was returned.

John halted the tape, looking closely at the image. *What was that?* He played the scene, rewound and played it again. *Something has happened there.* John had paused the shot. The still image covered the whole room making it impossible to identify people. A woman in a black dress caught his eye as she appeared to be involved in an incident with a man. He looked closely. *No, a guard! That guy's wearing a uniform.* He played it again and sat back laughing. *The silly cow's just backhanded someone.* John re-wound and laughed again at the comedic nature of the video. He paused the shot, and checked his watch, realising that he'd have to pack and leave. Leaving the USB drive in he closed the laptop and placed it back in its case. Jacket now on, John tapped his pockets and spoke aloud.

"Cigs, wallet, lighter," he chucked his overnight bag on the bed, "clothes, laptop." He tapped his laptop bag and stopped. The image of the lady in the black dress played across his thoughts. He moved to pick up both bags. *Woman in a black dress. Security guard.* Suddenly, the footage appeared to be not as amusing.

"She's the bloody distraction," he said aloud. *Time to move. I need to get somewhere where I can take a good look at this.* John left his hotel room with a grim look on his face. The first decent bit of information that he had uncovered. John barely remembered leaving the building as he headed to the hotel car park.

* * *

Jack walked slowly along Threadneedle Street admiring the architecture of the area as pedestrians whisked by him chasing their busy lives. The bank, known as 'The Old Lady of Threadneedle Street', stood majestically overseeing the monetary flows of the city and ultimately the world, her footprint stamped firmly within the international monetary systems. *No wonder she's never been done,* he thought staring up at the four columns dominating the main entrance. The building was positioned upon a rough granite plinth standing upon its island within the city. *Formidable*, thought Jack. *Undoable? No. Nothing is unachievable.* It was a mindset that had got Jack through life and put him where he was today.

He stepped back, looking at the building's architectural line and the towering glass structure dominating the skyline behind. *That's possible, definitely possible.* Jack continued walking the circumference of the building as he had done many times during the past week. Watching the comings and goings at both front and rear, looking for patterns, anything to give the team an edge. Nothing at ground level had materialised and any opportunity at night was extremely unlikely. The beginnings of a plan were formulating in his mind. He believed it could work but he needed to speak with Jane and Ronnie.

Checking his watch he flicked them both a text requesting a meeting tonight at Ronnie's and offered to bring a takeaway with him. He received an affirmative from both and headed back to Bank underground station to head home, change from his suit and hit the sports centre for practice on the climbing wall and some gym work.

* * *

As the front door opened Jane and Ronnie were overpowered by the scent of patchouli and orange emanating from the house. An aproned figure peeked around the door conspiratorially and beckoned them inside maniacally.

"Quick. Get in," she said, pulling them into the hall and quickly checking the street before closing the door. "You can't be too careful."

"Marge," stated Jane, as if that was the only explanation required for the lady who had opened the door. Ronnie took it in her stride, unflinching at Marge's behaviour just as Marge was unfazed by Ronnie's attire. She put her hand out.

"I'm Ronnie," Marge shook her hand.

"Marge," replied Marge, reciprocating the handshake. *My type of person,* thought Ronnie, as she removed her hat and glasses.

"Where's Jo?" asked Jane.

"Kitchen," came a prompt reply from Marge, who was now peering around a netted curtain covering the left window beside the door.

"This way," said Jane. Ronnie followed, the scent of the soap drawing her forward.

Two people worked within the kitchen standing at work surfaces on either side of a central bench table. Ronnie smiled as she entered seeing the 3D-printed moulds which she had developed sitting in neat rows on the table.

"Hi guys," said Jo. "I'll need you out the back soon. Dangerous chemicals here." Jo looked like a quintessential baker, rotund in figure with a tight bun of hair positioned at an angle on her head, Her ruddy cheeks dimpled as she smiled at them both. Wearing a patterned apron, goggles balanced on her head, and a surgical face mask dangling around her neck she portrayed a confusing image. Recognising their confusion she clarified.

"It's all chemistry, ladies." They looked around at various drying racks, jugs, liquids, powders and waxes, accompanied by weighing scales, three microwaves, whisks, spatulas and spoons. "Chemical compounds working together to create soap. We're just mixing the next batch. Nip out the back and you'll see Gav with the finished product." She ushered them through the kitchen and out of the back door into a yard where a large garden shed was standing.

"Bollocks," said a man's voice from within the structure and with a rattle of the lock and shuffle of foot, a tall man walked from the shed bumping his head on the way out. The male wore blue overalls, yellow marigolds and had a curly mop of hair. He was wearing spectacles. The right lens appeared to be coated with gold paint. The paint also covered half his nose and right cheek.

"Gav," stated Jane, again clearly feeling that no further explanation was required. Ronnie nodded at Gav who removed his spectacles and attempted to clean the lens with his yellow-gloved hands. "How's it going, mate?"

"Good, Jane," he smiled in greeting. "Just had the nozzle the wrong way round, that's all. Take a look," he nodded towards the shed.

"Is it safe?" asked Jane.

"Oh, yes. It's fine. Don't breathe too deeply though. I'll wash these off," he indicated towards his spectacles. Jane turned to Ronnie.

"Let's take a peek." They walked towards the door and Jane opened it allowing Ronnie to enter first.

"Yes," Ronnie exclaimed. "I knew it would work." Jane joined her. Both women were confronted with three neat rows of wooden shelves upon which stood neatly placed bright gold soap bars. They stared, raised their hands and high-fived.

Gav returned to the shed with marigolds now removed but traces of gold still on his face and spectacles.

"You've missed some," said Jane, pointing to his face.

"Oh, I know. No worries. It's a bugger to get off though. What do you think of the soap?"

"Look's great. We just need to keep going."

"Jo's a hard taskmaster so we will." The women left the shed and Gav to his spraying responsibilities. Jane knocked on the back door and opened it slightly.

"Safe to come in?"

"Yes," replied Jo, "the dangerous part is done."

"What's so dangerous?" asked Ronnie.

"We use caustic soda as our lye and when you combine that with water it produces an intense heat and the mixture is corrosive."

"And that's what we use on our skin?"

"The soap then needs to be left after it's formed so that the residual caustic soda can evaporate. Then the solid bar is safe to use after two to three weeks." The second lady in the kitchen was whisking a golden-coloured liquid. "That's all the ingredients being whisked together and Judith's waiting for the batter to reach the point of trace. Just keep the door open, stay there and you'll be fine," Jo clarified, "When the batter starts sticking to the sides, looking more solid, then it's ready to pour in the moulds on the table." The kitchen table had a row of rectangular boxes with silicon moulds within them. Half were full of the golden mixture and half waited to be filled. "We leave it twenty-four hours for the soap to harden, remove them from the moulds and dry them further on racks for two to three weeks, a process called 'curing'. Midas then puts his touch on them."

"Are the moulds working well?" asked Ronnie.

"Yes, they are. It took us a little while to get the mixture right so they'd set correctly. I've made them fragrance free as requested."

"What's the beautiful smell then?" asked Jane.

"That's one of the scents for my soaps that I sell. I call it "Summer Meadow."

"It's lovely," said Jane. "Can I ask a favour?"

"Yes, lovey." Jane reached into her handbag and produced some slim black silicone templates. "Can you place some of these in the middle of the new bars? Suspended in the soap." Jo took one template and examined it.

"Don't see why not. Can I ask why?"

"Best not to know." Jane handed over the rest of the templates which depicted a running black hare.

* * *

Barry was in pain both mentally and physically. He'd checked his body in the mirror this morning and the bruises around his ribs were beginning to fade. The family had called him in and given him a real grilling about what had happened at his arrest. He knew that Roper was behind telling them but he couldn't blame him. Mainly because Roper was right. In fact, Roper was right in every way that he could be. Not only was Barry in the mire with the police, but he was also up to his neck with another unknown criminal network. The reality was that he had nothing to tell anyone. His 'new associates' seemed to believe that he was a top tier criminal or spy but he was just Barry and Barry was hurting. His telephone rang.

"Hi, Barry here."

"Baz, I've got a possible job for you."

"Whose this?"

"Terry, you dimwit." *Terry ringing me!*

"You free for a bit of grafting?"

"Does it pay well?"

"Will do if you're good enough for it."

"What's it involve?"

"Best not said, but it's driving. Fast driving." Barry smiled. Driving was his thing.

"Sounds good to me. Where and when?"

"This afternoon so we can discuss it. Will and Ted will be there too."

"Competition?"

"Maybe. I'll text you the time and location."

"I'll be there."

"Good lad. Don't forget your car." The phone line went dead. *I'm in enough shit already*, thought Barry, *May as well earn some money whilst I try and work my way out of this mess.*

* * *

At one o'clock Barry rolled into the Lee Valley VeloPark car park, its Pringle roof dominating the skyline. Terry was standing behind a white van with its boot doors open and he spotted Ted taking a bicycle out of the rear.

"You've not got us doing bike trials have you?" Barry said to himself. He knew that Ted certainly wasn't up for that. Ted was about five-eleven and in his late fifties. He was a white van driver and his beer-bellied physique was topped with a thin sprinkling of curly white hair. Barry pulled up beside the van just as Ted appeared to be taking an old-school Raleigh Chopper from the back. Barry climbed out of his car and walked around to the back of the van which he saw also contained a BMX bike and a further cycle with Grifter written on the side.

"Terry," Barry shook Terry's hand noting that he looked well and was sporting a healthy tan. "Looking good, mate."

"Cheers Barry. You OK? Had a rough night?"

"I'm fine. Just working hard."

"Good lad," he tapped Barry on the shoulder. "Look what old Ted's brought with him."

"Classics," said Ted in a deep resonant voice.

"We're not riding these, are we? I don't think you could!" said Barry, laughing.

"Cheeky boy," replied Ted. "I could show you a thing or two." He squatted on the Grifter sucking in his stomach as he did so. "Once round the velodrome."

"Not unless there's medics on hand," said Barry.

"Now, now boys. Calm down. Here's Will."

An Audi Q4 entered the car park and Will raised his hand in greeting as he parked the vehicle. He stepped out of the car and walked around to the men.

"Boys. Nice to see you." He shook all of their hands. Will was in his mid-thirties with dark brown hair, a beard and was wearing aviators. He was dressed in a smart long-sleeved shirt and Chinos and beamed a bleached smile at them. He looked at the push bikes which were now all standing in a line. "Nice collection. Yours Ted?"

"Yes, mate."

"Quality." Will looked at Terry. "What we here for then?" he asked.

"A time trial," said Terry.

"Interesting. What's the job?"

"Can't say." Will's eyebrows raised and the other men frowned. "Hang on. Not because I don't trust you. I'm keeping it tight and it's in your interest not to know." Barry was listening intently. *Maybe I will have something to tell,* he thought. "You'll have to trust me," said Terry. "You know I'm good for it."

"Is the pay good?" asked Ted.

"The best payout that you've ever had or likely to have," Terry paused looking at the men. *They're interested*, he thought, as he gauged their faces. "I need three of the best drivers that I can get and you are them. I need confidence, know-how and speed and I think that you all fit the bill."

"What are we driving?"

"You won't know until the day."

"Where?"

"In the city."

"Getaway drivers?" asked Barry.

"You could say that. However," Terry held his hands up, "let's not get ahead of ourselves. I need to know that you are up for it first." He received three murmurs of assent. "OK. Here's the course for today." Terry took a map out which displayed the area of the city in which they were in. He pointed to a red cross. "That will be your starting point. Finish point is here," he gestured to the carpark.

"What are we driving?", asked Will.

"The vehicles that you've arrived here in." Will and Barry laughed. Ted studied the map ignoring them both.

"No way," said Will, "Ted doesn't stand a chance!"

"Don't you worry about me lad," said Ted, his fingers moving on the map.

"What are the rules?" asked Barry.

"Two simple ones. I need to see you at the start but I'll be waiting here. Whatsapp or Facetime me so I can see that you are there. I countdown from three and you're off. One car at a time. The next car sets off after the first has finished."

"And the second?" asked Will.

"Get from there to here as fast as you can and don't get stopped by the cops."

"Right then," said Ted. "When do we start?" He closed the rear doors of his van and started moving the cycles to some bike stands at the front of his vehicle.

"Anytime, make your way across there. Let me know when the first car is ready." Will and Barry moved to their vehicles.

"See you this evening," said Will to Ted, receiving a two-fingered reply. Terry walked back to his vehicle retrieving a stopwatch from within. *I've got a good feeling about this. They're already competitive.*

* * *

Three hours later the four men were sitting in the biergarten of a local pub.

"How'd you do it?" asked Will in exasperation.

"Same way as you, Will. Picked my route and floored it," replied Ted.

"But you're in a van!"

The time trial had been completed and all vehicles had finished within a minute of each other. On paper, the Audi should have been a clear winner but Terry had chosen Ted for his knowledge.

"I drive for a living," explained Ted, "Yes, it's a white van but there's thousands of us out there. We're known for driving wherever we like, and parking wherever we like. We rarely get done for it as everyone, business or domestic, wants their parcels delivered. Roads are roads, mate. There are throughs all over the place, wider paths that you can squeeze down, a no entry is not always a no entry.

Rules are there for bending, my son."Terry could see Will's mind going through the route and the pennies began to drop.

"There's always another way, Will," said Terry. "The hare and the tortoise." Barry was sitting enjoying the conversation. He had not had this much fun in ages.

"What next?" he asked.

"Well, I'm happy with you all. Fancy a treat?"They replied in the affirmative. "Then I'm taking you to a track tomorrow. We're gonna work on speed and trust. Believe you me, we're gonna need both for what I have planned."

* * *

"Who the hell are you?" said John, looking again at the image of the woman in the black dress. There was a knock at his hotel door. He threw a shirt over his laptop, approached the door, looked through the security peephole and saw the incandescent smile of Ricco looking back at him. John opened the door, allowing the man in.

"Thanks for coming."

"No problem, my friend. Let me take a look." Ricco followed John across to his desk, where he showed him the image of the woman directing the security guard and the subsequent revelation of the diamond.

"It is not right. She is a distraction. She's involved."

"That's what I thought. How do we find out who she is though?" Ricco ran the footage again then turned around and looked at John studiously, clearly contemplating something.

"I feel that I must trust you, John," he concluded.

"Well, thanks!"

"Wait," Ricco held up his hand. "I received a call yesterday. If I tell you the content of the call then you must keep it secret. If you tell anyone," Ricco paused for effect, "then you will be killed. Simple as that."

"OK," replied John, "you know I can be trusted."

"I think so too," Ricco smiled, although his eyes didn't. "I received a call from a client yesterday. A client from back home. Take a seat, John. Have you a drink?" John handed him a bottle of sparkling water from the hotel fridge. "Perfetto," he cracked the seal, took a sip and sat in the desk chair facing John. "My client has reported a robbery to me. He is extremely angry and has lost a significant amount of cash and property." John looked at him in confusion. "So what's that got to do with us, you say," said Ricco, anticipating John's next question. "What it has to do with us is that the burglar left a calling card."

"You're joking."

"I never joke about such things."

"The hare?"

"Yes, the black running hare."

"When, where?"

"My client had a large party. The theft occurred during the party."

"One of the guests?"

"Maybe. Someone with skill though. It was not an easy job to do. A professional, in my opinion."

"Let's start with the guest…"

"Already obtained. I have brought it with me." Ricco produced some sheets of paper from within his jacket and handed the guest lists over to John. He started looking through the list. "Many names you will not know but I have highlighted one that you may." On the second page circled with a black pen was the writing Thomas Lomax +1.

"The woman?"

"Maybe. Who knows? Maybe we'll ask Barry."

"Yes, we could do, but the little shit seemed to know nothing of any value to us. There's got to be a handler, someone moving the stolen goods onwards. What did your client have nicked apart from the cash?"

"Watches, jewellery."

"Right. My boss must be able to give me some details of some decent criminals who could move on stolen watches. Also, we need a Lomax family tree. This woman might be in there. I'll ask for both to be provided. That won't compromise your client's position will it?"

"Not at all. I'll keep working on the guest list." Ricco held out his hand for John to return the list. *Trusted my backside,* thought John, as he handed it back and watched Ricco leave the room. He returned to the computer and studied a rerun of the incident at the museum.

"We're onto something here, Johnboy," he said aloud. John was under no illusion that Ricco's 'client' would be connected to the Mafia. Whomever the burglar was, the net was closing. The combined might of the mafia and the Masons together, with some assistance from the Met Police, was sure to turn up trumps.

"The net is closing, mate. The net is closing." He picked up the phone to dial Fortescue and ask him to obtain the information that he needed.

* * *

Now back at home Ronnie felt relaxed, though she'd be lying to say that she hadn't enjoyed her outing. Jane had made all the difference with her aura of confidence and cheerfulness and today had been a milestone for Ronnie. A step forward from which she refused to retreat. For the first time in a long time, she felt useful.

Ronnie was sitting surfing the net whilst waiting for Jack and Jane to arrive. Mrs Pilcher had enjoyed her day and had returned home buzzing with excited chatter. However, the day had taken its toll and she had retired to bed at eight o'clock exhausted but happy. She was confident that her mum would sleep through the night. Ronnie clicked on a YouTube link and was presented with a clip from a black and white film 'The Day They Robbed The Bank of England' (1960). She sat back and watched it, smiling at the antics of the erstwhile robbers.

"I've got to send this out." Using her encrypted phone she sent a group message to the team. There was a light tap at the front door. *That'll be Jane.* Ronnie answered the door to Jane who was looking at her phone and chuckling.

"Nice one, Ronnie." She handed Ronnie a Sainsbury's bag containing a couple of bottles of wine and some crisps. "Just to keep us going," she clarified.

"Thought you were driving?"

"Oh, I'll get an Uber or maybe Jack will give me a lift."

"I bet you he will," said Ronnie.

"Oh, stop it! We're just friends. Work colleagues."

"For now," said Ronnie. The doorbell rang. "That'll be him." She opened the door where Jack was standing with a four-pack of beer. "It's not a party, you know!"

"I thought it would be rude to turn up with nothing." Ronnie quickly grabbed the four-pack off him and ushered him into the hall where Jane was waiting.

"Where's the food?"

"I'll order it in."

"Hi there," said Jane, smiling at him.

"Jane," he smiled back. Ronnie walked between them.

"Come on you two. We'll go to the lounge. Mum's gone to bed so she won't disturb us. I'll grab some glasses." Ronnie entered the kitchen, reappeared with a selection of glasses and placed them down on a table. "Grab a seat, I'll pour. What's your poison?"

"White wine," said Jane.

"Red for me," replied Jack who was looking around the room. "There's some old stuff in here, Ronnie. It's great."

"Ancient you mean. I don't like to change things. Mum seems comfortable with them."

The walls were painted in magnolia with a couple of old paintings on one wall and an old dark oak dresser standing against another.

The shelves on the dresser contained various ornaments, postcards and an old pewter mug containing an array of pens and pencils. The top shelf held some outward-facing dining plates. The carpet was an old red and gold medallion-patterned Wilton which showed thread bared areas at the kitchen and living room doorways. An old Ercol Windsor three seater sofa and matching chairs with pale patterned upholstery provided the seating, apart from one large comfortable chair which was situated next to the electric fire with a good view of the television.

The television stood in contrast to the rest of the room as being the only modern item. Jack lowered himself into an Ercol armchair and was pleasantly surprised by its comfort. He couldn't help but run his hands along the wooden armrests as he was sure many people had done before.

"There you go," said Ronnie, passing him a glass of red wine.

"Thanks," said Jack looking across at the Wally dogs holding guard at each end of the mantle. To the right side of the mantle was a large framed photograph depicting a man standing next to a car.

"What's the car?" asked Jack, recognising it as a classic and pointing to the picture.

"Oh, that was Dad's pride and joy. An early Citroen" Jack stood up and walked to the photograph where a curly-haired male in his forties was standing next to a pale blue Citroen.

"The Tin Snail," he said, "produced for the farmers of France. A popular and affordable car in its time."

"How do you know so much?" asked Jane.

"I've always loved old cars. I've got one myself," Jack sat back down.

"What type?"

"You probably won't have heard of it. A Gordon-Keeble. Very rare. I'll take you out for a spin in it one day if you'd like?"

"Would love to." Ronnie pulled the ring pull on her can breaking into their conversation.

"OK, guys, ready when you are." Jane blushed and Jack laughed.

"Sorry, Ron. Cars are my thing."

"I'm sure they are. Shall we get down to business though or we'll be too drunk to discuss anything." She took a large slug of lager.

"Right, I've got the beginnings of a plan that I think can work," said Jack, who had the ladies' undivided attention. "It's risky but then the whole job is. I've done a lot of recceing and from ground level, the bank looks impenetrable."

"I agree," said Jane.

"So," continued Jack, "that leaves us with subterfuge and a roof attack. Probably both." Ronnie slurped from her can as Jane sipped her wine, both enthralled.

"To consider either, Jane, we need to empty your head again. I've had some further thoughts. Tell us again about the bank." Jack sat back with the room's attention now focused on Jane.

"Okay. The building sits on an island made of granite. There are ground level and upper floors. The Governor's and Senior Officials' offices are all situated above ground. Their offices are known as The Parlours. There is a central quadrant in which the Governor has his gardens. Only he, and his guests, are allowed in there."

"Good, I may come back to that. Continue," said Jack.

"There are three floors below ground. Over two of the floors, there is a system of eight vaults containing the gold. The place looks like a prison with solid metal doors, caged doors and concrete as thick as you can imagine. It's like a maze with endless corridors."

"Good," said Jack. "What else is down there?"

"The library, gym, Dr and dentist offices. Oh, also the maintenance team is based down there."

"Anything else?"

"Just that it's an old building. There's lots of corridors, hidden doors, even hidden stairs, but it's been modernised. As you'd expect the security of the vaults is top spec."

"You have the blueprints, Ronnie?"

"Yes, Jane got them for me. We've been working hard on routes to the vaults and on penetrating the security systems. I'm confident I can get in, open any electronic doors, and mess with CCTV, movement and pressure sensors. We don't need to change anything they have. I just need to hack into their systems. I've been in there a couple of times already and there have been no security scares so far."

"I can confirm that," said Jane.

"Do maintenance wear their own uniforms, Jane?"

"They're employees of the bank so it's a corporate uniform."

"Can you get one of their uniforms if needed?"

"Yes."

"Good. What about door locks? They can't all be electronic. Who maintains all the locks?"

"Oh, that would be Bob."

"Bob?"

"Bob the Lock. They have their own locksmith."

"You're joking?" said Ronnie.

"Not at all," said Jane, "He has his own office. There are keys everywhere. He can break into anywhere."

"Maybe we could recruit him?" said Ronnie.

"Not a chance. He takes the security of the bank very seriously. We'd never bend him."

"Bob, maintenance, civilian staff, all nine to five?" interjected Jack.

"Yep, clock in and out. All staff come in via the doors at the back of the building."

"Yeah, I've watched them," said Jack. Ronnie topped up Jane's glass. Jack had not drunk much of his wine.

"What about the cleaning staff? The offices and corridors must all be cleaned."

"Like the maintenance staff. Cleaners are all directly employed by the bank. They have their own uniforms." Jack raised his eyebrows. "And yes, I can get hold of their staff uniforms too."

"Back to The Parlours then. Secretaries etc. Who looks after the senior officials."

"The butlers."

"Butlers?" said Ronnie. "What age are they bloody living in?"

"I know, Ronnie but traditions are maintained. The butlers all wear a uniform too. Pink jackets." Ronnie choked on her beer.

"Nine to five too?" asked Jack.

"Mostly. It just depends if anyone is working late."

"Security teams out of hours then?"

"Minimal. They rely heavily on their technical security. Four to man the upper floors, a couple in the CCTV room, a couple in the vaults, one security manager on call in the event of an issue."

"The roof then. What's the security like up there?"

"No rooftop gardens and no access allowed to any staff except for security members. All windows and doors are alarmed. CCTV cameras positioned in strategic locations. The threat from above is deemed low. There's no way of getting up there as it's on an island. There are no buildings close enough to climb across to it. It's all netted though with the biggest threat being the local pigeons."

"Can we have a look at the blueprints please, Ronnie."

"I'll grab my Mac." Ronnie returned a couple of minutes later with her laptop and a small projector. "Sorry, Dad." She moved the framed photograph exposing an area of wall where she could project the images from her screen.

"I want to see if we can identify the locations of hidden doors and stairs, Jane. Do you think you can do that?"

"I'll give it a try," said Jane.

The group worked late into the night working through the blueprints floor by floor.

Chapter 10

"I want a progress report, John. I've supplied everything that you have asked for," said Simeon. Dressed in his master's robes, Fortescue sat in his private offices within the Freemasons Hall with Harrison standing beside him like an obedient dog. Digby was sitting at the other side of the desk, unimpressed by their fancy dress or demeanour.

"Things are progressing well."

"What do you mean well?" asked Harrison. Digby ignored him. He'd met the likes of Harrison when he was in the job. A man promoted beyond his abilities who had garnered the support of senior colleagues along the way. Digby had never been asked to join the Guild. He was not the right type of character, didn't have enough money and was not of enough importance to even register on their radar. He didn't care. All he cared about was getting his wages. He may not have respected the guild but would have been a fool not to realise how influential they were. However, he still ignored Harrison.

"Well, I hope you are doing better than the Met enquiry team," said Fortescue, "What a bunch of buffoons." He looked up at Robert. "I'm sorry Robert, but it's true. Your team is only good for pushing pieces of paper around and gathering data. If Smith doesn't get his finger out of his backside he'll be looking at demotion not promotion." Digby tried not to laugh aloud at the dejected look on Harrison's face.

"It's going well, Simeon. I feel the net is closing. We have a good lead on a woman who could be the key to it all," *Doesn't harm to embellish the truth,* he thought. "And we're looking for a handler of stolen property. Your paperwork," he held up the folder on his lap, "will help with that."

"Who is 'we'?" asked Fortescue

"I'm working with some European colleagues. They're proving very useful."

"I told you, Robert. This is what gets results." Simeon slapped his hand on the desk. "Not you peacocks strutting around your offices, holding meetings that achieve nothing. This is how things get done and this is why the brotherhood is as strong today as it has ever been. Do we have any names yet, John?"

"No, but we will."

"Good man. There will be some more money put into your account tonight. You may go."

"Thank you, Simeon." John stood up and walked towards the door, opened it and was closing it slowly behind him as the men continued speaking.

"Is Smith coming tonight?"

"I believe so, Grand Master."

"Well, I'll be having a word with him if he does, believe you me." *Pompous fools,* thought Digby as he walked out of the building.

* * *

"Right, we go at 3.30. Everyone understand?" said Tyrone.

"Yes."

"Yes."

"Yes" replied the three men standing in front of him in the washhouse.

"You'll be with me, Jimmy," said Tyrone.

"Right ya are."

"I'll see you tonight, lads," said Tyrone. The men split from the area and headed off to their cars. Taking different routes, they would travel from Manchester across the M62 to York where tonight Jimmy would be shown how to use gas to take out an ATM. Jimmy had been sent up the road after Pat had made the arrangements. Pat had volunteered his services for free and although there was some risk, at least he would gain the knowledge about the procedure.

"We'll head on over there, Jimmy. I'll call on Titch on the way and pick up the gas and welding gear." Jimmy nodded. He'd been talked through the whole plan, so understood what was required.

"Jo will pick up the Audi later on. They've got it stashed across there."

"Where's the car from?"

"Aw, we nicked it a couple of weeks ago in the city. It's on false plates now but the York lads have got another stashed which I can ask for if we need to. The muskers haven't found it yet. As far as we know." Tyrone grinned at Jimmy. "It's gonna be a right laugh. I'll go over the plans again as we travel."

* * *

Five hours later, Jimmy was sitting within the passenger seat of a Nissan Navara with Tyrone next to him. Tyrone's phone vibrated and he checked it.

"It's time." Two roads up from them was a Morrisons supermarket, their target for tonight. "Caps and gloves, mate." Jimmy put his baseball cap and some blue polythene gloves on. "You wanna swig?" Tyrone held up a silver hip flask which Jimmy accepted. He took a mouthful of neat whisky. "Good lad. That'll warm your insides. Let's go." The gas canister and tubing lay in the back seat. Tyrone started the engine and drove ahead, moving out of the street towards the store. A man stood on the corner of the next street, smoking a cigarette, giving Tyrone a discreet hand sign as he entered the road and headed to Morrisons. "We're on." The four-by-four entered the store car park at speed. The interior store lighting was on. The car reversed up to the machine.

"Out," said Tyrone. Quickly jumping out, Jimmy reached for the gas cylinder, and Tyrone for the rubber tubing and a tyre lever. They moved to the machine. Tyrone dropped the tubing. He rammed the lever into the machine's side. "Tubing in!" he shouted. Jimmy picked it up and fed it through the small gap.

"What are you doing? Shouted a male in a green shirt who had walked out of the store.

"Get back in. We're not here to hurt anyone," shouted a member of the team.

"I'll call the police."

"We're just here for the money. Stay inside and you'll be safe," the same male shouted. Tyrone threw the lever in the back of the truck.

"Gas," he instructed. Jimmy turned the gas valve gently with a shaking hand.

"On full. Empty the bastard." Jimmy opened it to full. Still holding the cylinder, he moved to Tyrone who was now standing behind a brick store pillar.

"Light her up," shouted Tyrone, covering his ears. Jimmy copied Tyrone as he watched a spark ignite when another of the team ran past the machine. The world slowed. His muffled ears numbed the noise. Tyrone's face was held in a rictus of excitement. Then, "BOOM!" an explosion. Air ripped past the pillar, buffeting Jimmy. The Navara rocked. Tyrone nudged Jimmy.

"Move, move." A man jumped onto the back of the Navara, throwing a metal cable attached to a mounted winch. Two of the team stood to the side of the machine, now partially dislodged, wrapped the cable around it and clipped it tight. Tyrone reversed the Navara. Jimmy collected the remains of the tubing and canister. Throwing them in the truck, he climbed in too. The winch powered and the machine was pulled on. Tailgate now closed, the team dispersed as Tyrone gunned the engine. He slammed the accelerator down and they moved.

"Whoooaaaa!" he screamed as they headed to a main road. Sirens sounded in the background and Jimmy found himself grinning with excitement. Two further cars screeched from the car park heading in different directions.

"Heading for the layup," shouted Tyrone. "Eyes open." Jimmy knew the layup was a quiet industrial yard where both the getaway vehicle and the men, who would safely open the ATM cartridges, would be waiting. The money would be removed and the Navara and its contents would be torched. Now away from the immediate scene of the store, Tyrone slowed as he headed down a country lane.

"Now that's how you do it, Jimmy my son. That's how you do it."

* * *

Barry eased off his accelerator as he turned into Bovingdon Airfield under the direction of Terry. Will and Ted were sitting in the back and had chatted all the way across London to the site. Barry had been fairly quiet but Terry just assumed that he'd had a late night and a busy day. Terry had arranged for the lads to meet in the late afternoon. He had booked some time at the airfield which had an area of the old runway set aside for private track racing events.

"They do a load of filming round here you know?" said Terry.

"What like?" asked Ted

"Loads of bits. I think they filmed some of *Rogue One* and that Bond film *Spectre* here."

"How'd you manage to get it?"

"I know a man who knows a man who helps run the track. Just paid him enough money so that we get to use it for a couple of hours."

"Nice," said Barry.

"Park over there mate and I'll nip out to the office. Toilets are over there. I'll fetch your drivers."

"Drivers?" said Will."

"Yes, I told you that this would be fun. Get yourselves comfortable. I'll meet you round the front." Barry halted the car and Terry jumped out and headed off towards the building in front of them.

Ted, Barry and Will climbed out of the car and stretched their stiffened muscles. All wore blue boiler suits at the request of Terry. No one had complained as they were getting paid for this. They also knew that Terry was keeping things close to his chest.

"We don't exactly look like Formula 1 drivers, gents. Do we?" said Barry.

"You certainly weren't acting like one on the way over here," said Ted.

"I'll beat you on the track though, mate."

"Maybe, maybe," replied Ted. The men used the facilities and then walked towards the trackside together where Terry and his drivers were waiting. Positioned on the track were three VW Golfs standing in a row. The drivers were chatting, all dressed in racing suits. Six helmets were positioned on the ground before them. Terry approached his team, leaving the drivers to chat behind him.

"For all intents and purposes, we are here as part of a film crew who need to get some professional tips on driving. That's what the lads behind me have been told so you need to keep to the script. It's just general practice for us, we haven't been booked for any film or series. We are just brushing up on our skills. Keep conversation light, and keep it all focussed on the driving. We only have two hours here. Any questions?"

"Do we get to race each other?" asked Barry excitedly.

"Not today. Today is about these boys teaching you how to drive safely together as a unit. I know that you can all drive and that none of you are scared of speed. The aim is about getting you to drive together as a team. Nose to bumper, in convoy, at speed." Smiles crossed all of the men's faces. "If you get the hang of it then you're on the job." His gaze swept across the men. "Off you go then, get acquainted and show me what you've got."

The men eagerly walked over to the drivers, made their introductions and with helmets in hand, walked towards their respective vehicles. *Three weeks,* thought Terry. *That's when we need to be ready. You need to nail this, boys.* Terry watched as the cars set off, the drivers wasting no time as they picked up their speed and took the first circuit around the three-quarter mile track. Three circuits later, the Golfs screamed towards Terry, nose to tail. *That's what we need.* His mobile phone rang, it was Ronnie. He wandered away from the track where the cars had halted so that Ted, Will and Barry could begin driving.

"Ronnie, how's things?"

"Good, Terry"

"What can I do for you?'

"I've been surfing the web and found a Citroen Classic Owners Club."

"Not a surprise. There's geeks for every type of motor."

"Yeah, but these geeks have planned to join a local rally. They're all meeting up with their prize cars."

"And that's important because?" asked Terry.

"The start point is in the city, Terry. Central London out to Lee Valley and North from there." Terry felt his heart quicken.

"When?"

"Two weeks on Saturday."

"Thanks, Ronnie. You're a star. I'll be in contact." He ended the call and turned as he heard the approach of the Golfs. They swept past at speed, not in formation, but they were flying.

"We have a date," said Terry to himself. He felt adrenaline coursing through his veins. This was an opportunity they couldn't miss, a gift and a piece of pure luck. *I need to make some calls.* He searched through his phonebook. *Dougal and Goose first, Jane, Keith and Jack. The timetable is tight. Bloody hell, Tommy as well. Meeting tomorrow. Set a schedule.* Terry made his first call.

"Goose, how can I help?"

"Goose, it's Terry. One week."

"One week!"

"I need the cars in one week." Silence greeted him on the other end of the line. "Goose, are you still there?"

"Yes, mate. Just working it out. Can you give us ten days?"

"Yes, but no longer. I'll make it worth your while."

"Done. Now let me get on."The phone went dead. Terry heard the cars looping again and watched as they passed him in a straight line, one car after the other. *Closer lads, closer. Trust each other.* As if on his instruction the cars pulled nearer to each other and Terry smiled. *Two weeks, two bloody weeks!*

* * *

Keith stopped on the pavement, looking at his reflection in the shop window of a local florist. *There you are again.* He was being followed. Keith had an instinct for trouble, a feeling for when things weren't quite right and always had an awareness of his surroundings. He wouldn't have survived in the 'antique' business without it and this morning his sensors had been triggered.

He watched in the window as the same lady that he had spotted three minutes ago stopped abruptly on the opposite pavement where he had halted previously, scanned her surroundings and was now standing in the queue at a bus stop, pretending to wait for a bus. Experience told him that she wouldn't be on her own and there would be at least two others. *Not old plod though,* he thought. Plain-clothed cops had a look about them, a walk, a presence, a tell. Keith had learnt this through his years of dabbling in the shady side of life. *Let me find the rest of you then.* He moved on, already having mapped out his route in his head.

Keith continued and waited at a pedestrian crossing, noting that his follower had also walked away from the bus stop. He aimed to cross to her side of the road. She'd spotted this and quickly shuffled into a small store. He smiled to himself, he was enjoying himself, believing that at some point today he'd end up chatting to whomever was interested in him. The lights changed and he crossed over with a large group of people knowing that one of his other pursuers would be amongst them.

Turning right, he kept pace with the morning commuters, heading towards a local Costa coffee shop further along the street. Deliberately, he removed his phone from his pocket, raised it to his ear as if taking a call, and entered Costa. *They won't be able to resist a chance to hear what I'm talking about. Might think I'm meeting someone.* Reaching the front of the queue he ordered and glanced towards the shop door as he heard it opening. A male walked in, backpack over one shoulder, already carrying a disposable coffee Costa cup. The man looked around and took a table with a view of the door. *That's number two then. Stands out a mile. Amateurs trying hard to do the right thing.*

"Flat white for Keith," called one of the baristas.

"Thank you, young man." Keith collected his coffee, turned and smiled at the male with the backpack, who made his best attempts to ignore him, and walked from the cafe turning left as he did so. *Shane's next.*

Shane was a legitimate second-hand dealer of vinyl records and had a small store just around the corner from one of Keith's antique stores. He was an old friend who did not allow Keith's dip into the criminal world to affect their relationship. Keith slowed, wanting to ensure that the foot team behind him didn't lose him entirely. He stopped at a street corner, checked his watch and then turned into the side street where the record shop was. He didn't bother looking back, believing that his pursuer's skills were proficient enough not to lose him. Keith halted outside the shop then entered, with the doorbell ringing as he did so.

"Morning, me old son," said Keith to a tall, lythe man behind the counter. In the background played the gentle tones of 'Here, There and Everywhere'.

"Keith! How are you doing mate?"

"I'm good but a bit busy. I've brought you a coffee though. Do you mind?" Keith pointed behind the counter where he knew that the storeroom had a door leading out to a different street.

"Of course. No problem." Keith placed the flat white down for Shane.

"Next guy entering your shop is following me, mate. Can you tell him that I'll be at my shop in about ten minutes?"

"Will do. Thanks for the coffee." Shane was unflustered by Keith's behaviour and accepted it as a norm. Keith scooted around the counter and disappeared into the store room.

Within a couple of minutes, a male walked into the shop, glanced around the small store and started looking through one of the record racks. Shane walked around the shop counter and approached the male.

"Can I help you, mate?"

"I'm just looking thanks," replied the male with a hint of a European accent. The man stood at the same height as Shane but was broader and looked like he could handle himself.

"I've got a message from Keith, mate." The man looked at him, a stern expression on his face. "He said he'll be at his shop in about ten minutes. He's happy for you to meet him there." Shane walked away and went back behind his counter. He smiled at the male who just stood looking at him. "I'm sure he'll have the kettle on when you get there. Nice cup of tea for you." The man made no reply, looked at Shane in disgust and stormed out of the shop, slamming the door behind him. Shane chuckled and raised his flat white.

"Have a good day."

* * *

"Visitors here soon, Sophie," said Keith as he swiftly walked across to the counter in his small antique boutique". Not sure who but I'll be in the back making a cuppa. Let them know that I'll be through in a minute and then nip out for your lunch will you?"

"OK, Keith. How will I know who they are?" The shop was only small and currently there were no customers. Keith paid Sophie to manage the store although both knew that footfall was always low.

"I'm sure you'll recognise them. They're bound to look out of place." He nipped behind a curtain covering a door aperture behind the counter and began to whistle. Sophie could hear the tap running as he filled the kettle. She went back to scrolling through Instagram on her phone. Five minutes later the shop door opened and two males walked in. One was tall, bald and tanned and wearing a well-cut blue suit. The other male was of solid stature and scruffier in appearance. The scruffier male approached and spoke with a local accent.

"Can I speak ..."

"Keith's expecting you. He'll be with you both in a moment. Just making you a cuppa." Sophie placed her phone in her back jeans pocket, grabbed her jacket and walked to the door.

"I'm off for my lunch break." The male in the blue said nothing and watched as Sophie turned the sign on the door to 'Closed', left the shop and walked away. John looked at Ricco who just raised an eyebrow in response.

"There you are, gents," Keith made his entrance from behind the curtain carrying a tray which held a china teapot and three cups. He scanned the males, recognising that neither had been the ones following him. "I thought it would be nice for us to have a chat over a nice cuppa. Shall I be mum?" Keith picked up the pot and started pouring. "Milk, sugar?" Keith finished serving, chose a cup himself and gently pushed the tray across the counter. "Don't be shy." He smiled at them both.

"You're a bit of a smart arse, Keith, aren't you," said John, reaching for the jug of milk and pouring it into a cup. He looked at Ricco who gave a slight shake of his head. John handed Ricco his black tea.

"I'd say I'm just careful," Keith raised his cup, "and civilised, of course. I didn't catch your name?"

"I didn't give it." Keith waited expectantly.

"John," said Digby.

"And your friend?"

"Doesn't matter," concluded Digby.

"Ah!," said Keith, nodding his understanding. "Well, you're not old bill, or at least not anymore. I am guessing that you are not here to buy anything from my lovely shop. I'm intrigued as to why you would go to the trouble of having me followed though and who for?"

"We want to talk to you. Who we work for doesn't matter."

"I'm all ears gentleman. Cigar?" Keith held out a wooden box and could see that the male in blue was starting to get irritated. However, John was a cool customer. Not easily riled.

"We'll pass, thanks," said John, "My inquiries have revealed that you are not averse to handling a bit of hooky material." John raised his hand halting any response from Keith. "We're all big boys here, so no need to tip-toe around each other. We're not here to cause you any trouble."

"Let's just say that within the antique world, many things come my way," said Keith.

"Good, I'll accept that."

"What are you looking for?" asked Keith.

"A burglar. A person who only targets high-value items."

"Like?"

"Jewellery, watches, not paintings, maybe antiques."

"There's plenty of them out there," replied Keith.

"Not this one there isn't. Travels all over the place. You been offered any top-quality watches recently?" Keith's face remained impassive as he answered.

"No. Not for a long time."

"Know any of your peers who have?"

"They would be unlikely to tell me but I'll keep my ears open." The male in the blue suit nudged past John, reaching towards his breast pocket. Keith stepped backwards. The man produced a photograph.

"Do you know this person?" he said. *European*, thought Keith. *Smart suit, tanned, watches. I'm betting Italian.* He took hold of the photograph and picked up a pair of thick-rimmed spectacles from the counter. Keith looked at the photograph and his stomach flipped, his pulse increased and he suddenly felt hot. *Calm yourself.* Pulling the photograph closer he squinted at it as if examining it closely. He looked at the figure recognising that it was Jane, speaking to a man in uniform.

"Never seen either of them before." He handed the photograph back and placed his hands on the counter to steady them, noticing outside movement at the shop door. The door opened and in walked Sophie. *God bless you*, thought Keith. She turned the sign to open.

"Oh, sorry! Am I disturbing?"

"Not at all," said Keith walking around the counter and placing his arm around her shoulders, "these gents were just leaving." He took John's cup from his hand. "Weren't you fellas?" Keith spread his arms wide ushering the men like chickens towards the door. They reluctantly walked in that direction, the blue suit opened the door and they stepped out.

"We'll be in contact, Keith."

"I'm sure you will, John." Keith closed the door and turned his back on them, ending the conversation. They watched as he walked back to the shop counter.

"Notice the change in him when he looked at the photo, Ricco?"

"Oh yes, John. We're onto something." Both males walked away from the store.

"Have they gone, Sophie?" asked Keith as he waited at the counter.

"Just walking away, now. Who are they?"

"Trouble, love. Trouble. I need to make some calls," he said, "you can go for the day. We'll close up early I think. It's not busy out there." Sophie didn't need persuading and headed towards the door.

"See you tomorrow, Keith."

"I'll try and call in," he replied, already scanning his phone as Sophie closed the door behind her.

Chapter 11

Terry had called Tommy yesterday and had given him the update regarding the proposed timescale. Following that he'd sent a text out to the team calling them to a meeting today. He now paced in anticipation of their arrival. There was a lot to talk about, preparations to be made and targets to hit.

Keith had provided an unoccupied house for today's meeting, having been asked to keep an eye on it whilst the owners were away on holiday. The dining room, where Terry waited, was modern, functional and large enough for the team to be comfortable in. Terry was on edge following the call that he had received late yesterday afternoon from Keith. Someone out there had an interest in them and was trying to identify them. He knew that their interest was concerned with the Italian job. Therefore, he had to assume that they were trying to establish who was behind the burglary so that they could seek retribution and recompense.

Terry remained stoic about their interest, determining that risk was part of his life and part of this job. They needed the cash to progress and knew the risks when they went to Italy. Within thirteen days they'd be in the B of E relinquishing her of some of her assets. Until D day the team would just need to lay low, make their final plans and keep everything crossed. There was no way that Terry was pulling the job at this stage.

He continued pacing as he heard the door being answered a couple of times. Keith would be gathering the team in the kitchen. They would be grabbing some drinks. Keith's head popped around the door.

"They're all here, mate. Ready when you are." Terry nodded, walked towards the door and forcing a confident smile on his face, opened it wide.

"Come in you lot. We have lots to discuss." Keith had been sworn to secrecy last night. Terry trusted him to keep quiet. *Might as well start with the bombshell*, thought Terry watching the team enter the room. He closed the door.

"One more, Terry," said Keith. Terry frowned as he heard the toilet flushing in the downstairs toilet, the dining room door opened and he smiled as he watched Ronnie enter the room.

"Nervous tummy, Tel. Nice to see you in the flesh." She tapped his stomach as she passed him. "See you're eating well." Keith laughed.

"Great to see you out and about, Veronica."

"Thought it was about time." Ronnie sat on a seat next to Jane and started connecting a laptop and equipment together. *This is it then,* thought Terry, moving to the head of the table. He surveyed the room which had now gone silent.

"Thanks all for coming, an important meeting today, and we have lots to discuss. I'm going to start with some interesting news." Ronnie stopped fiddling and looked towards Terry. "We all know that this is a risky business and that we are all placing ourselves in the line of fire by going for it. To keep it simple, it seems that we have created a bit of a stir doing the job in Italy."

"A bit of a stir?" asked Jane.

"Yes. We've created a bit of an interest in that job from some private investigators."

"Oh, shit!" exclaimed Jane.

"Nothing to panic about. Keith's kept them at bay and they have no idea what we're planning. Just a lucky punt in Keith's direction and he's happy that he's covered it."

"What do they know?" asked Jack.

"Nothing really," said Keith. "They just asked me if I had, or knew someone, who had recently acquired the watches. I said no. It's not that unusual for me to be approached. Anyone who is anyone knows that the antiques business is not squeaky clean." Ronnie nodded her agreement and continued connecting a projector to her laptop. The tension in the air seemed to abate. "They also had a photo. Showed it to me. Wanted to know if I knew someone."

"Who was it?" asked Jack.

"It was Jane," replied Keith with a grin on his face.

"Me!" Jane's hand flew to her face covering her open mouth, her eyes wide in shock.

"Yes, love. You wouldn't know it was you unless you'd met you. The image of your face is unclear but it's clearly your body and hair to me. Of course, I said nothing to them. They walked away empty-handed." Terry interjected.

"It's all in hand, Jane. Nothing to worry about," Jack squeezed her arm in reassurance. "There is no reason to think that they'll ever identify you. You are completely unknown to anyone but us. You're invisible within the criminal world, a nobody."

"I'm not sure that's a compliment," said Jane, laughing nervously.

"It's your safety net though, love. Your get out for the Italian job. Nothing's going to get traced back to you."

"He's right, Jane," reassured Jack. Terry clapped his hands together.

"Right, bad news over. I need a pee and a cig. Keith," Keith turned to look at him, "descriptions of these two amateurs who visited you to the team please," Keith nodded. "I'll let all that sink in and we'll reconvene in five minutes. I'll be out the back if you need me." Keith swept out of the room, light on his feet, with the feeling that he'd unloaded some weight from his shoulders.

* * *

"Right, back to it. I take it that we are all still on board." Terry didn't wait for an answer. "Good. Let's start with the easier stuff first. Jane, how's the soap coming along?" Jane smiled, reached into a bag at her feet and placed a gold bar of soap on the tabletop.

"You tell me?" Terry lifted the bright gold bar. Jane produced two more from her bag, handing one each to Keith and Jack. Keith sniffed the bar.

"Odourless," he stated.

"They've cut down to the bare essentials. No need for it to smell nice."

"Nice and light," said Jack.

"Looks good, Jane. They've done a great job. How much have they got?" asked Terry, turning it around examining it thoroughly.

"A shed full," replied Ronnie. "They're still making it. How much do we need?"

"As much as they can do in eight days. We need it delivered and ready in nine days."

Everyone looked at him. He smiled, his eyes bright with excitement.

"We have a target date. We do the job in thirteen days. Everything needs to be finalised in nine days." The room was silent. "Yes, thirteen days. One week on Saturday." Keith sat back and chuckled as he looked at the faces of Jack, Ronnie and Jane. "Nothing like a bit of pressure to focus the mind."

"I'd guessed it might be then," said Ronnie, "hence tearing myself away from my house." She pressed her computer and a poster advertising the Classic Car Rally was displayed on the wall.

"The perfect cover people. The rally is on in thirteen days. We can't not take this opportunity. Now let's get to work."

Keith produced an enlarged map of the city and unrolled it across the dining table, holding the corners down with redundant coffee cups.

"Keith, you're in the chair." said Terry. Keith had been primed by Terry to manage the meeting whilst the team got down to discussing the nuts and bolts of the operation. He stood up, removed his jacket and placed it reverently over the back of his chair.

"Right! Let's start with the cars. Terry, where are we at?" Terry started talking as Keith produced three model cars and placed them on the table.

"Three Citroen, green, white and red. Hope, Faith and Charity. The cars will be race-ready, there's a lot of work gone into them. Three cars with three drivers. Jack, Jane and I will all be passengers."

"Who's driving?" asked Jack.

"People that I trust," replied Terry, knowing that it wouldn't be questioned. "They have been training and they're looking slick. You'll meet them on the day. They don't know you and you don't know them. That's how it will stay." None of the team complained.

"The cars will be parked in strategic locations, not far from the bank. We do the job at night, load the cars ourselves and leave them in situ. Jane attends work early on the Saturday, on the pretence of a security check, thereby ensuring that all is well. The rally starts at 10. We meet our drivers at 9.45, join the rally and tag along. At identified locations, we split from the convoy and follow pre-planned routes out of the city. I've got your routes here." He placed some paperwork on the table. "You will be the driver's navigator. You direct them. They find out the route when you tell them. Keep your route to yourself. The least we all know the better."

"You have oversight of it all though, T," said Jane.

"True, but someone has to. I brought you all together and you know I'm tight. If I get caught the cops get nothing from me."

"Why split the cars?" asked Ronnie.

"Triple our chances of getting away with some, or all of the gold," said Terry. Jack was sitting back looking at the map and the model cars. "Concerns, Jack?"

"Yes, mate."

"What?"

"The cars. They're too small."

"What do you mean?"

"We can't get enough gold in them. Don't get me wrong, they're a good little car, renowned for their strength. However, even if your mechanics have done an outstanding conversion on them, which I'm sure they have, I'd guess they'll take a full load capacity of maybe 500kg. Do the maths." Terry looked confused. Ronnie interjected as she typed on her computer.

"500 kg of gold comes in at approx. £250,000 in each car." Terry slumped back in his chair, deflated.

"I never thought. I, I… just assumed they'd be fine. It's not enough! Not for the risk we are taking."

"But we're taking the cash too aren't we?" asked Jane.

"What do you mean the cash?" said Keith.

"I just assumed," continued Jane, "Well, it was just obvious to me. I mean, you do all know that the bank also holds the biggest cash deposits in the country? All stored in the vaults next to the gold." Terry sat up straight. *Thank you, Jane. Thank you.*

"Great, Jane. Tell us more," said Terry, looking towards Keith who nodded in agreement. Jane had thrown Terry a landline, unbeknown to her, and he intended to grab it with both hands.

"The vaults contain crates of notes. Packaged and ready for distribution. Some are older notes and some are brand new. They're stored in vaults adjacent to the gold. Same security around the cash as the gold."

"Good, good," said Terry. "We just adapt the plan. Keith, you'll be driving too." Keith's jaw nearly hit the floor.

"Hang on, mate, I ain't no Lewis Hamilton."

"You don't need to be. White van man. Steady drive out of the city. You take the cash, we'll take the gold. Good man. You'll do terrific." Terry turned back to the others.

"Right, that's agreed then. Thanks, Jane. Keith, take a pew." Terry gestured to a chair next to him. Keith sat down. "Let's get down to the nitty-gritty. What's the plan?" He looked expectantly at Jack. Jack nodded to Ronnie.

"I'll start us off. Chip in anytime you need to," said Ronnie. Terry nodded. "OK. I've infiltrated and integrated into the bank's technical systems. Jane installed the device I needed and now I can just about play around in there as much as I want. The building is extremely secure with CCTV, motion sensors, heat sensors, weight triggers, and everything that you would expect. I doubt whether there is another hacker in the country who could accomplish what I have. They don't know that I have opened a back door to the system, don't know that I'm there and won't, even after we have done the job."

"Nice one, Ronnie," said Terry. "How do we get in?" Terry again looked at Jack.

"Two ways. Stealth and subterfuge," replied Jack. Ronnie pressed a key on her computer and the screen displayed an image of the rear entrance to the bank. "Jane." On cue, Jane spoke.

"All staff, employees, and dignitaries arrive at the grounds of the bank via this back entrance." Jane pointed to the entrance. "Walk, cycle, drive, they all go through here. Once inside they are required to provide a security pass, a card, which is swiped digitally allowing them through a door. Any bags are placed on the security desk where a guard will check them. Then there's a walk through a human metal detector and a walk past a further security guard. Guards are allowed to randomly stop and search any persons entering the bank at their own discretion."

"Thank you, Jane," said Jack. "The key to success in this job is for us to infiltrate the bank and to break out, not in. We'll do that in four phases." he continued.

"Phase one. Jane returns to the bank in her role as security adviser to overtly complete a spot check of the offices and systems. One guard controls the gate during the evening. She'll enter in his full view and advise him that she'll sign herself out if he's doing his rounds when she leaves."

"Why does she need to do the check at all?" asked Terry.

"It's expected and it's my turn," said Jane. "The check hasn't been completed this month and it would look unusual if I don't do it."

"It also confirms for us which security guards have turned up for duty. May be priceless information if things don't go as planned," clarified Jack.

"OK, I'm with you," said Terry, "continue."

"Jane will actually leave the building but will re-enter covertly. The system and CCTV will have clear imagery of her leaving. However, when she walks back in, Ronnie will have full control," resumed Jack.

"I'll scan her card out remotely," said Ronnie. "For all intents and purposes, she won't be there."

"Jane will move through the bank unseen with Ronnie's help and at some point head for the doctor's office," said Jack.

"Where will you be?" asked Keith.

"Patience, Keith. I'll get to that. You all with me so far?" The team nodded as one.

"Phase two. Insertion of Terry into the bank. The Old Lady employs its own cleaning and maintenance staff. Below ground level, there is a library, gym, doctor's and dentist offices which are all available for use by employees. Clocking into work is via the security gates. Terry, Ronnie already has you registered within the back of the system as a member of maintenance staff. She has a card printed for you." Ronnie held up the card with a smile on her face.

"Where'd you get the photo?" asked Terry in surprise.

"Borrowed it from the passport agency databases," she replied.

"Can we do the same for Keith, Ronnie?" asked Jack.

"Yeah, no problem."

"Let's create him one for a security driver."

"Will do."

"Terry, you will turn up for work for the late shift. Cleaning and maintenance work above ground level is mainly done during the evening. We'll go through what you need to do when you get in there but suffice to say that you'll be waiting in the doctor's office until I collect you in the early hours. A little bit of role play and nerve to get in but you are more than capable."

"Why the doctor's office?" asked Terry.

"One, there's an easy route from there to the vaults. Two, there are no CCTV cameras, sound or motion sensors in there. They have to comply with patient confidentiality. You can relax there, even make a cup of tea. Ronnie will be controlling the door lock so no one's getting in. You just need to keep fairly quiet."

"That'll be the challenge for you," joked Keith, referring to Terry.

"Phase three," interrupted Jack who was now well into his flow. He nodded to Ronnie.

The projected image on the wall changed to that of a large glass tower. "This is Angel Court, a twenty-six-floored, three-hundred-and-thirty-foot-tall office building within walking distance of the Old Lady. On Thursday before the job, I'll enter the building as part of the maintenance crew and make my way up to the twenty-sixth floor. On that evening I'll parajet across to the bank, land on its roof, stow my gear and gain entry to the building."

"You're joking?" said Terry.

"Not at all," replied Jack.

"Why Thursday?" asked Keith.

"Simple, mate. You need me for the vaults. If I can't get in then the whole job is off. You'll know whether it's on for Friday night. If it's not, then you can call it off. We rethink and plan again."

"How do you get from the top floor to the bottom?"

"I've studied the blueprints carefully. I'll be working with Ronnie to move through the building unnoticed." Ronnie nodded her agreement. "Don't worry, Terry. I'll be there." Terry checked his watch.

"Let's take a break. I need a drink."

"I'll make us a coffee," said Jane.

"I'll help you," said Ronnie.

"Lovely. Jack, with me." Terry walked towards the back door and out into the garden. Jack followed as instructed.

The back garden provided privacy for them both and its small lawned garden, with burgeoning flowerbeds, contradicted its central city location.

"Very nice," said Jack.

"It is. They've done a good job." Terry looked at Jack. "You sure you can do it, son?"

"Yes," replied Jack with no hesitation. "Terry, I've taken big risks in my 'career'. Take Italy for example. You trusted me there."

"I did."

"Then trust me here. I've planned it meticulously."

"You're not James bloody Bond though, mate. Parajets and all that."

"No, Terry. He's a figment of Fleming's imagination. I'm the real deal and I'm good."

"And do you need a wheelbarrow to carry around those balls of yours?" said Terry. Jack laughed.

"No, mate. My ego's big enough to carry them for me." Terry chuckled.

"It's exciting though, ain't it," said Terry.

"Pure adrenaline. I can't wait." He placed a hand on Terry's shoulder. "I'll see you back inside." Jack entered the house as Terry looked to the heavens. *A bit of help here wouldn't go amiss,* he thought, although doubted the criminal fraternity would be supported by heavenly intervention. The team gathered back at the dining table with coffee cups placed in the middle.

"Everyone grab one," said Jane.

"Are you always so cheerful?" asked Keith.

"Always helps to have a positive mindset, Keith. We're going to pull off the heist of the century. What is there not to be happy about?"

"Back to planning then," said Terry. "So, we're all in there, except for Ronnie and Keith. I'm in the doctor's room, Jane will join me, Ronnie at home and Jack floating around in the bank somewhere. What next?"

"Below ground level are a series of vaults," said Jack. "Jane's described it as a maze, corridors with solid doors and barred gates. The gates are controlled electronically, some biometrically, and a mixture of each to deter any attack. Pressure pad sensors are positioned throughout the corridors, at each gate. They cycle in a random pattern when the vaults are in full lockdown, during the night, so an attacker would never know which pad was active on which gate. There are also pads randomly distributed within the corridor floors, they also cycle in a random pattern."

"How do we deal with that?" asked Terry.

"I'll deal with it, T. We know where the pads are distributed. I'll be able to disrupt the pattern to our advantage," said Ronnie flicking up a blueprint of the first basement floor.

"What about biometrics?" asked Terry.

"Again I'll be involved with that," said Ronnie. "For the scanners to work correctly they need to have a person's biometrics, such as fingerprint, retinal scan etcetera, stored on a database. The scanners need something to reference the scan to, so that it can make the identification. I have access to that database."

"Is there anything that you don't have access to?" asked Keith.

"Not really, apart from maybe the codes to your lock up on Chandler Street." Keith's eyes widened. "Calm down mate, I'm only joking." Keith visibly relaxed. "I've had them for ages." Ronnie smiled at Keith as Jack interrupted.

"As a fail safe we have Jane with us. She has an appropriate access level which will get us so far. I'll get the Governor's fingerprint when I'm there. Hopefully, between us all, that'll be enough." Keith raised his eyebrows. Jack ignored him and continued. "We'll work on the timings, but essentially I meet with Jane and Terry. We all then move as a unit through the vaults. We take our time and keep our nerve. Remember, it's still an old building but with modern security measures inserted. However, no one has ever broken in and they're not expecting anyone to either. As much as they try to be on their A game they are bound to have relaxed." Keith took over the conversation.

"So, you've made it to the vaults. What are you faced with?" The projected photo, on the wall, changed to that of an image of the Queen walking amongst blue shelves stacked with dozens of gold bars.

"Pretty much this," said Jane. Keith whistled, and Terry grinned.

"Beautiful," said Terry.

"Indeed," continued Jack, "which brings me to phase four." He looked at Keith. "White van man. Delivery of the soap and extraction of the cash, some of the gold and all of us. Over to you, Jane." All eyes turned towards Jane. Jane looked to Ronnie who pressed a key. The wall now displayed a bird's eye view of the bank and its surrounding area.

"There's a reason why the bank has never been successfully breached and why their deliveries in and out have never been intercepted. That is because there has never been an 'inside' woman or, indeed, a man in the right position. Nobody has been privy to how it all works. The bank stands on its granite island and you can watch it all day and never see cash or gold move in or out. You could sit for months and still never see it, but it does move and it moves regularly. How does it move, you ask?" Jane was warming into her role enjoying the vacant look on Terry and Keith's faces.

"It moves in and out via an underground tunnel. Transported in white vans, no livery, just plain white vans. Security within them of course but no escort to draw attention, just driven away from the building and taken to their respective destinations. This is where Keith will be involved. Keith, you'll drive the van and its contents in and drive all of us all out."

"How?" he asked.

"A quick history lesson. The bank," the photo on the screen was annotated by Ronnie, highlighting each building as Jane spoke, "underwent a substantial rebuild in 1734. At that time the architect was tasked with incorporating a tunnel from the vaults away from the building. This brings in Mansion House."

The building was now also highlighted on the map showing it as diagonally across the road from the bank. "As some of you may know, historically this was the Lord Mayor's residence. What you may not know is that the building was constructed in 1739, and has a basement which contains eleven prisoner-holding cells and an annex to the Bank of England tunnel. When empty of prisoners, the cells were used as a temporary store for gold which was shipped in and out of the bank."

"You thought of being a teacher?" asked Keith, totally captured with Jane's delivery.

"Never," she replied and continued, "This brings me finally to Walbrook House." The large building was the third to be highlighted on the map, and was positioned directly behind Mansion House. "Three townhouses originally stood at this location and yes, historically were used for distribution of money. The construction of Walbrook, the redevelopment of these properties, started in 2007 and was completed in 2010. The bank took this as an opportunity to reinforce and expand the tunnel. The tunnel now ends in the basement of the Walbrook building where it exits into the building's private underground car park."

"Sneaky little bastards," said Terry.

"To be fair, you'd expect them to be," said Jack. "However, we have the inside knowledge which gives us the upper hand. Keith, Jane will go through how the deliveries and collections are made with you but essentially you'll be driving us in and out."

"Back to the gold, and the cash for that matter. How do we move it from the vaults?" asked Terry.

"The vault has its own hoists, as do the vans. We use the bank's own equipment, vehicle and exit route to break out and take the gold to our cars," concluded Jack. "In a very broad nutshell… that's it, folks!" Contemplative looks surrounded the table. *There's still a lot to be ironed out*, thought Terry, *but it's a plan*.

"Break for a bite to eat, guys. Back here in half an hour," said Terry, pushing his chair back and standing. "Lots to do, lots to discuss and the clock is running."

* * *

The weekend had flown past for Terry, who felt that he had either been in meetings with the team or on the end of his mobile phone resolving last-minute issues regarding the job. This morning had culminated in a phone call received from Frank Roper who had been tasked to ring around the family and warn them of a general concern about Barry Lomax.

Terry had been advised that Barry was being pressured by the police, and by another crime organisation, to spill his guts about anything he knew about the Lomaxes. 'The family' was looking into it all and would update everyone as they learnt more. It seemed that Barry had come clean to Angelo in desperation that Angelo would understand and help him. Terry had spent the last hour contemplating the predicament that this put him in.

Barry was a good driver. He'd grasped what was needed quickly on the track and probably picked it up quicker than the other two. Could Barry drive them out of trouble if needed? Undoubtedly. He didn't know what the job was. *Is he a grass though? Can I use him? Trust him?* Terry had concluded that he needed to speak with Angelo himself which is what he had done half an hour ago. He was now waiting for Barry to arrive. The cafe door opened and Barry confidently walked in and up to the table.

"Hi, Terry," he slid into one of the seats. "How are you doing?" The waitress walked over. "Just a can of coke please love, no glass." She walked to a fridge and returned with the can, handing it to Barry. "Thanks."

"Barry. How's things?"

"Good, mate. Good. Any news on when you need me?"

"Not yet, but be ready. You carrying your phone?"

"All the time, mate. All the time. What did you want me for?"

"Just wanted to check about your feelings on the other two. You think they're good enough?"

"Yeah, man. Wasn't sure at first. Thought Ted might be a bit slow but I was wrong. He can certainly shift a car along."

"Good, good. You heard anything that I need to know about? Anyone talking about the family or me?"

"Nah, I'd let you know if I did. You know that." Barry's complexion had paled.

"It's just I've heard some rumblings about something going down. Can't get the details though. You're probably better connected than me." Barry perked up.

"What you heard, mate? I can put some feelers out." *I hope you can mate,* thought Terry.

"A murmur about something next weekend."

"In the city?"

"I'm guessing."

"Whereabouts?"

"Not sure." Terry leaned forward and lowered his voice, causing Barry to lean towards him.

"All I've heard is a group that needs some money and the mention of ATMs. There's something big planned." Barry nodded as if he fully understood. Terry leaned back again and looked at his watch.

"See what you can find out, Baz. I need to shoot." With that, Terry stood up, chucked a tenner on the table and walked out of the cafe onto the street outside.

"I didn't enjoy that," he mumbled to himself. Terry felt little remorse for the travellers. After all, he was using them as a distraction anyway and family came first

However, the seed was now planted. This was Barry's test. Terry hoped that he passed the information to the gits that were squeezing him, but most of all he hoped that Barry got Angelo's approval before he did it. Terry knew that there were all types of grasses. The nasty little bastards who would grass on their own grandmothers, and the others who were deliberately used by the crime families to spread misinformation to law enforcement and criminal networks. It may not be the way that Barry wished to work for the Lomaxes but it was his only choice. That or an early grave.

Chapter 12

Barry looked at both of his phones as he sat in the driver's seat of his car. Life had thrown some curveballs at him recently and he now had a decision to make. In his position, either decision was crap. Be labelled a grass by his family, god knows where that would take him, or work as a grass on their behalf. Either way, he would be controlled for the rest of his foreseeable future. *Flip a coin?* he thought. *Some decisions are too important to trust to luck.* Barry picked up one phone, dialled and waited.

"Frank, it's Barry. I have something for Angelo."

"I'm with him now, I'll put it on speakerphone." Barry relayed the information that he had received from Terry. There was no response from the other end.

"Frank, you still there?" asked Barry.

"You're off speakerphone," said Frank. "Angelo says to pass the information on."

"Who to?"

"The Old Bill."

"Not the others?"

"No, let's see if they get to find out."

"OK."

"And Barry…"

"Yes."

"You've made the right decision. I'll see you tomorrow."

"OK. Thanks." Relief flooded into Barry's body. *Decision made,* he thought, knowing that at least he now had the protection of the family. He picked up his second phone and sent a text requesting a call. It didn't take long for the cops to ring.

* * *

Ali Smith knocked on the Superintendent's door.

"Come in," said Robert Harrison. Ali walked in to find Harrison in conversation with Commander Gillespie. Both were sitting enjoying a coffee and looked comfortable in each other's company.

"Sorry to interrupt, Sir," said Ali, "Ma'am," he nodded to Gillespie, "I've just had a bit of an update from the source unit."

"Which is?" asked Harrison.

"I'm not sure how much it will enhance our enquiry."

"Spit it out, man!"

"Intelligence has just come in from our source that someone might be planning a job at the weekend. Maybe looking at ATMs."

"Is that it? Any mention of our burgling friend?"

"No, but it's from the new source, so it may be tentatively connected."

"You mean that it's from Lomax?" Smith looked hesitant. Source's real names were not supposed to be mentioned, indeed on most occasions, the bosses weren't even provided the details. However, arrogant as ever and with a flagrant disregard for covert protocols, Harrison always had to display that he knew all. Harrison smiled at Gillespie hoping that he had impressed her with his insider knowledge. Ali Smith made no reply.

"Oh, make sure it's recorded properly, Smith, and keep a watching brief on it. Any news on 'The Hare'?"

"Quiet for the moment, Sir but I'm confident that we'll get there."

"Make sure that you do." Harrison looked away from Smith and turned back towards Gillespie, "As I was saying, Serena ..." Taking it as a clear dismissal, Smith left the room, closing the door behind him.

* * *

"Cheers, mate." Terry terminated his phone call which he had just received from Roper. Barry had passed the test by providing the solicitor with the information that Terry had given to him. *Two birds with one stone,* thought Terry. Now the cops now knew that something was going down at the weekend. They didn't know what but when events kicked off they would realise that Barry's information was legitimate.

This would begin the process of the cops trusting Barry's information and for the family to commence the long process of infiltrating the Met Police. The Lomaxes would use Barry, provide him with legitimate information regarding their criminality, he would pass it to the police and they could act on it. The Lomaxes may have to take a few small hits to their empire but, whilst the cops acted on the small stuff, the family could plan and progress their larger criminal enterprises. Positive results would increase Barry's value to the police. Barry in turn would be trained by the family, tasked to listen, question and probe, find weaknesses in the cops looking after him, weaknesses that the Lomaxes hoped they could take advantage of in the future. *Wouldn't be you for the world, son,* thought Terry.

"Afternoon, Keith. How are you doing?" Terry asked as he entered the house where the team had based themselves.

"I'm good, mate." Keith handed Terry a drink.

"Where's everyone at?"

"Ronnie and Jane are just checking on our soap order. Jack's gone into the city for a last recce of the bank and the tower, and we're here. Digestive?" Keith offered a packet to Terry.

"No thanks. Struggling to eat at the moment."

"Nerves?"

"Suppose so. You not nervous?"

"Absolutely shitting myself."

"You don't look it. You seem cool as ever."

"Nice of you to say but no, I'm bricking it."

"You happy with your part?"

"Yes. It's just pre-match nerves. Once we're going for it, I'll be fine. Jane's taken me through what I need to do, a dozen times may I say, and Ronnie's got my ID sorted."

"She's a good un ain't she."

"Who?"

"Ronnie. Well both of them. Jane's new to this game, however long she's been preparing for it, and Ronnie ... well she's pushed her boundaries and what can't she do with a computer!"

"Yeah, the team's good, mate. You can trust them."

"How are our travelling friends doing?"

"Primed and ready. They know it's this week and are gathering all their troops together. Just waiting for my call."

"Good, good. The cars?" asked Terry

"They've got them finished a day early. We'll collect them tomorrow and take them to the warehouse. Last meeting there tomorrow?"

"Yes, then we'll ship everything out from there. Ronnie and Jane are picking up the van and soap tomorrow and will bring it over. False plates ready for everything?"

"Yes, all ready to swap them after we've done the job."

"We're just about there then, Keith. Who'd have thought, eh?"

"We'll be rich men and women by the weekend."

"Let's hope so. It's the last push now."

* * *

"You will have to come to Italy so that I can give you proper coffee," said Ricco, "not this rubbish." He looked disdainfully at the pale and insipid contents of the mug in front of him. John was sitting opposite him enjoying a bacon roll, lavishly coated with ketchup. "Tis not good for you, John."

"Tastes great though," said John, his speech muffled by his full mouth. He sipped on his tea, washing the food down. "What are we going to do then?"

"You have not heard from him?"

"Barry? Not a jot."

"But something is going down at the weekend?"

"That's what I have been told."

"Do we think Barry is involved?"

"No idea, mate. I'm guessing that he has provided the police with the information though. I've tried ringing him but it's not even connecting."

"His phone switched off?"

"Could be."

"So Barry, an Uber driver, has his phone off. He's told the police about a job at the weekend. We cannot find him. He's layin' low. He's up to something."

"Agreed."

"I'll have my team watch his flat. We'll grab him if we can. Any news on the girl from the photo?"

"Nothing. She's a ghost. The Lomax family tree is massive. With nothing else to go on, I'm struggling. There have not been any more burglaries. The Met seem to be getting nowhere with their enquiries."

"We have Barry and Antiques Keith then. That's it?"

"So it seems."

"My boss ain't gonna be happy."

"Nor mine."

"We need to pressure them. I mean Barry and Keith. Let me find Barry. I will deal with him. You pay a visit to antiques. He definitely knows something."

"I'll trawl around his shops until I find him."

"Good, I need to report back by the weekend. We need something by then."

"Agreed," John drained his tea mug and stood up. "Let's get going."

* * *

"Here's the beauties. Hope, Faith and Charity. He tapped each car in turn. Green, white and red. Call signs for each car when they are being driven. As passengers, we will have radio comms. The drivers won't."

"They look terrific," said Jane.

"Wait until you hear the engine," said Terry, climbing into Hope and turning the ignition key."The engine thrummed powerfully and then idled.

"Nice," said Jack. "Which one's mine?"

"Take your choice," said Terry, having switched the engine off and climbed out of the car.

"Jane?" asked Jack.

"I'll take Charity," said Jane. "She looks lovely."

"You've got the keys for Hope, Terry, which leaves me with Faith."

"That's sorted then."

"Happy with your van, Keith?"The white transit stood next to the cars with its rear doors open. Sitting within the back was a pallet containing the gold soap bars in a large block, wrapped together and held in position by clingfilm."

"She'll do fine," he replied.

"We've come a long way, in a short period," said Terry, addressing the team. "All our pawns are in place. Two days and we start. That's two days to get any personal business sorted and out of the way. When we do this, and we will, we'll need to keep our heads down. Let the dust settle for a while. That means no contact with friends, family, or anyone. All except for Ronnie who is looking after her mum."

He looked around their faces, ensuring that they fully understood. "You all know what you need to do. We all do our part of the job properly and we'll be rich people by Sunday." Smiles of anticipation and nervousness spread across the team. "Any questions?" Everyone remained silent. "Take your cars from here. Hide them, stash them, until Friday. You all know the plan. Ronnie, Keith will drop you in the van at your gaff." Ronnie nodded.

"Lastly, from me," He walked to each person and shook their hands, "Good luck. You get caught, and you keep quiet. Your gold will be waiting for you when you get released. You have my word on it." He finished and turned away and walking towards a side door called out loud. "Now, let's get out of here. Ten minutes between each car." Terry continued walking, his moment of infamy now within his grasp.

* * *

Keith was idly polishing a large brass paperweight, resembling a gold bar, which was positioned on the counter within his shop. The doorbell of the shop chimed, indicating that a customer had entered. He looked up and smiled. A smile that froze on his face when he saw that the customer was John. *Alone this time*, he thought.

"Morning, Keith,"

"Good morning. John, was it?" asked Keith, "What can I do you for?"

"That yours?" asked John, nodding towards the bar.

"Nah, nicked it from the Bank of England," said Keith, receiving no reaction from John, "Only joking." Keith gave a nervous laugh. John reached across the counter and taking hold of the bar dragged it across the wooden surface.

"She's heavy," he said looking at the item. John then reached into his pocket, retrieved a packet of cigarettes and lit one. "Thought we should just have another chat. You know. Just me and you."

"There's no smoking in the shop. The signs ..." Keith pointed to a sign as his voice faded. John ignored him, inhaled deeply and blew the smoke out.

"Just called in to see if your memory has improved."

"About?" John slammed his hand on the wooden top.

"DON'T PISS ME ABOUT, KEITH." Keith jumped in shock. John's voice quietened. "I think you know something. Something about the watches and I think that it's in your interests to tell me what you know." John produced a metal item from his pocket and placed it down with a clunk Keith stared down at a metal knuckleduster.

"Ahh, I see," said Keith. *This isn't looking good.* "No need for that though. I was waiting for you to call back. Where's your friend?"

"None of your business. What do you know?"

"I may have heard something. Not much mind you. Just a name."

"And the name is?" John placed his hand on the knuckleduster.

"Scrimshaw. Ian Scrimshaw."

"And who is he?"

"He's a handler up north. Birmingham based, I think. Your people will have heard of him. Whoever your people are." John gave no response. "I've heard that he's trying to shift a couple of top-quality watches. Don't know the make. Not my specialism, you see." John picked up the duster and placed it back in his pocket.

"That's a start." John walked back to the door and opened it. "Have a nice day, Keith. I'll be seeing you soon." He walked away from the shop.

Keith walked over and locked the door. He'd have to contact Terry and let him know. *Head down now Keith. Lay low until Friday,* he thought. John may take a while to find Scrimshaw, who was indeed a handler of stolen goods. Scrimshaw had fleeced Keith a couple of years ago for which Keith had never forgiven him. Birmingham was far enough away to keep John busy and after Saturday no one would be seeing Keith the Quiff for quite some time.

* * *

Jack had prepared all of his equipment for his afternoon visit to Angel Court. Keith was due to collect him later and drop him off in central London, close to his destination. His outfit and pack were placed neatly on the bed, ready for him to change and collect but first, a job to do.

Now, dressed in his joggers and hoodie and carrying a small package, Jack walked on the Boundary Estate. The streets were quiet as he approached the block where his sister lived. Graffiti adorned the bottom of the stairwell which also stank of urine. Jack was glad that this would be one of his last visits for a while and possibly forever. Electing to use the stairs he climbed quietly, eventually stepping out onto the landing where his sister lived.

Approaching cautiously, he gently placed the package outside of her front door and knocked on the door, walked swiftly away and secreted himself around a corner. Peering around the stairwell wall he watched the door open and a child's hand reach out, taking the parcel. Jack ducked back as he saw Chris' head bob out, looking up and down the corridor. Jack walked quietly away with a smile on his face.

* * *

"Can you get the door please, Chris," yelled Tania who was sitting on the toilet texting her friend. "I'll be there in a minute." Tania finished her ablutions and opened the door to see Chris standing with a package in both of his hands.

"It was just this mum. No one was there!" Tania looked at the package which had Chris and her names neatly printed upon it.

"Give it here love." Chris handed her the package as they both sat down on the sofa. "It's addressed to us. Let's open it," she said excitedly. Tania carefully opened one side of the package, looked in with confusion and as she opened it fully, they both watched bundles of tens and twenty-pound notes tumble onto the floor. Chris laughed at his mum's shocked face as she stared at the hundreds of pounds before them.

"Look, mum," said Chris, reaching into the package and taking out a black object. He held up the silhouette of a running hare. Tania took hold of Chris and started crying tears of joy, knowing that this would give her her chance to get out.

* * *

Ronnie checked in on her mum who was watching her favourite afternoon soap opera. Tomorrow Mrs Pilcher was being collected early by a patient transport team and was being taken to her annual holiday at a Cotswolds Retreat. The holiday was something that Ronnie ensured happened every year and was a place that her mum recognised and enjoyed. Although not due to visit there until next Wednesday, Ronnie had been able to secure a few extra days for her. The break would do them both good and would allow Ronnie to fully concentrate on the job at hand. Further, should the need occur then Ronnie could disappear for a few days away from home. Ronnie was looking forward to the excitement of the next few days and went to double-check that her equipment was ready for the task at hand.

* * *

Jane looked around her apartment. Everything was neat, as it should be. She moved one of the cushions on the sofa, swiftly placing it back in a different position. She felt tense. Jane had everything ready for work tomorrow, had had it ready for hours in fact, but she was fretting. Unused to the nervousness within her she was scared that she couldn't pull it off, and that she couldn't to work and act naturally. She had the full day to contend with, knowing that Jack was in the building with her but not knowing where. If he was caught then she would have to get involved, speak with her bosses, and speak with the police. Hang him out to dry. The job would be called off and her years of self-sacrifice would be for nothing. Jane moved the cushion again before walking towards the hallway and the kitchen to prepare her tea.

* * *

The Angel Court entranceway stood before Jack, the glass tower thrusting towards the sky, dominating the surrounding architecture. Keith had dropped him off as close as he was able and now Jack had wheeled a sack barrow carrying a large package onto Throgmorton Street. Dressed in a plain polo shirt, workman's trousers and wearing a cap, he had moved smoothly through the pedestrian traffic largely unnoticed by busy commuters striding by.

Previous access to the building had brought him to this point. In the entrance vestibule an escalator transported attendees to the second floor where they would be greeted at the reception. The reception was grand in itself with a double-height ceiling and a seating area which gave fantastic views into the cultivated dense woodland that had been created outside. The 'Diorama' housed trees up to nine metres tall which provided a beautiful canopy to the setting. However, today the reception was not Jack's target. On the ground floor behind the escalator, his recce had discovered a service lift, his ingress to the building.

Jack halted in the street, close to the doorway, and prepared himself. The culmination of his plan started today and he was feeling the pressure. The team were reliant on the first stage going well as there would be no job without it. He calmed his nerves. *Come on, Jack. You're ready.*

Taking a deep breath he took hold of the trolley, tilted it and walked confidently towards the door. The automatic doors slid open with a hiss, Jack walked into the air-conditioned coolness of the lobby and straight towards the rear of the escalator. He was aware of the CCTV cameras covering the entrance, hence the cap, but his years of experience had taught him to act naturally. *Behave as people would expect you to.* The customers and staff should see a confident maintenance man going about his daily business, walking through the building as if he belonged there.

The theatre of the act would allay most questioning eyes, and prevent unwanted conversations but, in the back of his mind, he had to be prepared to deal with any person or situation. Despite his outward appearance, Jack's paranoia was high. He pushed the lift button to call it and waited whilst he watched the floor indicator showing the lifts descent from the second floor. *Could have been so much worse*, he thought imagining the wait should the elevator be positioned on the top floor. Jack checked his watch which displayed four-fifty. The lift pinged and the doors opened.

"Mind yourself there, buddy," said a large male dragging a trolley, containing red and blue mailbags, from the lift. Jack smiled and stepped to one side, moving his barrow with him.

"You pulled a late shift?" asked the male, huffing as he pulled the load.

"Just a quick job on the tenth floor," replied Jack.

"On a Friday!"

"I know, mate but it won't take me long."The man continued walking towards the elevator.

"Have a good one," he called, disappearing from view. Jack entered the lift and pressed the button for the top floor. He felt calm after his interaction and was now in role. He watched the floor buttons illuminate as he passed the seventh floor, climbing steadily through the Sky Floors. He had gambled on the building quietening after five o'clock and anticipated that any late meetings would be held on the Garden Floors and the Roof Gardens.

The Gardens terminated on the seventh floor and he was well beyond them. Jack's luck held as he reached the rooftop with no persons calling or using the maintenance lift. He stepped out into the bright sunshine, lifted his encased parajet from the trolley and, leaving the trolley within, sent the lift back down to ground level. He knew that the trolley would be discovered by a member of staff at some point but thought it was likely that they would just move it onto one of the landings and forget about it.

The air at the top of the building was markedly cooler. The white caged covering, over almost the entire roof, provided a small degree of protection from the wind. Jack surveyed the area, looking for a location to secrete the parajet so that he could explore the rooftop. Large metal ducting wormed its way over metal boxing, white pipes and guttering. Jack lifted the parajet and stashed it underneath one of the convection pipes. There has to be a hatch to allow me to get onto that mesh, he thought as he carefully manoeuvred himself around the metallic architecture.

"There you are." Jack saw a small set of stairs which moved from rooftop to mesh, at the top of the steps was a hinged hatch cover. He moved closer, noting that the hatch was padlocked. He turned back, retrieved the jetpack, carried it over to the base of the stairs, unzipped the side pocket of its carrying case, and took out his lock picks. A quick check of the lock and he had opened it. Jack tentatively lifted the hatch and peered out over the vast expanse of solid metal caging. "Looks good," he said, lowering it and returning to the base of the ladder. "Right, Jack. Orientate yourself. Where's The Old Lady?" Jack spent the next thirty minutes exploring the rooftop and, having located the Bank of England, was happy. He looked at his watch.

"Better check in with Ronnie." He returned to his pack and dialled her.

"Jack, how's things?" she asked.

"Good, I'm on the roof and ready. No complications."

"WHAT'S THAT?," shouted Ronnie, "THERE'S A LOT OF WIND NOISE. YOU ON THE ROOF?"

"YES, I'LL TEXT YOU." He terminated the call.

Jack:- On the roof. No issues.
Ronnie:- Good man. I thought so.
Jack:- Next check-in when heading to target.
Ronnie:- OK. Good luck, Gabriel. You like that?
Jack:- Genius!!!!!!!!!

Jack chuckled to himself. Ronnie would let the rest of the team know that he was ready. He opened the pack and retrieved some overalls and something to eat. It would be a long wait now until darkness and the early hours of the morning. Jack secreted himself and his equipment out of sight but with a view of the maintenance lift doors.

* * *

He's in position. Update later.

Terry looked at the received text. *Good lad. Good lad.* He was sitting on the sofa nursing his only whisky of the night, hoping that a dram would help him get to sleep later. Terry switched on the television and channel hopped halting on a rerun of The Dark Knight and waited for his next text to arrive.

Jane jumped as her phone pinged indicating that she had received a message. She felt on edge and even after her tea couldn't settle. In the bathroom, the taps were still running as she prepared a bath. She smiled after reading Ronnie's text.

"A real action man," she said aloud thinking of Jack's activities this evening. She walked towards the bathroom to try and relax.

Keith stood at the counter in his shop when his pocket vibrated. He'd locked up early and was just tidying up. He read the text.

"Go for it, son." His eyes moved to the polished brass bar on the counter. "Real gold by Saturday." He touched it for good luck.

Chapter 13

Darkness had now descended upon the city as the ebb and flow of daytime activity had changed to that of the night time economy. Angel Court reigned over the surrounding architecture as Jack crept and negotiated its crown towards the edge of the skyscraper, behind him the black package that was his parajet waited for his attention. The night was balmy with a gentle breeze pushing against his side, accentuated as he approached the side of the building with the forced updraft caused by the building.

Looking across from the Angel, the Old Lady squatted stolidly, her rooftop illuminated with carefully positioned security lighting. One area appeared to be darker than the rest and was the area in which Jack intended to land. *It's time*, he thought. He moved back to the parajet and slowly removed its component parts.

Powered paragliding was Jack's favourite sport. The Maverick was the ideal model for his flight across to bank. The lightweight titanium alloy frame could be assembled in minutes. He worked swiftly and smoothly as he snapped the frame together, adding the netting system as he did so, and soon had it attached to the engine. Jack climbed into the harness and looked behind him where the wing was spread out behind the machine. With the jetpack holdall now neatly folded and fastened to his chest, he was ready to launch. Now using his covert radio Jack transmitted.

"Jack to Ronnie."

"Go ahead."

"Ready to go."

"OK." Then silence. Jack knew that Ronnie was taking over control of the rooftop cameras. After a sixty second wait she announced, "Clear to go."

Jack pressed the electric start and as the engine gunned into life he walked slowly forward feeling the wing pulling upwards. He engaged the throttle finding the point between drag and lift, stepped closer to the precipice of the roof and applied more throttle, allowing the parajet to propel him, and the wing to engage and take his weight. The updraft from the building pushed him skywards. He used the controls and adjusted his body and couldn't help but smile with the elation of flight swamping his senses. Jack orientated, adjusted his speed and descended towards the Bank of England. As the motor thrummed through his body he glided confidently on his approach to the bank. He focused on his landing area, the dark patch looming quicker than expected. With practised ease Jack adjusted, glided in, and landed, cutting his engine as he did so.

The roof was covered in netting. Jack turned and dropped to his knees for stability, swiftly pulled in his wing, gathered it and held still. Before him, the outline of a dormer stood starkly against the luminescence of Angel Court and would be his entry point to the building. Jack moved. Slipping out of the harness he crawled slowly over the netting touching the rooftop as his hands and knees pressed against it at different points. Jack reached the small valley before the dormer and now in darkness caused by its shadow waited whilst his eyes adjusted. Before him the outline of a roof doorway with a small long window to its side, revealed itself.

"Ronnie, I'm on the roof."

"You OK?"

"Yes."

"Nice one. What are you looking at?"

"As planned I'm in the southeast corner. Looking at a rooftop door with a small window to the side." He switched the light on his phone illuminating the door. "It's full metal with a lock and has no markings."

"Can you see The Angel behind it?"

"Yes,"

"You're at door three. Standard lock, it's alarmed, there's no CCTV once you get through."

"I'll be ready in five."

"OK." Jack terminated the call and retraced his route to the parajet. Climbing back into the harness he carried his equipment back to the door, disassembled it and stashed it back within its pack. He looked around the roof and identified an area to hide it. A place where it would stay forever and hopefully remain undiscovered. Leaving the pack and now carrying all his equipment in his hands and pockets he returned to the door, lockpicks ready.

"Ready, Ronnie."

"Okey dokey. I've got the schematics before me. Give me two minutes." Jack waited imagining Ronnie tapping on her keyboard as she worked. He waited patiently. "All done. Over to you. You've got a free run of the stairs to the next landing. I'll text the team. Call back when you're happy."

"Will do." Jack examined the lock. Choosing two implements he inserted a wrench bar and probed with a Peterson Reach, offset hook. Gently working he felt the pins move as he manoeuvred the hook and with a satisfying last click, defeated the lock. Jack gently pushed against the door, which swung smoothly inwards. Looking up he saw the alarm plates on the door and frame and, now releasing his breath, was confident that Ronnie had done her job.

He produced two magnetised metal plates joined by a long wire and attached them to the door alarm plates. The equipment would allow Ronnie to reset the door alarm but still allow Jack to enter and exit through the door without setting off the alarm. As long as the wire between the magnetised plates remained in place, the system would not detect that the door had been opened.

Jack had discussed the tactic with Ronnie and this would be his means of moving through the building. Defeat a door, place the magnetic plates in position, and move on to the next door. As he defeated a door he would return to the previous one, remove its magnetic plates and Ronnie would reset the alarm. Using this method he could move steadily through the building, always have an escape route, and hopefully leave no trace that he had been there. He moved downwards towards his next challenge.

* * *

It was three a.m. when Terry was awoken by the sound of his mobile phone pinging. He reached to his bedside table and squinted at the screen. A message from Ronnie.

The eagle has landed

Sitting up and he rubbed his eyes before rechecking the message. *We're on*, he thought knowing that the rest of the team would be receiving the same information. He replied with a thumbs-up emoji, climbed out of bed and headed to the toilet for his nightly visit, a curse of the over-fifties. Terry had booked a hotel for the night so he could be in the city and knowing that he now wouldn't sleep, jumped in the shower before putting the kettle on. Over the next forty-eight hours, he knew that his body would be running on pure adrenaline and an hour or two's extra sleep tonight would make no difference, even if it was achievable. His phone rang,

"You awake?" It was Keith.

"I am now. You get the message?"

"Yes, he's in."

"He certainly bloody is."

"Game on, Tel. This time tomorrow we'll be rich."

"All things being equal we will."

"I can't sleep now."

"Me neither. We need less at our age anyway."

"Just as well. I seem to be running for a piss all night."

"Join the club, mate."

"Which one?"

"The millionaire club." They both laughed. "You contacting Pat?"

"Will do. I'll wait till after eleven."

"Cars to park up this morning. Everyone's briefed."

"Yeah. I'll park Jack's for him."

"Good," Terry looked at his maintenance uniform hanging in the wardrobe. "All ready then. Good luck."

"You too, Tel. We're gonna do it, you know."

"See you on the other side." Terry ended the call and made himself a strong coffee.

* * *

Jane walked away from Charity, having ensured that the car's doors were locked. She had received the text in the early hours of the morning and had not slept since. Now dressed in a dark suit, she had travelled into the city early to secure her parking on Lower Thames Street and was now walking to work.

It would take her about fifteen minutes which should give her time to calm her nerves in preparation for the day ahead. Jane wasn't sure how she was going to get through the day but knew that her challenge was minor compared to Jack's, who had to move through the building and remain undetected for the duration. She walked along Lower Thames Street, heading towards Fish Street Hill where her route would eventually take her to Threadneedle Street. *Just follow your routine*, Jane reassured herself. *Grab a takeout coffee en route, calm your nerves and act naturally. It's just a normal day.* She continued briskly walking, enjoying the early morning sights and sounds of the city, an atmosphere that, following tonight, she would not experience for some time.

Twenty minutes later, armed with a flat white, she scanned her staff card and approached the security desk at the bank.

"Morning, Martin. How are you this morning?" Martin looked at her as he unzipped her handbag to check it inside.

"Morning, Jane. Fine, thank you," he replied, his face remaining impassive.

"You're always so serious," she said, smiling at him.

"Guarding the biggest financial institution in England is a serious business."

"Indeed it is, Martin. Indeed it is." Jane walked through the screening detector, collected her bag at the other side and headed towards her offices, smiling at the second security guard as she did so. *So far so good. I hope you are OK, Jack.*

* * *

Jack had rested for a few hours in one of the upper-floor offices. Reliably informed by Jane that it was unused at this time it had provided him a safe location to relax and recharge his batteries. The rest had also allowed Ronnie to relax and get some sleep if she could. They had arranged to contact each other at ten o'clock. The bank should be fully occupied by then with staff going about the business of the day. Jack checked the small map, that Jane, Ronnie and he had created and called up Ronnie.

"Jack. How's things?"

"Good. Did you get some rest?"

"Rest but no sleep."

"Same here."

"Jane's in the building. She clocked in at about five to nine. She'll be in her office."

"Good. The others?"

"Everyone is on the move. Just doing their final checks."

"Great. We move on?"

"Yes, it's all go. The CCTV cameras start at the next floor, The Parlours. All the corridors are covered. None of the offices. Staff changing on your floor. Watch out for cleaning and maintenance teams. Some of the senior staff are in. The Governor hasn't clocked in. He's probably out at a business meeting or press event."

"OK. I'll set off in five. Comms seem clear."

"Cool. The radio's working well. Good luck."

"Cheers." Jack checked the room over to ensure that he'd not disturbed anything, wanting to ensure that he had left no trace that he'd been there. Thin celluloid gloves protected his hands. He removed his earpiece, fitted a new battery in it and heard the blip in his ear as it powered and connected.

"Jack with a comms check."

"Loud and clear," came the reply from Ronnie who was monitoring at the other end. The team had agreed that communications would remain between Jack and Ronnie only. No one listening in, or chirping in with suggestions that may distract the burglar. They'd have to trust him to do his job, collect Jane and Terry as planned and get the job done. He altered his radio to whisper mode which would allow him to speak quietly though Ronnie would hear him clearly.

"Moving forward," said Jack.

"Received," replied Ronnie.

Jack walked towards the door of the office and listened intently as his hand moved towards the door handle. He took hold of it, turned it gently and cracked open the door. Peering out he saw no one, heard nothing. Slowly, he pulled the door inwards, checked the corridor, which remained clear and stepped out. He pulled the door to and shut it behind him. Turning left he crept swiftly down the corridor to where it turned sharply right. Jack calmed his breathing, the inhalations sounding loud in his head. He approached the corner but heard footsteps in front of him, someone opening a door around the corner! He froze and looked back. The corridor behind remained empty. The office door he had exited was too far to retreat to. He waited. Prepared himself. *Get out of this one, Jack,* he thought.

The door reopened. Jack stood ready. *Going to collect my uniform mate, but I got lost.* The door closed. Footsteps walked away. Jack peered around the corner seeing the back of a tall man turning left at the end of a straight corridor. Jack followed, identified the door he needed, opened it and walked in.

A quick scan revealed it to be a changing room. Grey metal lockers were situated in neat rows around the walls surrounding a central bench with a metal coat rack and rails attached to it. A toilet door stood open, the room was empty. Uniforms of the bank butlers were neatly hanging from the rails ready for use. Jack checked them quickly, looking for a suitable size to fit him, found a jacket and tried it on. *A good fit.* The trousers were slightly tight but they would do.

A laundry chute was positioned on one wall which he used to discard his own clothing, knowing that they would be put through a wash cycle before anyone discovered that they weren't standard uniforms. A pair of white gloves to cover his own finished the outfit. His small amount of equipment was placed in his pockets and he was ready to descend into The Parlours.

"Moving down, Ronnie," he transmitted.

"Received," the reply. *Time to hide in plain sight,* thought Jack, *Act as if you belong.* He checked his map, tucked it into his pocket and moved out of the room onto the corridor following the route that he had observed the other man take.

"Stairwell to my left, Ronnie."

"Empty at the moment, Jack. You can descend."

"Loud and clear." Jack opened the door to the stairwell and casually walked down the steps towards the lion's den.

* * *

Jane walked out of the Monday morning meeting with the security staff management team.

"Another boring hour out of the way," said one of her colleagues. "Roll on the weekend. You got any plans, Jane?"

"Not particularly," replied Jane, "I'll probably just binge-watch some Netflix." She threw her car keys down onto her desk as the male walked past.

"New car? You upgraded?"

"What do you mean?"

"That's a Citroen fob," he nodded towards the emblem showing on her key fob, "thought you had a 500?"

"Oh, that!" Jane quickly snatched the keys up. *Damn,* she thought, "just trying out a rental, see if I fancy one."

"Good little car maker. Try a C1. Nippy little cars. Anyway, back to work." The man walked off to his office. Jane put the keys away in her handbag kicking herself inside for making a mistake. She started scanning her emails to see what needed immediate attention. The meeting had gone smoothly, no incidents to report during the past week and the bosses seemed happy with everything. Next Monday's meeting was sure to be different, although Jane wouldn't be there to witness that.

* * *

"Hi, Pat. Your lads all ready?" asked Keith.

"Just waiting for the nod from you, mate. They're getting a bit twitchy waiting though."

"Well, they need to wait no longer. We're on for tonight."

"Great. They're getting on my nerves hanging about here. Agreed time and place?"

"Yes, as discussed, Camden, early hours onwards. Keep them busy."

"Don't you worry. They will be. Good luck, Keith. Whatever you're up to."

"And you. I'll tell you one day." The telephone call ended. Keith texted Terry to let him know that he had put the plan in action.

Keith had been busy this morning. First, he'd parked Faith on Upper Thames Street ready for later, then he'd finished checking in with his shops. His staff knew that he'd be off the radar for some time and knew that it wasn't unusual for him to be so. He now sat waiting in one of his garages, looking at a very unfashionable uniform and a white van. He had decided that he would just sit tight all day until he was required later.

* * *

Jack walked down a long corridor passing various office doors, some open and some closed. The financial business of the day seemed to be in full swing with the sound of secretaries typing, whispered phone calls and occasionally suited men and women walking with determination.

Within all the activity Jack wandered through unknown and unseen. A natural piece of the environment who was ignored and unnoticed by the employees of the bank. In his head, he knew where he needed to go and navigation through this area was necessary for him to get there. He moved casually but with purpose, a man with a goal.

"You there," stated a voice. Jack kept walking. "I'm talking to you, butler," he turned to see a suited man, carrying a tray holding a carafe of water and two glasses.

"Me, Sir?"

"Yes, you. Apologies. I don't know your name."

"Biggs, Sir."

"Apologies, Biggs. Are you new?"

"Relatively, Sir."

"Well, never mind. Do you know where the Governor's rooms are?"

"Yes, Sir. I do indeed." Jack had memorised the location whilst studying the building's blueprints.

"Good man. Here you go." The male handed Jack the tray and contents. "The Governor will be back this afternoon. Take this to his office and place it on the sideboard. There's a good chap." *A stroke of luck,* thought Jack.

"Yes, Sir. Straight away." Jack turned and walked away with the tray, struggling to hide the smile on his face. Jack continued on the corridor, turned left, then right and headed towards the Governor's private corridor. He pressed his radio transmission button.

"Just heading to the Governor's office, Ronnie."

"You are bloody joking!"

"Not at all."

"It's too early."

"No option." Jack continued walking and saw the large office doors before him. Ronnie was sitting watching him on CCTV and realised what his interaction with the man in the suit must mean.

"You make your own luck, mate. Nice one," she said to herself.

* * *

Terry walked along Byward Street having travelled into the city in Charity. He'd swap keys with Jane later. She'd park up Hope for him. The car would stay there now, until tomorrow, when she would join in the Classic Rally with the others. He'd checked in with Ronnie and so knew that the team's tasks were being completed with no hiccups so far. Tommy had received his last update early this morning and was no doubt currently sipping champagne. Well, maybe just a beer. Hopefully, he'd save the champagne for tomorrow.

Terry knew his route through the city and walked casually along, in his maintenance uniform, carrying a small bait bag over his shoulder. He planned to arrive at 4.30 p.m. but was early so decided to stop for a coffee beforehand to pass the time. He couldn't sit still at the hotel so had decided to get parked up early and be ready in plenty of time. He took the security pass out of his pocket for the umpteenth time and examined it. *You'd better work,* he thought. Confident in his abilities he knew that once through the security measures he would be fine. He knew where the maintenance crew were stationed, knew where the doctor's office was. He could bluster his way through anything but he also knew that luck always played her hand and hoped that today she played in his favour.

* * *

John was fuming. Sent on a wild goose chase to Birmingham, a trip that had proved to be fruitless, by a smart-arsed 'Keith the bloody Quiff' had not helped his mood. A trawl of Keith's known shops had proved negative, John was now in the mood to punch someone. It hadn't helped that the snivelling little shit Simeon had just called him and blown his stack regarding Digby's failure to obtain results.

Ricco was getting nowhere, despite having broken into Barry's flat to try and find him. Barry was lying low and was nowhere to be found. John reflected that it was probably good for Barry that he hadn't been found, as he was John's likely target for use as a punch bag. The police were faring no better, only working on a rumour that something may happen this weekend. John didn't even know if it had anything to do with the man he was after.

Sitting staring at his half-drunk coffee, he looked up as a middle-aged man wearing a security uniform and carrying a small shoulder bag, walked in and ordered an Americano.

"Lucky bastard," John mumbled to himself as he stood up and walked out, wishing that he had such a simple job in life.

* * *

Jack walked along the red-carpeted hallway as he approached the large dark oak doorway which led to the Governor's sitting room. The hallway decor was plain and pale except for gold-painted lines which ran along the skirting boards towards the door frame, itself painted white and gold. Jack approached the door, knocked, and hearing no reply opened the door and entered. Before him, a round coffee table stood with a comfortable three-seater sofa behind. A large chandelier hung from the architrave ceiling and large windows gave a view outside to the Governor's private garden. He stepped into the room, gently closing the door behind him.

Jack scanned the lavishly furnished room with its period pieces. In themselves they must have been worth a small fortune. Remaining at the door, Jack looked at the gardens outside which were also empty. Jane had advised him that the gardens were for the use of the Governor and his guests only and the stillness outside reflected this. Looking left there was a further door which would take Jack into the Governor's office. He approached, knocked to be safe and, hearing no reply, entered.

A large desk dominated the room, which had a seating area to one side and again, windows giving a clear view of the private walled courtyard with its neatly trimmed hedges. A sideboard occupied one wall where a redundant tray of glasses and a water jug was situated. Above the sideboard hung a painting of Sir John Soane. On another wall, a large piece depicting Her Majesty the Queen. Jack placed his tray down, next to the used one, and moved swiftly to the Governor's desk.

The desk had a large, light blue, ink blotter to protect the beautiful walnut top. A set of pens, neatly laid out, adjacent to a paperweight, and a half-empty glass of water. Jack smiled. The paperweight was fashioned in the shape of a small gold bar and was immaculately polished. Jack retrieved the glass in his gloved hands, poured its contents into another glass and carefully placed the used glass to one side. The Governor's fingerprints were likely on the glass. Jack used specialised equipment to identify and retrieve the Governor's thumbprint as a fail-safe, in case Ronnie came into difficulty with the bank's security measures. *Always maximise an opportunity*, thought Jack. He retrieved his map from a pocket, oriented himself and moved to a wall.

Jane had advised him that throughout the bank there were several hidden staircases allowing movement secretly through the building for senior staff if ever required. Although never expecting to gain entry to this room, Jack was aware that a secret corridor led from the room downwards. A large tapestried freeze adorned the wall and pulling it gently away Jack could see the outline of the hidden door. He pushed gently, heard a click, and the doorway was fully revealed. *One last job,* thought Jack.

He moved back towards the desk and removed an item from his back pocket, gently lifted the gold-coloured bar, and placed his calling card underneath it with a white corner sticking out. Jack moved back to the hidden door, gently opened it and stepped into the stairwell, pulling the door behind him. Darkness shrouded him. He reached for his phone, activated the light and looked down a thin corridor which led to a descending staircase.

"Ronnie, you there?"

"Yes, mate. I watched you enter the office. Everything seems good. No alarms. How are you doing?"

"I'm fine. In the hidden corridor that leads from the Governor's office."

"What's his office like?"

"Size of your house and probably worth twenty times as much."

"Not his though, mate. Owned by the bank."

"True."

"It's 4 p.m. now. Terry will be entering soon. What's your plan?"

"Keep heading down. Find somewhere to rest up and wait."

"That staircase leads directly down to the vaults. There's a branching corridor off it in a couple of floors. You'll be at the basement level there."

"I'll take a look. This area has not been used in months. A thin layer of dust on the floor and webs galore. I'll check it out."

"OK, I'll let everyone know that you're fine and that we're on target." Jack moved onward, intending to find somewhere to settle on the staircase. He was conscious that his only known means of egress in an emergency was into the Governor's office and that he may need to find an alternative route. He stopped as a deep rumble echoed from below and was sure he felt a tremor in the walls. Jane had warned him of the sounds within the building of passing tube trains. Good for dampening any noise he made but may also hide the sound of anyone else who should enter the secret stairwell. The tube train passed. Jack listened intently. *No sound from anyone*. He moved downwards.

* * *

Big Ben chimed the quarter hour as Terry negotiated his way through the city towards Threadneedle Street. Ronnie had provided the team with an update regarding Jack's progress and everything was looking good for tonight. Terry's insertion into the bank was the next play on the board and he was feeling nervous. *Nerves are good though*, he thought, knowing that he would be a fool not to be.

He took his staff pass card out of his pocket and checked it over. It would be enough to fool him and Ronnie seemed confident that it would get him in. He pressed it to his lips, kissing it for good luck, and clipped it onto his chest pocket. The colossal building loomed before him, the Union Jack flying at its crown.

"Here goes nothing," Terry mumbled as he approached the staff entrance joining some of the other maintenance crew. All ignored him, accepting his uniform as they entered. He slipped into line feeling the coolness of the building. Jane had explained what would happen as he went in and Ronnie had ensured that he knew his route to the doctor's office. He knew that Ronnie would be watching him but he carried no radio communications, as they may be discovered by the security guards. He had to trust that she would look after him. He approached the desk, handed over his mobile and scanned his card. The guard behind the desk looked at him. Terry smiled.

"First day?" asked the guard.

"Yes," replied Terry, "should've been yesterday but I couldn't make it." The guard looked at the screen and back towards Terry. *This is worse than airport customs*, thought Terry, his smile fixed on his face.

"A late shift, on a Friday! You've pulled a crappy one there," said the guard, "just follow the others, they'll show you the way." Terry exhaled in relief. "Through the gate." The guard nodded towards the metal detector. Terry turned and walked towards it.

"Hey," the guard shouted. Terry turned, adrenalin pumping, ready to run. "You forgot your phone." The guard held Terry's phone in his hand.

"Sorry. My bad," Terry replied and collected his phone.

"No problem, mate. Welcome to the Bank of England." Terry turned again as the guard checked through another member of staff. Placing his phone on a small table to the right he walked through the metal detector with no alarms and retrieved his phone. *Thank you, Ronnie.* He then followed a group of maintenance staff to a stairwell where they descended one flight and turned right down a long corridor. His phone vibrated in his hand.

Take the next left corridor.

It was Ronnie. She clearly had him in view. Terry looked ahead where the corridor ended in two double doors. There was a corridor to the left just before the doors. He checked behind seeing that it was clear and closed in on the back of the group of five people before him. The first reached the doors, scanned his staff pass and a buzzer sounded. He pushed the door, and the others followed, Tommy stepped swiftly left and stopped. He looked down the corridor and saw a camera pointing directly at him.

* * *

Ronnie was sitting looking at two computer screens before her. Both displayed the corridor in which Terry was currently standing; however, one showed him there, looking like a rabbit caught in headlights, and the other showed an empty corridor. The security office within the bank would see the empty corridor only. She changed the right screen to view sixteen different locations and the left to view two, Terry's corridor and the corridor beyond the doors. She flicked him a text.

Keep calm. I've got this. Go to doors. Use your pass.

She watched as Terry looked at his phone, read the text and gave the camera a thumbs up.

"Now would be nice, Terry," said Ronnie out loud, as she watched more staff exit the initial stairwell and walk towards his location. He turned and walked to the doors, used his pass and passed through just as the group crossed the corridor junction. Ronnie could see that his route to the doctor's office was clear. She texted.

Quick

Terry responded and moved along the corridor, counting doors as he did so. He stopped and reached for a door handle.

"Not that one," said Ronnie aloud, knowing that Terry couldn't hear her. She quickly typed on the keyboard attempting to access the security for the door that he was reaching to. Terry's hand stopped. He looked back up the corridor, retraced his steps and began counting the doors again. Ronnie stopped typing and watched. Terry walked past the door at which he had halted towards the next one along. He reached out. Ronnie pressed a key. Terry turned the handle and walked into the doctor's office. Ronnie sighed in relief, slumped back in her chair and pressed a further button, locking the door behind him. Her phone rang.

"Ronnie, I'm in," whispered Terry's excited voice.

"Nice one, Tel."

"I mean, I know that you know that. But I'm bloody in, Ronnie. I'm bloody in !"

"Calm down, mate. You've done well."

"What a rush, Ronnie. I was bricking myself." She smiled but knew that now was not the time to take the piss.

"Jane next, mate."

"You're bloody brilliant, Ronnie. Couldn't have done it without you."

"I am and you couldn't," laughed Ronnie. "Now, take a chill pill and I'll check back in with you on the hour. You're safe in there."

"Will do. I'll tell you something though,"

"What?"

"We're gonna bloody do this. I can feel it."

"Good. Now, I am feeling the call of nature. Text you in an hour."

"Righto." The call ended. Ronnie stood up and headed to the loo, running through her checklist on her fingers as she walked.

"Jane next. Check-in with Jack. Check-in with Terry. Update Keith.

Chapter 14

Earlier, Jane had watched Terry enter the bank on the security cameras within the CCTV suite at the bank. Ronnie had reassured her that things had all gone smoothly and that Terry was now safely ensconced in the doctor's office. Now, it was Jane's turn. She knew that Brian was on as she'd passed him on his way to work so things should go smoothly. The city remained busy with both cars and pedestrians and Jane was just another face in the crowd as she returned to work. With the staff entrance door now being locked, Jane pressed the door intercom awaiting a response. Brian's Welsh voice boomed out.

"Hello, there. What can I do you for?"

"Brian, it's me," Jane looked up at the security camera, smiling, "Jane, from security."

"Ah, Jane," he said, "I can see you now. I take it you need to be in."

"Yes, please. Just a spot check of the offices. You know what the bank's like."

"Of course." Jane heard the click of the door security lock releasing. "Come on in, door's open." Jane pushed on the door and entered. Brian was sitting behind the desk drinking a cup of tea.

"How are you, love?" he asked.

"I'm good. Doing your rounds soon?"

"Cup of tea first," he raised the cup, showing it to Jane as she placed her handbag on the desk. "No need, Jane. I trust you. Detector's off too. Go on, I'll buzz you through." Jane felt a pang of guilt but not believing her luck, walked onwards.

"I'll check myself out if you're on your rounds later."

"No problem, Jane." She continued walking. Brian had been an evening security officer for many years and it was clear to Jane, in her professional role, that his standards were slipping. His overfamiliarity with procedures and friendliness with staff would cause the bank's security team nightmares and unfortunately for Brian may prove his undoing as an employee. However, Jane steeled herself. Tonight, she had no room for sympathy. She was here to do her job and would walk away from the bank tomorrow and never return. She headed towards her offices, spot checking in other offices on her way, knowing that all would be monitored and recorded on the bank's security systems.

Two hours later, having done a sweep of the offices, Jane left the ladies' toilets having donned her covert radio and earpiece. She now had communication with Ronnie.

"Loud and clear," replied Ronnie. "You are good to go. Brian is on his rounds." Jane locked up her office and retraced her steps through the building to the staff entrance. Walking to the door she pressed the release button and stepped through. "Keep walking, Jane. Away from the building. That's it. Stop in one, two, three." Jane stopped. "Right. Ninety seconds. Brian's heading back."

"On my way." Jane returned swiftly to the door knowing that Ronnie now had control. The scene was set. Her spot visit had shown her diligence in her job and luck had shown a weakness in the bank's security. Unsurprisingly, that weakness was human error, and tonight the error was called Brian.

Jane walked to the door, heard the lock release, now controlled by Ronnie, and swiftly entered the building. She walked beyond the desk and detector, heading to the flight of stairs which Terry had descended earlier.

"He's approaching the doors on your left, Jane. Move!" Jane spun around, looking for cover. *The desk,* she thought. She crouched low and ran back to the desk. Dropped behind it and tucked in tight under it, just as the doors opened. Jane held her breath, her pulse throbbing in her head.

"He's in the room." Jane heard quietly in her earpiece. Brian was humming Men of Harlech quietly to himself. She heard his segged footwear clip towards the desk and gently released her breath in an attempt to calm her body. "At the desk." Jane could see the two polished toe caps of well-buffed shoes before her. A weight leant on the desk above her as the shoe leather creased. Ronnie was silent. The humming stopped. *Reaching for something*, thought Jane. She heard the scrape of a solid item on the desk above.

"Don't mind if I do," said Brian aloud. The toes spun away and the heels clicked across the flooring.

"Coming around. Sit tight. Kitchen." Jane heard the doors of the small kitchen, situated to the side of the desk, open and close. "Move, move, move." She uncurled her body and in a comedic parody of an adult playing horse, shuffled around the desk and through the gates, towards the stairwell. The muffled sounds of a kettle bubbling and the Bank of England's own Welsh tenor reached her ears. She pushed on the doors which Ronnie had unlocked and squeezed through just as Brian reentered the reception, looking around the room suspiciously.

"Stay still," said Ronnie in Jane's ear. Brian stood still looking and listening and seemingly satisfied with everything, returned to the kitchen. "Stairs down," said Ronnie. Jane followed her instructions and headed for the lower corridor. "Clear all the way. Head for the doctor's."

"Yes, yes," Jane responded, her heart ready to leap from her chest, "On my way." Jane had made it safely back into the building with the security team unaware of her presence.

* * *

Terry lounged back in the doctor's chair, staring up at the ceiling, his heels resting comfortably upon the doctor's desk, contemplating his lot. This would probably be the only time in his entire life when he was at the doctor's and not complaining about having to attend. Although a clinical setting, with patients' bench, height and weight scales and various implements neatly placed on a Formica work surface, the doctor had still managed to secure himself a beautiful mahogany desk and leather office chair.

"I bet that you earn a fortune, mate," said Terry aloud. His phone vibrated.

Jane's at the door

Terry lowered his legs and was sitting up straight when Jane entered the room.

"I'm sorry, madam. Did you book an appointment?" Jane looked at Terry sitting comfortably behind the desk and laughed.

"Well doctor, as this is a bank, I'm actually looking to make a withdrawal."

"Lovely, I'm sure that can be arranged." They both started giggling. Jane held up her hand, showing Terry how much it was shaking.

"Actually, I'm terrified." He took her hand in both of his.

"Me too, but I feel alive. It's dangerous, ballsy, and exhilarating but we're doing it."

"I nearly ran into the guard!"

"Did he see you?"

"No, Ronnie talked me through it."

"She's a good one." Jane pressed the transmit button on her radio.

"I think he appreciates your skills, Ronnie," said Jane.

"I know, I know," she replied.

"When do I get my comms?" asked Terry.

"Jack's bringing them," replied Jane. "What now?" Terry sat back down.

"Now we wait for Jack."

* * *

Jack checked his watch. *Nearly midnight. Time to get going.*

"Ronnie, you there?" he transmitted. Ronnie had kept Jack on his own radio channel and would switch the team all onto the same channel when they were grouped together.

"Here, Jack. Ready to go?"

"Yes."

"Terry and Jane are waiting for you. They're safely in place."

"Waiting over then. I'll go and find them." Jack had taken the opportunity to rest whilst Terry and Jane had infiltrated the bank. Sometimes sleep was out of the question in his profession but he had grown used to maximising rest time in order to preserve strength. He stood slowly and stretched. Folded neatly and now placed in a small alcove was his butler's jacket, his dark clothing now allowed him to blend with the shadows. Jack exited the stairs into an adjoining small corridor.

* * *

"Jack will be with you in a minute," said Ronnie to Jane on the radio.

"He's on his way, Tel," said Jane. They turned to face the main door of the room and waited expectantly. The minute seemed to drag by. Terry looked at his watch.

"He's taking his bloody time," said Terry.

"Do you think he's OK?" asked Jane.

"Check with Ro ..." The bathroom door behind them opened, Terry jumped in alarm and they both turned around.

"Hi there," Jack smiled at both of them, "Mind if I join you?"

"Bloody hell!" said Terry, holding his chest. Jane ran to Jack and grasped hold of him.

"You OK?" she asked, interrupting Terry's expletives.

"Never better." He returned the hug, removed Jane's arms and stepped fully into the room. Terry walked towards the bathroom.

"How the hell did you?"

"Governor's staircase. Secret back stairs so he can visit the doctor anytime he wishes with no-one the wiser. Wouldn't want anyone to know that the Governor's not feeling well would they?"

"Brilliant," said Terry, peering into the room.

"Jack, Keith wants a call with you all. He sounds worried," said Ronnie.

"Tell him to call me. I'll stick him on my phone speaker. I'll make sure that I transmit the call live to you, Ronnie." Terry's phone vibrated.

"Keith, what's up?" said Terry.

"I'm worried that the job's blown, mate. One of those blokes came back to my shop, they're chasing after the watches and now I can't get hold of Barry. I've got a bad feeling."

"Barry?" asked Jack.

"Your driver," said Terry. Terry checked his watch and looked at the others. "What do we do?"

"No mention of this job. We're here. The plan's good, so we trust it. Trust each other," said Jack. Keith looked at Jane.

"I'm out of here tomorrow, whatever happens. I'd rather have the gold and cash when I leave. Let's go for it?"

"Ronnie, what do you think?" asked Jack on the radio.

"We've come too far. Go for it?"

"Ronnie's in. What about you, Keith?"

"I'll go with whatever Terry wants." Jack and Jane looked at Terry.

"We only have this one chance. We are here now and doing it. I say we keep going. Let's get this done. Keith, keep the wheels in motion with Pat. Keep trying Barry and keep calm. We're going to be fine."

"Will do. Good luck." The call terminated.

"Here's your equipment, Terry," said Jack, handing Terry his covert equipment. "Get that on. I'll tidy the bathroom. I'm dying for a pee." Jack disappeared into the bathroom as Terry put his radio set on.

"Right, we all set?" asked Jack reentering the office. Terry and Jane both nodded. "Let's go over the plan once again." Jack pressed his transmit button. "Ronnie, let Keith know that he can prepare himself and set off within the hour."

"Will do," came the reply. Jack took a map out of his pocket and opened it on the table. He pointed to an area.

"We're here."

* * *

Pat was sitting comfortably on an office chair, his elbows resting upon a small desk. Both items of furniture had been bolted to the floor in the rear cargo space of a van. Upon the bulkhead of the compartment was displayed an enlarged map of the area of the city that they were targeting. The desktop held his mobile phone, a police scanner, a walkie-talkie and a marker pen. The sides and floor of the van were carpeted and the rear windows of the van were mirrored glass preventing anyone from outside seeing in. On the floor of the van a square of carpet could be peeled back to reveal a small hatch. The hatch would allow him to stash map, phone and radio quickly. In an emergency a lever could open the base of the metal compartment, discarding its contents onto the road or ground underneath.

Pat had commissioned the alterations to the van when he started planning the job. He needed a legitimate vehicle in which he could run the job but should the police stop/check it, or in the worst case chase it, then he needed to dispose of any evidence quickly. With an opening door in the bulkhead, he could also swiftly climb through to the front if needed. All the work had been completed by one of his lads. If the vehicle worked well for them tonight he could put it away in a lock-up to use another day. If it didn't, then they'd just torch it.

Tonight, Pat wanted to be part of the action and in control. However, he wasn't a fool. Screwing cashpoints was a young man's game. Pat had nothing to prove and as he got older had fashioned himself into a facilitator rather than a perpetrator. Everyone would take risks tonight but Pat's was a calculated risk. Would the police be suspicious that he was out and about in the city in the early hours? Probably! Would they pin anything on him? Not if he could help it. He looked at the map, checked his watch and pressed the transmit button on his radio.

"From Pat. Go, go, go."

* * *

Robert Harrison was standing within the Force Control Room, in the middle of his night shift, covering the city centre role as the Force Commander. He enjoyed his stints on nights, away from monotonous daytime meetings and posturing peers attempting to impress those in the higher echelons of the service. The night shifts were relaxing for him as he watched the Control Room in full swing, coping with the vagaries of the night time economy. Drunken louts, domestic disharmony, missing people, car thefts and reported burglaries. All in a normal night's work for the Metropolitan Police.

He enjoyed seeing his staff working and wasn't adverse to taking the opportunity to chat with the team members, especially if female and considered to be worth his effort. Harrison had never really given much thought to the staff's view of him, never noticed how busy they suddenly became when he wandered near them. How someone would suddenly stand up from their station and visit the loo when he came near, or how they gathered around in support when he singled a person out. Oblivious to his effect on people, he just felt that he was popular and 'one of the team'.

Robert had received his handover at 8 p.m. and now at 1.30 a.m., he felt more settled. The informant, on this occasion, was wrong. No mysterious 'big job' had been committed. 'The Hare' had not raised his head. Robert fully intended to have a good talk with Ali Smith tomorrow. Smith had failed to deliver the goods and however much Simeon wished the burglar to be found, it appeared that Smith wasn't up to the task. Robert had a mind to close down the enquiry team and to recommend Smith's demotion within the lodge. Robert smiled to himself before sipping from his coffee mug.

* * *

Pat listened to affirmative replies on the radio.

"Fred."

"Daphne."

"Thelma."

"Shaggy."

"Scooby."

He chuckled to himself having named each team with the only quintet he could think of. *That makes this The Mystery Machine*, he thought as he looked around him.

Each team knew their role and would deploy in ten-minute intervals, starting with Fred. Pat would be told when the first team was on target and ensure that the next team deployed as per schedule. Any problems and he would give them instructions as to what action to take. He'd monitor the police frequencies and sit back and enjoy the mayhem.

"Fred, on target."

"Good luck," replied Pat. "Prepare yourselves, Daphne."

* * *

The control room manager had been supplied with limited intelligence about the anticipated criminal activity today. The day shift managers had briefed the night shift and Robert, confident that the information would dilute with the telling, felt reassured that he, at least, was present to deal with any issues. He looked over to where the manager sat behind two computer screens, on a raised platform, with an overview of the whole room. *She's working well*, he thought. As if sensing his stare, the manager scanned the room and, on seeing him, beckoned him over. Robert placed his cup down and casually strolled over to the officer, climbed the five stairs up to the platform and smiled.

"How can I help?" he asked.

"ATM attack, Sir. I was told you needed to know." Robert's interest was piqued.

"Where?"

"Kilburn High Road." The manager was listening to her headset. "Explosives used at the Lloyds Bank. Dispatch twenty has it," she pointed across the room towards a desk with a number twenty on it.

"Have CCTV got it?"

"They've been notified."

"When did it happen?" The manager held up her hand palm out in an instruction for Harrison to wait. She listened on her headset and spoke to someone at the other end of the radio. Robert looked at her perplexed, turned, descended the stairs, and walked to desk twenty. The control room dispatcher was also talking to someone over the radio. Robert leaned over and started reading the text on the screen which detailed what was happening. He looked back towards the manager to see her again beckoning him and, turning swiftly, he ran back to her. Everyone else in the room remained calm and casually watched Harrison's panic.

"What is it?"

"Another, Sir. Finchley Road. Allied Irish Bank."

"Who has it?"

"Desk five." Robert looked for desk five.

"Best stay here, Sir. I'll keep you updated. Grab a seat." Another member of staff rolled a seat over to Robert inviting him to sit. "There's enough panic out there, Sir, without having any in here." The manager smiled, pointing to the seat and started typing on her computer. Robert sat down, like a naughty child, gripping the arms of his chair to dispel his anger.

* * *

"OK, Ronnie. We're going to get moving."

"Right with you," she replied. Jack, Jane and Terry were standing in line by the door ready to leave.

"I have control," said Ronnie. "The corridor is clear. Go when you are ready." Jack cracked the door and slowly opened it. They had checked over the office behind them making sure that they had left no trace that they had been there. They stepped out into the corridor and walked cautiously forward, listening for any sound of other persons in their vicinity.

"You're passing the library on your right," said Ronnie in their ears. "First door on the right, after the library, is the stairs. The lock is deactivated." Moving swiftly beyond the library they entered the stairwell and continued down.

"We're doing well," said Jack, turning to the others. "Just keep calm and we'll get there."

"The vaults next," whispered Jane. Terry gave them a thumbs up.

"Let's go," said Jack. "Moving ahead, Ronnie." Jack again led to the door, inched it open and stepped through. He scanned the corridor, seeing barred gates at either end, turned and beckoned the others through. Stark-white painted walls surrounded them, with black iron prison gates at either end. Jack pointed right and up to the ceiling where a CCTV camera was aimed down towards them.

"I can see you. They can't," reassured Ronnie in their ears. The team moved to the gate on their right.

"Looks like a prison," said Terry.

"Wouldn't know," said Jane.

"Let's hope you don't get to find out," replied Terry. Jane smiled nervously at him. He grabbed her shoulder and squeezed it reassuringly, then froze as he heard a deep rumble. "What the hell!"

"It's the tube passing. Don't worry. Happens quite frequently," said Jack, now having some expertise, having rested for hours within the building. The trio continued walking towards the barred gate, and as they neared it, heard the lock mechanism release. Jack pushed the gate and it swung inwards silently on well-oiled hinges. They slipped through, shutting the gate gently behind them, and continued.

"Heading to 'Bob the Lock's' office next," said Ronnie, "I'll just check it." Jack held his hand up indicating for the other two to wait.

"Stop there!" said Ronnie. "He's not clocked out of the building." Jack remained frozen with his hand held up. Jane looked at Terry who held his arms wide as if asking what to do. "I can see him now," continued Ronnie. "He's in his office. Little bald bloke with a goatee. Looks like he's tidying up some bench tops." Jack turned and gestured for Terry and Jane to stay where they were, a finger to his lips telling them to remain silent. He received a thumbs up in reply. Jack walked slowly forward along the corridor. He moved to the left side, improving his viewing angle. The corridor was illuminated by a light coming from a raised barred window, the door to the room looked to be solid steel and was closed. Jack returned to the others and beckoned them towards him.

"We're going to sneak past, Ronnie," he whispered.

"Received." They crept along taking slow measured steps, ears alert for any sounds and copied Jack's crouched posture as they did so.

"He's locked something away. Moving to the door," said Ronnie. Jack increased pace. Now under the window and passed the door "towards the door." Jack and Jane were now beyond it. Terry, immediately outside. "Reaching for the door handle." Terry stood poised. Flight or fight, not an option. It would be a fight. His heart hammered in his chest. "Wait, he's back to the bench. Forgotten something." Jack gestured frantically for Terry to move. Terry crouched and hurried. Jack and Jane were moving ahead. "Back to the door. Door open." Terry could hear the door behind him. Before him a right turn in the corridor. He squeezed against the wall. "Light switched off." Terry couldn't see Jack or Jane. He dove forward, skidding across the floor. Hands grasped him. Pulled him right into the corridor. The team clutched each other tightly.

The locksmith's head popped out as he looked up and down the corridor. He scanned carefully and stepped out to listen.

"Must be hearing things," he said, as he moved to close the door. Ronnie watched him on the screen.

"He's in the corridor. Door closed and locked. He's walking away." Jack could hear the muffled shuffle of footsteps moving away. "Through the gate and away," said Ronnie. Jack looked at the others, signalled for them to remain quiet and moved slowly down the corridor with both following. Ahead of them the route to the vault door. They rested.

"That was bloody close," said Terry, "I thought I was going to have to smack him."

"Poor Bob," said Jane.

"Poor Bob, my arse," said Terry, "I wouldn't have had any other option." Jack interceded.

"Well, we are through. No one was hurt, nothing damaged."

"Speak for yourself, mate. I was terrified!"

"Incontinence, Tel?" asked Jane, giggling.

"Very nearly, love." He tapped his chest in imitation of his heart hammering.

"Let's keep going," said Jack. "This door, a small corridor, then the vault. Ronnie, can you do the honours, please?"

"Yes. Bob's on the floor above you now. Took the lift. Next corridor has movement sensors and pressure pads. I'll sort the pads one at a time but keep low. The light array will still be active but altered. Hands and knees unless I say differently. Jack first."

Jack got on his hands and knees. Jane pulled gently on the door. Before them was a small dark corridor. At the far end was a secure metal door with a keypad entry. Jack knew that the room had a pressure pad floor at this end and also a light beam security array which randomly changed patterns. Ronnie would have disabled the pad by now. She had managed to find a technical solution to raising the floor height of the light beams up to waist height, without breaking the random light pattern. This would provide the team with a crawl space in which to navigate the room.

"Jack, five seconds. Ready … Go!" Jack shuffled quickly forward aiming in a direct line. Head down and with quick movements, he doggy crawled across the space to the far side and stood up. The beams didn't cover the door area.

Ronnie could only interfere with the sensors for seconds. Jane crouched. Got in position and waited.

"Jane, five seconds. Ready … Go!" Jane copied Jack's movements. He grabbed her and pulled her upright, their bodies pressing together as he held her. She looked into his eyes. He smiled. Terry coughed and they looked to see him on hands and knees ready. They released each other and watched him as he followed the process. He stood up in between them, smiling at them both. The door at the far end of the small hall had closed behind him.

Now, working in a tight space Jack moved to the keypad. He sprayed a solution on it revealing greasy finger marks on all nine displayed numbers.

"Nothing obvious, Ronnie," he transmitted, knowing that the number code changed each day.

"I've been working on it, Jack. No joy so far. Hoping you could help."

"There's a key slot next to it too," said Jack.

"Manual override?"

"Could be."

"Locksmith?"

"Probably!" Both were thinking alike. The likelihood was that any key would be in Bob's office. Jack would need to return to it. He explained his thoughts to Jane and Terry.

"Do you want me to come?" asked Terry.

"No. I'll go alone. You and Jane stay here and see if you can come up with anything with the numbers. I'll go back and see what I can find." Jack checked his watch, "Keith will be setting off," then crouched down in position. "Ready, Ronnie." Terry squatted, his back to the vault door.

"Ready. Go," said Ronnie. Jack moved.

"DROP!!!" shouted Ronnie in his ear. Jack dropped flat onto the floor.

"What's up?" asked Terry.

"The beam has lowered. "Stay down, Jack." Jack remained still.

"Wait there," said Terry, repositioning himself. "Hold still, Jack. I'm gonna push you." Terry pulled his knees to his chest and braced his back against the vault door. He gently placed the soles of his shoes against the bottom of Jack's. "Move your arms slowly up and forward, mate," continued Terry. "When I say I'm going to launch you. You reach for the door. OK?"

"OK," replied Jack.

"Three, two, one." Terry pushed with explosive power forcing Jack's body forward. Jack reached for the door. His hands moved wide and braced the door space. He pulled, and pushed with his toes, his head gently thudding against the door. He pushed again and nudging the door open pulled himself through.

Jack turned to see Terry breathing hard and Jane beside him. Jack stood up and grinned.

"Back soon." He disappeared from view.

* * *

"That's a third one just coming in," said the control room manager.

"Where this time?" asked Harrison.

"Hampstead High Street. Barclays Bank." Harrison looked at a map displayed on a screen.

"Is there a pattern? Where are our lot?"

"They're travelling towards them, Sir. It's a busy night. All in a similar area. All seem to be banks."

"It's got to be an organised job."

"Undoubtedly."

"I need to make a call. I'll be back soon." Robert strutted through the control room and out into the glass-sided corridor beyond. The manager watched him as he paced up and down with his phone to his ear.

"Smith? Is that you Smith?"

"Yes, Ali Smith," said a tired voice at the other end of the line.

"It's me, you blithering idiot. Robert Harrison. I need you here."

"Where's here, Sir?"

"Central control room. Get here as soon as possible."

"Anything important?"

"Of course it's important, you fool." Robert terminated the call and next rang the on-call informant handler.

After venting his spleen at the poor detective who had unfortunately answered his call Robert felt much better with himself. He pondered on whether he should call Simeon but decided that caution was the better course of action. He'd ring him at eight am, it being a more sociable hour.

"So much for a quiet evening," he said aloud, walking back into the control room.

"Another one on Abbey Road," greeted him as he approached the manager.

"Get some extra resources out there. This is bloody ridiculous," said Harrison.

* * *

Keith trundled along steadily in the quiet traffic, preparing himself for the task ahead. Usually a calm character who remained unflustered, Keith was feeling nervous. It wasn't often that he was directly involved in the commission of a crime. Well, not at the sharp end anyway. His talents lay in passing on goods once they had been stolen, not in stealing them outright. Tonight his role was different, delivery driver and getaway. With a security badge safely on his chest, he now drove towards the car park entrance of the Walbrook Building. A gated barrier raised before him as he entered an area which was occupied by several cars. He followed his memorised route to the rear of the car park.

"On my approach, Ronnie."

"Drive towards the doors. The number plate recognition will read the registration plate on your van. Good luck."

"Thanks." Keith drove steadily towards a metal roller door which started to lift as he got near. He took a deep breath as he looked down the throat of a dimly lit tunnel and entered, seeing the security door closing behind him. Ahead a further barrier was manned by one guard, who appeared to be snoozing, within his guard hut. The vehicle headlights illuminated the structure, disturbing the guard who peered forward into the beam. Keith switched to side lights so as not to dazzle him. He rolled forward to the gate and stopped the vehicle, the idle of the engine reverberating against stark concrete walls. Keith lowered the driver's window.

"You're an early run," said the guard, tucking his shirt into his belt in an attempt to hold his voluminous stomach in place. He rubbed his eyes and straightened a half-fastened tie.

"Morning," replied Keith. "I pulled the short straw."

"Me too, mate." Keith flashed his security badge to the guard who raised a hand in acceptance. The man produced a security inspection mirror which he used to check the underside of the vehicle as he walked around it. Seeming satisfied he returned to Keith.

"Delivery or collection?"

"Both," replied Keith, "shouldn't take too long." The guard stepped away from the vehicle and, pressing a button, raised the barrier. Keith drove forward.

"See you soon," said Keith. "I'm through, Ronnie. Heading to the transit bays," he transmitted.

"Nice one. Jack's just sorting out a quick complication. They'll be with you soon. Nothing for you to worry about." Keith switched on the van radio to hear, 'Well, it's one for the money. Two for the show' being sung in the resonant tones of Elvis. He relaxed and tapped his left foot as he continued.

* * *

"Now within 'Bob the Lock's' office, Jack faced the back wall which was painted white and had large bunches of keys hanging from hooks on the walls. Some held labels, some did not. Hundreds of them. *Surely, far too many for this building* thought Jack. Below the hanging keys was a workbench with paperwork, books and yet more keys strewn across it. *Bob is not a tidy man! Where to look?* Two safes were situated underneath the bench and various types of locks were placed on a further workbench. These locks were cleanly laid out, and ordered by size and quality. The locksmith was a practical man, disinterested in the red tape of paperwork and procedure but keenly interested in defeating locks, practising his skills in being the best. Jack could have spent hours playing in this room but hours he did not have.

"Any clues, Ronnie?" he asked, now back on a separate channel with her.

"The bench that you are next to. He reached under it before leaving." Jack squatted down and, using a torch that he'd found in the office, illuminated the area as he looked. A small box was attached under the work surface. He reached for it, pulled, and its magnets released with his hand pressure. Jack stood up, placing the small metallic box on the surface, opened it gently and revealed a small key fob within. *No key though.* He pressed the fob button and heard an audible click above his head where there was a small shelf. Looking around, he retrieved a chair. He used it to climb up and discovered a small safe box with its door ajar. *Sneaky beggar*, he thought, *people rarely look up.*

It's why he favoured rooftop burglary. People rarely look up when walking, running or searching. They almost always look at things ahead of them or, if walking, down to hazards that may trip them. A simple ruse by the locksmith but Jack knew it would be effective.

He gently opened the door to the safe, to be faced with a blank plate. He tapped it and pushed against it. Nothing. The safe box was secured to the shelf. *This has got to be something,* thought Jack. At least, he hoped it was. He had little time for messing around. He checked the fob and pressed a second button on it. The black plate moved back presenting him with what looked to be a digital scanner.

"I've got a scanner on a small safe here, Ronnie. Can you access it?"

"I didn't know it was there. With time, yes, but not quickly." Jack reached into his pocket as he was talking, retrieving the Governor's print that he had lifted. *Nothing ventured,* he thought and placing it over his thumb pressed it to the black plate. The safe opened and sitting securely inside was a singular key.

"I may have it," he transmitted. "Heading back." Jack left the office and retraced his steps to the vault door.

"Keith's approaching in the transit," said Terry as Jack stood up next to them.

"We'd better hurry then," replied Jack. "Any luck with the number lock?"

"None," said Jane.

"Let's try this then," he held up the key. Fingers crossed on his left hand, he inserted it in the lock and turned it to the right. A loud hiss escaped from the door and the clunk of a mechanism ensued before the door opened centrally and the right and left doors swung silently backwards. Jack, Jane and Terry looked into the vault of the bank. Terry's face broke into a smile.

"We're in, Ronnie," said Jane.

"I can see you. Gold to the left side and cash to the right. We need to get moving. I'll contact Keith."

All three walked into the vault and turned left towards the gold vault, following a small corridor and turning into a large room resembling a warehouse. Dark concrete walls and flooring secured the rows of shelving which tracked down either wall. Jack reached for the light switch, flicked it on, and all watched the austere strip lighting trigger from their end down the room. Beaming back at them were innumerable gold bars stacked precisely on blue-racked shelving. At the far end of the room, before a secure hangar door stood a forklift.

"Bingo," said Terry, placing a hand on each of his colleague's shoulders and squeezing. The team gazed at the sight before them, frozen in an instant of time which would be burnished in their minds forever. "The cash, Jane?" Jack and Jane moved into motion.

"Next room over," she replied.

"Let's go and check," said Terry. "Jack, keys and let's get Keith in here."

"On it," said Jack, to moving the forklift and loading doors. Terry and Jane headed to the second room.

"How many corridors hold all this?" asked Terry.

"You don't want to know," replied Jane, "but everything we need is in these two. This way."

Jack ran to the forklift and checked the ignition for the keys which helpfully were in position.

"Ronnie, the outside shutter?"

"I've got the alarm sorted. Interior button for you to press and it will raise." Jack ran to the shutter, located the green button and pressed it. The door began moving smoothly upwards.

"Good morning," said Keith as his coiffured hair poked under the rising door, followed by his head and body. He crawled through on hands and knees and raised a hand to shake Jack's. Keith looked up and froze in position gazing open-mouthed at the room. "Bloody hell !"

"I know, but we need to get moving."

"I got hold of Barry. Said he'll be ready."

"Great, Now, come on."

"OK," Keith turned to the open door where his van stood with the boot doors open, turned back to the room of gold, and back to the van. "What first?" He heard the sound of the forklift. Jack came whizzing past and down a concrete slope to the vehicle loading bay.

"First the soap," he yelled as he drove past Keith.

"Right," Keith replied. Still in shock, he shuffled down the slope, trying to catch up with Jack. They both moved to the van where the golden bars of soap were waiting.

"We'll take these in first," said Jack as he manoeuvred the forklift into position. The soap was all piled on one pallet, all one hundred gold-sprayed bars of luxury. Keith entered the van and directed Jack as the bars were gently lifted out.

"Easy now, mate," he yelled as the load jolted. "We've got time." Jack reversed gently and repositioned to move gently up the slope into the gold vault. Keith walked swiftly behind, feeling a tension in his chest which could either be his asthma or plain old stress. As Jack drove into the vault, another forklift travelled towards him, containing a large grey plastic box, with Terry driving and Jane riding shotgun on the side. They passed each other, grinning their heads off. Keith stopped, turned and walked quickly back down the ramp to oversee the loading of the van.

"Stay down here, mate, or you'll give yourself a heart attack," yelled Terry. Keith gave him a thumbs up in reply as the load entered the vehicle. Jane ran from the bay back into the vault to assist Jack. "Two more," yelled Terry, holding up two fingers to clarify his meaning. He turned the forklift and returned to the vault.

Jack had positioned the machine and was lifting the first tray of gold. The shelving split into trays, effectively acting as metallic pallets, allowing him to lift the bars as one. On the forklift before him was now positioned seventy-two bars of solid gold. Driving slowly, he headed towards the vehicle bay. The gold tray had been selected from the centre area of the shelves and Jane turned to select the last twenty-eight bars that they would steal, each singular bar being a fortune in itself.

"Over the axle, mate," yelled Keith, as the load was moved into the van and gently positioned.

"Another half load," called Jack as he drove away.

Next came Terry with another box. Keith checked his watch. The timings were good. Jack returned to the building and drove towards Jane, who gestured to a half-empty shelf.

"This one," she said. He positioned the forklift and removed the bars, then headed to Keith. Terry, seeing him coming, reversed off the bottom of the ramp, making room for Jack to pass before reentering the bank.

"Last load," called Terry, passing Jane. Jack returned to Jane and positioned the forklift to lift the soap.

"Where the full one was. Best we can do." She pointed to the central gap in the shelves. They would have to leave the half-shelf space empty. Not ideal but she knew they had no choice. Jack gently placed the soap in position and reparked the forklift in its original place. He jumped out, smiling with his face glowing with exhilaration.

"This is a blast," he said, running to Jane. "Where's Terry?"

"Last crate," she heard the forklift coming. They turned as Terry drove at speed towards the dock doors, with a look of determination and concentration on his face.

"Cash vault, Jane. Help Terry there. I'll check in here," said Jack. Jane ran back towards the vault where Terry would return with the forklift.

The crates in this room were stacked two up centrally in a large square. Terry had removed three crates from the outside edges so on his return he would need to move some crates to make it less obvious. Jane was not sure how much time any of this would buy them but it was worth a shot. Terry returned, moved the crates and parked up the forklift.

"Time to go," he said, as both ran from the room back to Jack, who was waiting at the roller shutter.

"Go, go, go," said Jack. Encouraging them through the door towards the van. He scanned the vault once more and was happy that it looked almost the same as when they had entered. He checked his pockets pulling the vault key from them. *Damn, I should have put that back.* He raised his arm, about to throw the key, and stopped. *Safer to ditch it in the middle of nowhere*, he thought. Jack switched the vault lights off, ran back to the roller door and pressed the red button to lower it, then ran to the van and jumped into the back with the other two. Keith secured the doors and jumped into the driver's seat.

"We're out of here, Ronnie," he transmitted on the radio, as he turned the engine on. He pulled away, feeling the extra weight in the vehicle, and gently turned towards the tunnel, following the exit signs.

"Security reset at the bank," replied Ronnie, "Keep cool, Keith. Walk in the park for you."

Ronnie watched the van on the screen as it entered the tunnel and disappeared from her view. She began typing rapidly, checking that she left no technical footprint within the bank's computer systems.

Keith took a steady drive, knowing that the team would be working feverishly in the back readying the gold for onward transit.

"Guard station in view," he transmitted to them. They would halt and wait, resuming their work after they had passed through. He spotted the guard in his hut, this time awake. Keith raised a hand in greeting. The guard raised his arm in reply and moved to press a button in his kiosk which raised the gate.

"Wouldn't be in your shoes when they find out," said Keith to himself. He drove under the barrier and headed up the slope to the underground car park and out onto the open roads.

"Out into the city guys. Heading to the cars," he transmitted.

* * *

"Twelve seventy-two to control."

"Go ahead," said the control room dispatcher.

"That's us at Kilburn High Road." Harrison listened to the transmission on a set of spare headphones. "Confirm an attack on the ATM. Gas used. A big hole in the wall and no ATM."

"Witnesses?"

"Plenty. I'm going to need some support here."

"Start taking details. I'll find some resources."

The call had been taken at one of the operator's desks and Harrison was patched in to listen only. Five attacks on ATMs had now been reported and resources were deployed all over the place. The organised attacks had put extra stress on the Met officers who were already trying to cope with the large number of reported incidents that were the forces usual for a Friday night.

Smith had arrived at the station twenty minutes ago and Harrison had sent him upstairs to CID to start planning the investigative strategy to investigate the offences. The source units had come up with nothing so far. No one had been able to find Barry, who was the only person who may have an inkling about who was behind all of this.

Harrison wasn't comfortable. His night shift had turned into a complete maelstrom and, more importantly, he had no intention of being blamed for it all. It mattered not to his bosses that criminals were unpredictable and that intelligence was lacking. They would just claim that it could and should have been foreseen. That was partly why Harrison had brought Smith in. He needed a scapegoat and Smith was a good start. Someone to blame if it all continued to go pear-shaped. If, by some miraculous intervention, things went well, then Harrison was there to take the credit.

"I'm going to check on the CID," said Harrison to the control room manager. "Try and sort this mess out," he continued. He threw his headset on the desk and stormed out of the room.

"What a tosser," said an officer who was sitting behind the manager.

"You're telling me," replied the manager.

* * *

Ronnie started packing up her equipment. She'd had a long day, was knackered, and her role in the heist was just about complete. Her last job was to get rid of any evidence on her side of the operation.

She'd closed down her access to the bank and terminated any technical connection which she had made with it. She was confident that they wouldn't be able to detect that she had been in there. On her final check of the camera, she was assured that the night security staff had no idea that anyone else had been in the bank.

Ronnie started dismantling her computer hardware having placed everything that she needed on a removable hard drive. The drive contained nothing from or about the bank. Just access to other more legitimate projects that she had been involved in. The screens, keyboards, and laptops would all need to be moved when daylight came along. She would just leave a bog standard Asus desktop monitor and computer here and her Playstation. Ronnie had arranged for the family to collect her about mid-morning in one of their vans. She would move the equipment then and they would safely dispose of it all for her at a local scrapyard.

Now in her bedroom, Ronnie put the hard drive in her backpack. Today she will leave home for a while. Her mum was safely in residential care and possibly would be happy to remain there. *Who knows?* thought Ronnie, looking at a photograph of her mother which she had in her room. A young lady with bright red hair and a big smile. Ronnie touched the photo gently with a smile on her face.

"Our lives are going to change Mum," she said, with a tear in her eye. Whether for good or bad, Ronnie didn't know. It was a big frightening world out there, one that Ronnie was going to throw herself into, at least for the next fortnight.

* * *

"Approaching Tower Hill," said Keith. A knock sounded on the bulkhead of the vehicle letting him know that the team in the back had heard him. They were still obviously working hard. "Pulling up to the car." Keith stopped the van with the side sliding door facing Hope, blocking any view of the vehicle with his van. The side door opened.

Terry stepped out of the van, now wearing his normal clothing, unlocked and opened the boot of the vehicle.

"Ready," he said. Jack started handing him gold bars, both counting as singular bars went from hand to hand from the van into Hope. Taking only minutes they both said 'thirty' in unison. Terry gently closed the boot and looked back into the van.

"Good luck," he said to Jack and Jane.

"Good luck," replied Jane.

"See you soon," replied Jack. Terry slid the door closed, ensured it was firmly shut and opened the passenger door. He looked in.

"That's me, mate. Get them there safely."

"Will do," replied Keith.

"Once you've dropped them. Wait for my word and get going. Don't stop for anything."

"You know I won't." The men looked at each other and shook hands. There was no need to say anything else. Terry closed the door and Keith drove gently away. Terry placed his hands in his jacket pockets and walked away from the car. He had organised somewhere else close by to get his head down for a couple of hours. Jack and Jane would be taken by Keith to Charity and Faith where the gold would be transferred. Keith would take the van to a lock-up and in a few hour's time the three cars would join the Classic Rally and all the gold and cash would be transported out of the city. Terry strolled away with a little skip in his walk as he did so.

Chapter 15

Jane walked towards the entrance of the bank feeling both nervous and tired. She had managed to get no sleep whilst riding the criminal roller coaster on which she was still clinging. Her task this morning was to go to work as usual. It was her turn to work the weekend and to ensure that all was in order at the bank. She entered the door and walked up to the security desk, placing her bag down.

"Morning. How are you?" said the guard checking Jane in.

"Good thank you. Everything fine?"

"Nothing to report." Jane walked to the security gate and passed through, collecting her bag at the other side. *I can't believe that I was hiding under that desk last night,* she thought. She continued through the building heading, towards her offices.

During the weekends, the bank only worked with skeleton staff with most of the offices being empty, though a cleaning crew would be working their way through the building. The medical offices and library were closed but the gym facility would be open with one member of staff working. Security worked twenty-four seven but again, at weekends, worked with a limited crew. Jane walked through to her office after greeting the one member of staff who was working diligently at their desk. Once in the office, Jane switched on her emails and the kettle, and sent a text to Terry telling him all seemed well and to continue with the plan. She received a thumbs-up emoji in reply.

Jane sat down at her desk and sipped on her coffee. She had diaried a planned meeting at 9.30 a.m. in her schedule, so the bank was expecting her to be out of the building by then. This would be her last hour of working for the bank. She looked around. *Will I miss this? Not at all.* The thrill of last night was still coursing through her veins. The phone on Jane's desk rang, startling her. She picked it up.

"Morning, Jane Swithens."

"Jane, it's Mick in CCTV. You got a minute?"

"Of course. What can I do for you?"

"Probably better if you come over here."

"OK. Give me two." Jane put the phone down, amazed at how she had sounded so calm. She felt sick though. Reaching for her bag, she fumbled for her mobile and dialled Terry.

"Jane?"

"I've been called to the CCTV room, Terry. Something must be up. They sound worried."

"Right. What are you going to do?"

"I don't know. What should I do?" Jane could feel panic start to build. Terry remained silent. "Terry, you there?"

"Yes, yes. Just thinking. Go and see what they're worried about. Take all your stuff with you. We need to know what they know but be prepared to get out quickly."

"How?"

"Whatever way you need to. I'll get our boys mobilised. You know the plan when you leave."

"Yes."

"Everyone will be ready if it's on the hurry up, trust me."

"OK."

"You're strong, Jane. You'll be fine."

"OK. I'll let you know." Jane terminated the call, checked her face in her hand mirror and grabbed her bag. She walked out of her office.

"Just off to CCTV," she said to her colleague who raised her hand in acknowledgement.

The CCTV office was located in the next corridor across from Jane's office, where a suite of cameras were dedicated to monitoring the building. Jane used her staff card to swipe the entry lock and walked in confidently.

"What we got, Mick?"

"Not sure yet, Jane. Look at the screen." Mick pointed to a monitor which showed the room holding the grey cash crates. "They look different."

"What do you mean?"

"They look like they've been moved. Look, here's a still from yesterday's recordings." He pointed to a further screen displaying an image in the vault. "Look there," he pointed, "looks like there's a gap in the middle."

"I can't see it, Mick. Not clear to me."

"That's why I've sent two of the team down to look." Jane's heart jumped.

"You've done what?"

"Standard procedure. Thought you'd want to be here to see. Look, they're just going in now." Jane watched as two of the security guards entered the vault and walked towards the crates.

"Mick to Rob, what have we got?"

"There's a gap in the middle of this square, Mick." Mick looked towards Jane who had a look of shock on her face. "Nobody's been in the vault for two days, Jane. Something's wrong!" His hands moved the keyboard joystick, he highlighted a small image and brought it to full size. The image displayed the gold vault. Mick peered at the screen as he leaned forward.

"What the hell, those pallets are wrong," he said. "That area's not blue metal. Looks like wood! What's going on?" He turned again to look at Jane.

"I need to make a call. Keep them there." Jane gestured to the screen, retrieving her mobile from her bag. "I'll be back soon. Don't say anything to anybody" Jane swept out of the room into the corridor. She dialled Terry. Now running towards the main entrance. *Answer, answer,* her mind screamed as she approached the doors to the front reception.

"Jane?"

"We're blown," she said. "Get moving." Jane ended the call and peered through the double doors. One security guard, talking at the kitchen door. Jane looked right at a red fire alarm. She smashed it with her phone. Immediately the alarm rang. Jane waited. Waited. Both security guards appeared. Water sprayed down from the ceiling soaking her. Jane held up her bag for protection. Pushed the doors. Hurriedly walked in. She screamed.

"Fire alarm. Everyone out." Jane ran through the metal detector to the exit. One guard opened the door helping her to leave. She ran.

* * *

Mick remained sitting looking at the screen as his world erupted around him. Water sprayed from the roof and he watched on his screen as the vaults were sprayed also. His colleagues crouched as the alarm brayed and water rained from the ceiling on top of them.

"Check the gold," screamed Mick on his radio. His colleagues would know that they were safe down there. The vault was impenetrable and the water would stop in two to three minutes. Just enough to dampen the rooms but not spoil anything. The rest of the building would get soaked. He watched as his men ran into the vault.

"Centre, row two." The guards moved and pointed at the wooden pallet. "Yes, that one." He watched amazed as one guard reached up, easily lifting a solid gold bar with one hand. Mick zoomed in and viewed the man bend the bar in his hands.

"He says that it feels like soap," said a second guard over the radio, "It's not heavy." Mick watched as the bar bent and snapped in two. Something stuck out from the bar.

"What's that black thing?" The second guard pulled on it and held it up.

"I dunno. A rabbit or something."

"Stay there," said Mick. "I'm going to have to get out. Fire brigade will be here soon." Mick moved quickly from his office and started making a call as he moved through the corridor. His grandfather would need to know, he'd been working in a senior role in the bank for years and would know what to do.

* * *

Gerald Sindbourne watched as Simeon lined up his shot for the first hole which was a par three. Both gentlemen had met this morning for their monthly round of golf where they could discuss business and leisure at a nice sedate pace. Gerald watched Simeon place his ball down and move into position with the club extended and his legs bent. *A nice easy hole to start with* thought Gerald as Simeon swung the club backwards. Gerald's mobile phone rang aloud. He reached for it quickly with a grimace on his face. *No points for ruining the Grand Master's first swing*, he thought. Gerald turned his back, missing the hooked shot and the scowling reprimand on Simeon's face, and answered the call.

"Michael, I'm playing golf." A muffled voice responded. "What's that infernal racket in the background?"

"We've been robbed," screamed Mick's voice, an alarm sounding in the background.

"Who has been robbed?" asked Gerald, straining to hear.

"The Bank of England."

"The Bank of England?" Gerald's driver dropped from his grasp. He turned to look at Simeon.

"Yes."

"You're joking. You have to be joking?" Simeon moved towards Gerald. "The bank's been robbed!" he exclaimed. Simeon snatched the phone from him.

"How much? Who did it?"

"I don't know. Gold, cash, both taken. What should I do?" Simeon passed the phone back to Gerald.

"Sort him out," said Simeon with a disgusted look on his face. Gerald took the handset as Simeon moved to make a call of his own.

"Digby, there's been a big job. Where's Barry?"

"What job?" asked Digby. "He was spotted him leaving his gaff this morning but they've lost him. They're searching for him now." Simeon pulled his phone from his ear, listening to Gerald.

"Soap?" said Gerald. "A black rabbit, what do you mean a black rabbit?"

"There's been a robbery, Digby. It's our man. Find Barry now. We need to speak to him. We need to find The Hare."

"What's he done?"

"He's only gone and robbed the Bank of bloody England."

* * *

Jane walked onto Threadneedle Street, crossed quickly over the pedestrian crossing and entered Finch Lane. She started running as she removed her work mobile from her pocket and disposed of it in a public waste bin as she passed. A steady run would take her ten minutes to Charity. Less if she could manage it as she now jogged Birchin Lane heading for Gracechurch Street and Lower Thames. Her driver would be waiting.

* * *

Terry had sent the text out as soon as Jane had got to work. Wanting to ensure that his team was ready he'd mobilised them into the city and had just sent them their meeting locations. Jack would be heading to his car, as would Keith to his van. The classic rally would be congregating on the ExCel already so, although earlier than planned, they should drift in nicely. Terry headed towards Tower Hill, scanning the area as he halted and looked. *There you are*, he thought as he saw Will confidently striding into his view, sporting his trademark chinos, shirt and aviators. Terry walked towards Will as he spotted Terry and adjusted his route to meet him.

"We on?"

"Yeah, you ready for the drive of your life?"

"Hell yeah." Terry threw the car keys to Will.

"Over here, mate," said Terry walking towards the green Citroen.

"A 2 CV!" exclaimed Will.

"Trust me, you won't be disappointed." Will climbed into the driver seat and turned the engine on, smiling at the satisfying purr of the engine. Terry went from boot to bonnet and ripped off the real plates, which had been velcroed in position, revealing cloned plates underneath. He climbed into the car and threw the originals in behind him.

"Set off when I tell you, mate. Steady drive. The fun doesn't start for a while." They waited.

* * *

Jack walked casually onto Upper Thames Street feeling relaxed and in control. The job had gone well so far and as long as everyone played their part today, things should go smoothly. Jane had needed to be inventive this morning but as far as he knew she had coped with the situation. He knew that he couldn't afford to think about her right now. His focus needed to be on his role today and nobody else's. Jack took a seat on a bench, enjoying his take-out coffee, with a clear view of Faith. He checked his phone which displayed an image of Barry, his designated driver. Terry had provided him with a description too. Jack was confident that he would recognise him.

Ricco was sitting in the passenger seat of a small white box van that was being driven by one of his colleagues. Barry had been spotted leaving his flat earlier this morning by the team, but they hadn't been able to get close enough to get hold of him. John had been in contact and told Ricco that he needed Barry bringing in today. Something had happened and it was in everyone's interest to get hold of Barry. The van was sweeping Upper Thames Street with further support vehicles nearby.

"There," Ricco indicated with a hand in his lap, his finger pointing in the direction of eleven o'clock. "Walking along by that row of cars. He's looking around."

"For us?" asked the driver.

"Not likely, but let us go. Pull slowly up. I'll get him." The vehicle moved and Ricco prepared to pounce.

Jack spotted Barry walking on the Upper Thames, towards the row of vehicles in which Faith was parked. A small white van was also travelling on the same road. *I'll wait for that to pass then approach him,* thought Jack as he stood up and started walking towards Barry.

Jack watched the van as it slowed and saw the passenger opening his door before the vehicle stopped. The van halted next to Barry and the passenger jumped out. The driver's door opened suddenly and slammed into Barry. He fell forward. The passenger jumped on him and pinned him down. Jack sidestepped next to a tree, hiding himself, and watched.

"The doors," he heard the passenger shout. The male driver climbed out and opened the rear doors of the van. He helped the passenger as they lifted and then threw Barry into the back. The passenger also climbed in. The driver slammed the doors shut, jumped back in and pulled away. Jack looked around the area. No witnesses were in sight. *Make a decision, Jack.* He ran towards Faith, quickly climbed in, switched on the engine and reversed.

Ricco piled onto Barry, pinning him down with the weight of his body. He looked out of the rear window looking for any witnesses. A car drove out of a parking space at speed. *An old Citroen.*

"E35 ... Damn, too far." Ricco heard Barry mumbling and turned to him. "What you say?" Ricco leaned towards Barry's head.

"I can't breathe," he gasped. Ricco eased the pressure off his body as he retrieved two cable ties from his jacket. "My friend, that may be the least of your worries." Ricco tied Barry's wrists behind his back and then also tied his ankles together, before banging loudly on the driver's bulkhead. The vehicle slowed and stopped. Ricco heard the driver exit the van with the engine still running and waited for the boot door to open.

"Everything alright, boss?"

"Fine." Ricco climbed out and slammed the door shut leaving Barry within. The men climbed into their respective seats and continued their journey. Ricco rang John.

"I got him."

"Where?" asked John.

"Upper Thames Street."

"Witnesses?"

"Maybe. I'm not sure. Person in an old white Citroen. E35. That's all I got."

"I'll get it checked. Head to the garage."

"OK. See you there." Ricco finished his phone call. "Where's the other cars?" Ricco asked his driver.

"Running parallel routes nearby."

"Get them looking for that Citroen. Something's not right here."

"Right away, boss."

* * *

Jane ran onto Lower Thames where Terry had parked Charity. She slowed to a walk, catching her breath, and tried to calm her mind as she headed towards the car. A man stood waiting and as she approached she checked the image on her phone, recognising the male as Ted. Heart still hammering, she approached him.

"Ted?" she asked, as she looked at the tall ageing man in front of her.

"That's me, young lady."

"You're my driver."

"It seems that I am."

"Let's go." She handed Ted the car keys and he followed as she led him to Charity. Calm and unflustered, Ted climbed in and started the engine.

"Where would you like to go?"

"A steady drive towards the Royal Docks, please. I'll direct you."

"Right you are," replied Ted. Jane reached into her bag, switched her radio on and smiled to herself. *You'll do just fine, Ted. Cool as a cucumber.*

"Take us across London Bridge, Ted." Jane reached for her earpiece and switched it on.

"Jack to the team. My driver's been kidnapped."

"What do you mean?" responded Terry.

"Bundled in the back of a white van." *Oh my god,* thought Jane, her hand moving to her mouth in shock.

"I'm driving myself," continued Jack. The sound of his car revving could be heard in the background.

"Stick to the plan, Jack."

"I will," he replied. "Heading for Tower Bridge."

"En route to Blackfriars," said Terry.

"London Bridge," said Jane over the radio.

"On the way to my van," said Keith, sounding slightly out of breath. "Good luck everyone."

* * *

"What's he said?" asked John, as he walked into the garage.

"We haven't spoken with him. Waiting for you," replied Ricco. John walked through the small office where Barry was sitting, restrained in a small wooden chair, with one of Ricco's team guarding him. John walked across to him and whipped the hood off Barry's head.

"Leave us," said John to the guard. The guard looked over John's shoulder towards Ricco, who nodded his assent. The man walked from the small office, closing the door behind him. Barry looked at John, his terror displayed clearly on his face. He never saw the blow coming. With a crack, his head whipped to the right following a slap from the man before him. The male forcefully grabbed Barry's hair and turned his face towards him. Blood trickled from Barry's split lip, tracking down his chin. He started whimpering in fear.

"Shut up and listen, Barry," said John quietly. Barry immediately complied. "I have no time for messing around," continued John. Ricco watched the interaction in silence. "What were you doing on Upper Thames?"

"I was ..." Barry's head whipped left, the force of the blow propelling it before Barry heard it. He screamed. His head was again turned forward and the man's face was inches from Barry's, his dead eyes looking at Barry. "Truth son, or I am going to carve you up." The male produced a bowie knife. Barry started crying. The man stepped back. "Why were you there?"

"I w-w- was supposed to meet someone."

"Who?"

"I don't know." John drew his hand back. "NO, NO!," screamed Barry. "I promise, I don't know. I wasn't told." John relaxed.

"Why were you meeting?"

"To drive him."

"Him?"

"Him, her. I wasn't told."

"Drive where?"

"He would tell me. Give me directions."

"What car?"

"Don't know," Barry's panic eased as he spoke. "I just know it was small. That's it. That's as much as I know." John looked towards Ricco and back to Barry.

"Who asked you to do it?"

"Come on, man. You know who. Family. I just get told and do what they say." John had heard enough, knowing that the Lomaxes fear and control over Barry was far greater than anything he could exert. He turned to Ricco.

"Let's go."

"What about him?" asked Ricco.

"Your lot can dispose of him."

"Kill him?"

"No, drive him from here and chuck him out on the road somewhere. Are your cars still out there looking?"

"Yes."

"Right. You're with me. I'll bring you up to speed."

* * *

"That's us approaching the Rotherhithe Tunnel," said Terry on the radio.

"You are the lead car, Terry. You have Charity in two and Faith in three," Jack replied. The cars were now positioned in the natural flow of traffic, interspersed between other cars but effectively in convoy as they approached the tunnel to pass back over the Thames.

"We'll lose our radio signal here. Keep your positions," warned Terry. The cars entered.

Five minutes later Hope appeared at the other side. Terry raised a hand to a workman in fluorescent overalls, who was standing watching the traffic pass. The workman raised his hand and continued watching as the flow of traffic continued. As Faith left the tunnel, Jack saw the back of a man wearing a fluorescent jacket.

"Which way, Terry?" asked Will, as they exited the tunnel.

"Right towards the Royal Docks, mate. The ExCel centre. Keep it steady."

"OK."

Jack felt surprisingly calm having witnessed Barry's abduction but felt confident in himself knowing that he was now solely responsible for his part in the plan. Unused to relying on others for his safety, Jack was comfortable controlling his own destiny. He could see Hope turn right three cars in front of him and so followed her direction.

Jane was enjoying herself. Ted was a calming influence and despite her excitement, she felt that she was being driven through the city by her favourite uncle. Ted had been very amiable, checked on her welfare, and even offered to stop off somewhere and buy a coffee for her if he could get the opportunity. She felt that he maybe didn't quite grasp the urgency of the situation but knew that Terry had chosen him for a reason.

"Heading for the ExCel then. What's there today?"

"We're going to join in the Classic Rally," replied Jane.

"Very nice," he said smiling. "When do we get to show off the engines?," he asked, "I can feel that she's got some oomph."

"In good time, Ted. Then you can show me your driving skills."Ted flexed his shoulders and shuffled in his seat, a behemoth in a small car and keen to impress.

* * *

"Right Smith, you need to get a grip of this." Harrison was pacing up and down in a small office in the station where he had called Ali Smith in to meet him. Simeon had been on the telephone, demanding immediate action by the Metropolitan Police. Fortescue cared not about the bank but did care that there was an opportunity here to catch The Hare. "Suggestions?"

"Ehmm, I'm struggling, Sir. If the bank won't officially report this, then our hands are tied." Robert looked at Smith in disgust.

"Our hands are tied," he mimicked back to Smith. "You tell that to the Grand Master," he hissed. "Think Smith, think. What do we know about that Swithens woman?" Harrison strutted to and fro. He was tired. The night shift had been horrendous and he was now having to deal with an officially unreported heist, based on information coming in from dubious third parties. Selena would have his life over all of this mess. He wasn't looking forward to that discussion which would undoubtedly happen later today. "The security woman from the bank's gone missing. The informant's gone missing. The gold's bloody missing. All we have is a suspicion about Swithens and a little white car."

"An old model Citroen, Sir."

"I know it's a bloody Citroen," shouted Harrison. "A car, it seems, that is currently on false plates," he said more quietly.

"The Force is dealing with the escort duties for a Classic Car Rally today," said Smith, nodding in the direction of the control room.

"There's got to be a link, there's got to be a link," said Harrison to himself. "What did you just say?" Harrison stopped pacing and turned to Smith.

"That the control room is dealing with the escort duties for a Classic Rally today." Harrison's visage altered as Smith watched him thinking.

"Right, set up a room. I want an analyst, an intelligence officer and you. Use whoever is on duty." Harrison's demeanour changed, enthused with energy. "I want a room with dedicated CCTV monitors and also a control room operator. I want it now, Smith. Now."

"Sir."

"She has to be the key, Smith. I want a profile on Swithens. Who is she? Where does she live? What does she drive?" Harrison walked out of the room with Smith next to him. They walked towards the day shift control room manager whom he knew personally. "Get it sorted, Smith." Smith scurried out of the way and started making calls.

"Morning, Sir. Bad night?"

"Not the best, Mary. I'm going to need one of your staff and some resources."

"Sure. You can have Debbie over there." Mary pointed to an operator on the main floor, "What resources?"

"A road crime team. I'll direct them if you get me their Sergeant's details."

"Can I ask what for?"

"You can but I can't say. Restricted intelligence."

"Right, you are. No problem. Take that room over there," Mary pointed to a dedicated incident room on the other side of the control room. "You need a coffee?"

"Strong as it comes. You are a ray of sunshine, Mary."

"I'll get it sorted." Harrison walked towards the room. Ali Smith was talking to one of the control room staff.

"Inspector Smith," Harrison called aloud, "this way." Smith followed Harrison into the dedicated room.

Chapter 16

Hope, Charity and Faith had halted at the Royal Docks where a stream of classic cars of all colours were wending their way from the ExCeL Centre towards the A12. The rally had started and was being led out by a marked police escort towards the main road which would take it north. The lead drivers of the classics could be seen with large grins on their faces, enjoying the excitement of their day. Terry's face was more determined. *So far, the plan is working. Keith should be just about ready to set off.* Although he didn't know what was happening back at the bank he had to assume that they now suspected that Jane was involved. Barry was an unavoidable casualty but he believed that Jack was more than up to the task at hand.

"Right, Will. Let's get the car into that convoy." Will nodded and slowly moved into the stream of cars. "That's Hope entering the convoy," transmitted Terry.

"Charity moving forward," said Jane.

"Faith moving forward," said Jack.

Ted started driving towards the give-way junction before him, poking the nose of the vehicle out. Suddenly, a uniformed officer stepped out before the vehicle with one arm raised, indicating for him to stop. Jane's heart leapt into her mouth. The officer turned to the main line of traffic, directing another vehicle. Jane's hand moved to her passenger door handle.

"Keep calm," said Ted. A police motorbike rode slowly beyond their junction as the officer walked to Ted's side of the vehicle. Ted wound down his window.

"Hi there, mate." The officer squatted down and looked across at Jane. "Ma'am," he greeted her.

"Officer," replied Jane.

"You joining the meeting?" the officer asked Ted.

"Yes. Just running a bit late."

"Hang on a minute, I'll get you in." The officer walked away towards the row of cars and again held up his hand, halting a white Citroen in the flow of cars. The front end of the convoy moved forward and the officer beckoned with his free arm, directing Charity into the convoy. Ted drove slowly forward, raised a hand of appreciation and slotted the vehicle in. Jane looked left to see Jack waiting in Faith, allowing them in, with a big grin on his face. Now that the red Citroen was in, the officer crooked his arm, swiftly encouraging Faith to move forward and the convoy to continue. Jack gave the officer a thumbs-up as he passed him by.

"Terry, in convoy."

"Jane, in convoy."

"Jack, in convoy."

Above the docks, a police helicopter circled, looking down at the snake of cars. Two marked vehicles led the convoy towards the A12, with police motorcycle outriders and marked vehicles shadowing it to clear their route towards the Lee Valley Velodrome. The pilot pointed as all of the convoy's car's hazard lights illuminated. Headlights also started flashing though they were thankfully saved from the incessant blast of vehicle horns. The co-pilot checked the helicopter computer where an alert had just been sent out from the control room. He laughed aloud.

"What's up?" asked the pilot, his voice reverberating with the motion of the aircraft.

"Observations for a white Citroen 2CV. Partial registration E35."

"Get the camera on. Maybe we'll get lucky," said the pilot, switching the helicopter's camera equipment on so they could try to hone in on the plates below them.

* * *

"There's no answer on her phone, boss," said Smith. "Seems like it's switched off."

"Is it connected to the network?"

"We've sent off that enquiry and are waiting for a reply. The road crime team are heading towards the convoy, there's a helicopter up and marked units shadowing the event."

"Her photograph?"

"Just sent by your contact in the bank." Harrison walked over to Smith's computer screen. "Anything else of relevance?"

"They haven't seen her since the fire alarm went off. Nobody seems to have spoken to her. They think that she drives a Fiat 500."

"Colour?"

"Maybe red. They think she may have bought a new car though." Harrison looked at an image of Jane Swithens looking back at him.

"Thin or not, she is the only link we have, Smith. She has to be involved. Get her photo sent out for sightings. Circulate her car. We must be able to find out its registration. Full review of her social media. Who is she friends with? What has she been posting? Traffic units continue to that Classic Rally. I also want to see what that helicopter can see. Get us linked up with them."

* * *

"Terry to Keith."

"Go ahead, mate."

"You ready to start heading out of the city?"

"Yes, ready."

"We're on the approach to the velodrome. You can start moving."

"On my way."

"Hope to Charity and Faith. You know the drill."

"Charity, yes."

"Faith, yes."

"Hope moves to the right of the car park. Come with me," said Terry. Hope turned into the velodrome car park away from the convoy followed in turn by Charity and Faith. All persons in the cars then put on plain black facemasks or head-coverings. Anything to make it hard for coppers or the public and CCTV to identify them.

"Close in. We're doing a circuit." He turned to look at Will who wore a black bandana. "Right Zorro, now we can start driving." Will checked his rearview mirrors, and seeing Charity and Faith behind, he slowly headed towards the entrance of the outdoor velodrome.

"Hold on tight," said Will.

Terry checked that his belt was secure and braced one hand on the dashboard.

* * *

"Helicopter images will be with us in a minute," said Smith pointing to a black and white screen on the right side of the wall before Harrison. Harrison looked up from a text that he was reading. "Also, Sir, we have an unconfirmed sighting of Swithens."

"Where?"

"In that convoy. Red Citroen 2CV which is being driven by an old man. Seen by an on-duty uniform."

"Registration?"

"Didn't get it." The screen went blank, flicked to a fuzzy picture, blanked again and then showed a bird's eye view of the convoy.

"Where are they?"

"Lee Valley Velodrome. Entering the car park." The staff in the room all looked at the image being streamed live from the helicopter.

"What are they doing?" Robert talked aloud as he watched three cars peel away from the convoy and move towards an entrance on the outside track. "Where's road policing?"

"Two minutes out."

"Get them to that track." Harrison watched as the three cars entered the track and turned onto the circuit. Their speed increased slowly, with the vehicles holding the outside edge of the circuit. He watched as they closed up on each other.

"Is this some kind of stupid stunt?" asked the analyst.

"It's got to be them, Smith. I want our cars behind them. Now!"

"Debbie, get traffic to enter the track," ordered Smith.

"Yes, Ali. Control to road policing, enter the track. Three Citroens, green, red and white. Control and contain."

"Received." The room watched as three marked police vehicles also entered the circuit and turned to follow the vehicles. The Citroens speed increased, and the police vehicles increased speed to match their pace.

"Road policing to control. Do we have permission to pursue?" Debbie looked towards Harrison who nodded.

"Yes, yes. Pursuit authorised now by Commander Harrison. Pursue and detain."

"Received." The blue lights on the police vehicles began flashing as the chase began.

* * *

Jack had seen the marked police cars enter the velodrome and observed them activate their blue lights.

"Jack to the team. I think we've got their attention."

"Loud and clear," said Terry in a raised voice. "Air support above us too. Let's give them a run for their money." Will increased his speed again, matched by the other two cars. The road crime team closed up on each other, like a chasing peloton, and increased their speed.

"Here we go, Jane," said Ted calmly. "You give me the directions and I'll keep you safe."

"One circuit, Ted, then we're out of here." The Citroens flew past a group of cyclists holding the centre line of the track.

"Good luck everyone. See you soon." Jack and Jane knew that was Terry signing off. Each car was on its own now. Keith would be heading sedately out of the city, safely transporting their cash and remaining gold load.

* * *

"They're splitting in different directions," said Smith, watching the screen.

"I can see that," snapped Harrison. He watched as the cars exited the circuit and separated. Two, red and white, travelled together as green headed in a different direction.

"Control to road policing. The cars have split," transmitted Debbie.

"Direction?" Debbie looked expectantly at Harrison who was chewing his fingernails.

"Decision, boss? We need a decision," said Ali. Harrison hesitated. The Citroens exited the car park.

"Direction?" asked the road policing ground commander. Ali Smith looked at Harrison who just stood watching the screen. He walked to Debbie who handed him a microphone.

"DI Smith to ground command. Split your team. Move with both groups. You have air support."

"Yes, yes." Smith looked at Harrison with disdain. On-screen, two cars went in pursuit of Charity and Faith. One raced after Hope.

"We need more support," said Ali to Debbie.

"The rally ends at Lee Valley. We can use their escort vehicles and bikes," suggested Debbie.

"Get them all on a dedicated channel, Debbie. I'm gonna get Mary in here to support you." He walked towards the door, passing Harrison.

"Snap out of it, Robert," he said quietly, "you are making a fool of yourself." Ali Smith went to fetch Mary.

Maybe so, thought Harrison, *but it's you who decided to split our resources. It all falls on you.*

* * *

"Head for Abercrombie Road," said Jane.

"Where from there? Give me something to aim for, Jane. I'll get us there. Faith's turned off." The engine thrummed as Ted accelerated.

"Head for the A12 and back to Docklands," she shouted, holding on tightly. Ted checked his rearview mirror, seeing the blue lights behind them.

"T junction," shouted Jane.

"Seen it," Ted looked right. Turned the steering wheel left. Skidded into the junction in front of a blue Tesla. The Tesla braked, tyres screeching. Ted accelerated, speeding away onto Temple Mills Lane. The first police car in pursuit braked harshly, avoiding the Tesla. The second skidded behind it, onto a footpath opposite, and collided with a tree. The first car set off as a police motorbike joined it. Ted accelerated. Jane held on tightly.

Faith turned right onto Olympic Park Avenue, slowed towards its junction with Westfield and seeing it clear, Jack accelerated across the carriageway on to Waterden Road. He looked up through the windscreen, seeing the police helicopter hovering above. His rearview mirror showed nothing behind but he knew that the copter would be directing resources his way. Ahead was his left turn. He checked his mirrors. Two bikes were closing, single blue lights illuminated. He slowed. Positioned for the corner. Turned left. Smoothly negotiated it and accelerated as the road opened up before him. He could hear the roar of the bikes approaching the corner. Jack looked ahead, spotting a back alley to the left. He turned in and stopped. In his rearview, the bikes sped beyond. *Too easy*, he thought. Then he heard the helicopter rotors above.

"Shit." The machine hovered above his location. In his rearview, one bike entered behind him and stopped. The biker used his radio. Jack put the vehicle in reverse. The biker watched. Saw the white reverse lights. Jack hit the accelerator. The Citroen charged backwards. The biker jumped from his machine. Jack slowed. Nudged the bike aside, then reversed at speed onto the road and headed towards Marshgate.

Hope drove at speed down the A12 with a marked police vehicle in pursuit. Will had a look of concentration on his face but he was in his element. He weaved the car through the traffic with ease, using the full width of the carriageway. Hope had got off to a quick start but Terry was no fool. He knew that further police vehicles and bikes would also be chasing them soon.

"They'll be trying to pool resources, mate. Expect some company soon." Will gave no reply, Terry didn't expect one. "Helicopter's still up too. Take the slip to Wick Road and head West." This was where Terry truly hoped to separate the Met Police resources. Three vehicle pursuits in one main area of the city would be hard for them to cope with. He knew that the helicopter would provide support but it had been up in the air for some time now and could only fly for so long before it would need to refuel. "Head for Mare Street, Will. Any route you like."

Ahead a junction appeared with an amber traffic light turning to red. Will could see blue lights behind him, chasing but still at some distance. He moved to the opposing carriageway, slowed as he approached the junction, checked for pedestrians and slipped his vehicle through red at a walking pace. He turned left and accelerated as the traffic behind moved in his direction. Will manoeuvred into the left carriageway.

"Nice one," said Terry. "The copter's hovering over to the left." Hearing that, Will accelerated.

"I need to get off here," he said, looking around him.

"There," pointed Terry, to a forecourt garage positioned between two adjacent roads. Will turned right. The vehicle's back end swerved out. He corrected the car and held it.

"Heavy load," said Will as he gritted his teeth and straightened. He entered the forecourt, crossed it and turned right onto the next road. "I can hear them closing," said Will. Terry could hear police sirens too.

"Keep going," said Terry. Will accelerated then suddenly braked as a blue and white police bike appeared from a road to his right. The biker slowed, skidded, hit Hope, and the biker launched over the bonnet. Both Terry and Will looked shocked. The biker stood up. Terry wound his window down.

"Sorry, mate," yelled Terry as the Citroen pulled away. "He's alright," clarified Terry. "We don't want to kill anyone."

"Two cars behind," said Will. Terry turned. Blue lights were closing in on them.

"Let's keep them busy. Head for Dalston Lane." Will pressed his foot down on the accelerator.

* * *

"What the hell's happening?" asked Simeon.

"I'm a bit busy, Sir. There's a pursuit," replied Harrison.

"Have you got him?"

"No, Sir."

"Well stop buggering around, Harrison. Get the firearms team on him."

"It doesn't meet my criteria, Sir. Let me do my job."

"If I let you do your job you'd have been sacked years ago. Now..." Harrison ended the call.

"Bloody idiot," he mumbled. "Smith, I'm leaving this with you. I have some calls to make." Harrison walked out of the room. He was tired. Needed to sit down. Needed some peace. He headed to his office.

* * *

Ted poked the nose of Charity out, looking right as Jane looked left. He'd held up in a disused warehouse when he'd spotted the opportunity, though they could both hear cars and sirens buzzing around the area.

"Do you think we're safe?" asked Jane.

"No idea. Only one way to find out." Ted moved the vehicle and travelled down a small alley towards the main road. Cars were stopped before them, held at the junction where a police vehicle with blue lights flashing had halted all the traffic. "Shit," said Ted, looking in his rearview mirror where a silver Audi estate had blocked them in. Behind that two other cars and then a police car. "Police, four cars behind us," said Ted. Jane turned to look.

"What do we do?" asked Jane. Ted looked left towards the pavement. In his rearview mirror, a police officer had climbed out of the driver's side of his vehicle. He was walking along the line of cars towards them.

"Nothing ventured," said Ted. He gently pressed the pedal and manoeuvred the car onto the pavement. The officer behind started running towards them, then stopped, ran back and stopped again. Ted laughed and then moved slowly along the pavement. He kept in low gears with the engine purring as he approached the corner, the officer ahead holding the traffic hadn't yet seen them. The officer behind remained undecided, and had forgotten to transmit his observations. Pedestrians walked towards the Citroen with concern on their faces but naturally parted to allow the car through.

"Thank you so much. Thank you. He's confused," Jane pointed at Ted and with her other hand rotated her index finger swiftly, in an attempt to make the public think that Ted was mad. At the corner, he edged onto the main road as a shopkeeper ran out and started yelling at them. The police officer turned, spotted them and yelled. Ted pulled away as the officer climbed into his car which was facing the opposite direction. The officer spun the car and started his pursuit.

"Hartmann Road," said Jane. We need to lose them before there though."

* * *

Faith entered the Bow Road roundabout with police vehicles directly behind. Jack turned left, slipped to the right and held the middle lane of the roundabout. Two cars chased. He knew a bike was near. The helicopter had veered away. He maintained his speed. Slipped to the outside. The police vehicles now held two lanes. *This is tight*, he thought. An engine roared to his right. A police bike appeared from the centre of the roundabout. Positioned directly behind him. Jack nudged his brakes and then accelerated. The bike followed him but now held back.

"Don't get too close," said Jack. "I don't want to hurt you." He checked his mirrors. A police car was closing in on his left. Another behind. He realised that the bike had pulled away to the outside lane. *They're preparing to try and stop me.* "Well, if it's good for you." The police cars closed in. Jack pulled the handbrake and turned sharply right. The nearside police car veered away and collided with a lorry. The lorry braked. Jack accelerated onto the roundabout, then over it and off the far side. He hit an exit and headed to East India Road. He pushed a button on his mobile. The text was sent. 'On my way'.

Hope turned into Shaftesbury Avenue with sirens wailing behind her. Will's concentration hadn't dwindled but the sweat on his face demonstrated the tension that he was feeling. Once again, Terry peeled his fingers from the dash in pain as lactic acid cramped his muscles.

"Left onto Chinatown Gate," shouted Terry. All politeness now discarded from his directions. He called them and Will responded. Hope turned sharply onto the road and slowed, weaving through pedestrians. Terry wound down his window, shouting for people to move. Both knew that CCTV cameras would be monitoring and recording. Caps now covered their heads in an attempt to hide their faces. A man ran at them, screaming.

"OUT OF HERE, IDIOTS!"

"Left onto Wardour. Head for Leicester Square."

"They're closing on us."

"Good. We want them to." Hope entered Leicester Square. "Police to the right." Will swerved left. Accelerated. The car gave chase. "Bike over there. Throwing a stinger out." Will mounted the kerb, took to the pavement, missed the stinger and continued. "Traf Square." Will glanced at Terry. "Trust me." They hit the square with Nelson towering over them. Sirens bounced from the architecture while pedestrians scattered. Nelson watched it all. "The steps." Hope shot forward and careened down the steps. Bounced when she hit the level ground and skidded.

Terry watched a police car attempt the same, overcook it and careen into a wall. Police bikes gingerly navigated the steps. A second car skidded at the top and tilted over the top step. Will selected reverse, stamped on the accelerator, shot backwards, pulled the handbrake hard and spun. "Right," screamed Terry. Will passed the column to his left. "That bollard's out," shouted Terry. Will headed for the only gap available. A removable bollard lay flat on the pavement. He cleared the gap and headed for The Mall. A wave of destruction lined their wake. Pedestrians ran, uniformed cops stood transfixed watching, and onlookers grabbed their phones to film the chaos. Terry and Will looked only ahead.

Horse Guards was a blur as they passed, as was Number Ten, which was secured by one officer who stood resolute. Terry saluted as he passed the Prime Minister's home, the PM being as ignorant to the activity on his doorstep as he was to the needs of the country.

"Victoria, mate." Terry couldn't help but fly past The Yard, grinning as he did so.

Charity careened into Hartman. Ted's face was red and he was grinning. Jane's adrenaline was coursing through her body.

"I think we're clear, Jane."

"Go to the City Airport. Easy in." Ted headed to the airport and navigated towards the building.

"Where?"

"The runway, Ted. I have a flight booked."

Faith joined the queue for the Rotherhithe tunnel. Before Jack, a large highway wagon was parked with its lights flashing. He could hear sirens behind him. He picked up his phone and dialled. The call was answered.

"I'm in the white Citroen 2CV approaching."

"I've got you. Slow it down and leave me space to get in." Jack followed the instruction and the large lorry pulled in front of him, manoeuvring towards the centre line on the road. "Come past me on the left. I'll leave you a gap ahead of me." Jack pulled left and moved forward negotiating through the small gap. Faith appeared before the lorry. "Right, leave the rest to me." Jack raised a hand to Dave Lomax who would deal with the pursuit behind. Faith pulled away from the lorry which was slowing. The lorry suddenly jerked forward and skidded then jacknived across the carriageway. The contents in the rear bounced out of the truck and littered the road behind it. Cars screeched to a halt, rear shunts occurred and Dave smiled. The Rotherhithe was blocked. Ahead Jack continued unhindered into the tunnel.

* * *

Digby was fuming as he felt his payday from Fortescue drifting away. He could feel the maelstrom of the city and had been sitting, listening to it all happening on a police radio that Fortescue had obtained for him some time ago. Three car chases going on, police officers in chaos and unknown bank robbers driving around the city as if they owned it. His mind kept flicking back to Keith. That brass bar on his shop counter. Digby couldn't help but think that he was involved. Digby had no chance of getting his hands on any of this team today. Too many police around and too dangerous. However, if he could just get a look at them then he could use that in the future.

He'd tracked their route as they travelled into the city. Plotted sightings on a tablet, a map of the city displayed before him. The green car was heading to an area where Ricco was waiting with his team. Digby didn't want to join in a car chase but if he could anticipate their moves and get ahead of them, then he may see them. At least that would be something. The police sirens were getting louder. Commuters went about their business, mainly oblivious to the bedlam around them as they accepted the noise as a norm for the city. At home people watched events unfold on their televisions. The press had hold of the story and were trying their best to obtain the coverage that the public craved. Digby waited patiently.

"Positive sighting of vehicle on Poultry," transmitted an officer on the radio.

"He's coming our way, Ricco." Ricco halted the car on Cornhill. "I'm getting out. I want to see what these clowns look like." Digby climbed out and strode towards the junction with Prince's Street. He never noticed a plain police car pull to the side of the road near to Ricco. Digby looked up, sighted the city CCTV cameras and noted where they were. He'd need Fortescue to secure images later for him. He was also sure that there would be plenty of private CCTV cameras in the area, shops which he could approach later and pay to secure any clear images of these fools. He could hear the police coming and so waited outside of Bank Underground Station where some workmen were removing some of the safety bollards. He waited, watching the traffic for a green Citreon. *Keep coming*, he thought.

* * *

"It's getting tight, Terry," said Will.

"For them too, mate. Slowly, up on the pavement. Sound your horn, let's clear these people." Will mounted the kerb as he approached the junction, hitting his horn. People ran to the sides, stepped onto the road, and into any nearby doorways. "The cops will struggle with this," shouted Terry. "There," Terry pointed out, "where the bollards have been removed."

"That's into the underground station."

"Go," The vehicle turned in. Terry looked out of his window where a large man stood pointing at them. Standing in a plain jacket and trousers he just stood looking and pointing. *Who the hell are you*? he thought. He saw a uniformed cop approaching the man. "The left gate will be open, mate. There's work going on here."

"Where we going?"

"Down." Hope moved forward, horn sounding as pedestrians moved aside, confused by the sight of a car in the station. Children pointed laughing, Terry waved back amiably, acting as if this was an event, a novelty. Hope squeezed through the gate. "Head for the escalator."

"You sure?" asked Will.

"Trust me. I've got us this far." In his mirrors, Will could see people scattering as police officers ran in, pushing people back in their attempts to secure the station. "Centre. There." Terry pointed to a small ramp which led up to the middle aisle of the escalator. Descending and ascending stairs continued moving on either side but the aisle was clear, a silver slide to the platform. "Up there and steady as we go down."

"You're mad, Terry. I can't run this on the tracks. You'll get us killed, man."

"It's in the plan. Come on. We're making history." Terry laughed. Hope crept forward.

"You owe me," said Will. Hope mounted the ramp.

"Steady, steady. Keep us central," said Terry, encouraging Will. The car perched on the steel aisle and Will slowly moved down, the people on either side with looks of terror and incredulity on their faces. Screams of 'idiots', and 'fools' were shouted. Terry lowered his window, leaned out and yelled, "Sorry, just filming. Won't be long. Sorry. You're all safe." He looked back. Behind him, the cops had reached the top of the escalators. The public were being cleared and officers were descending. He checked his watch. The automated station tannoy announcement sounded.

"The next train to arrive at Bank is the …" Terry listened as the timing and stations were called out and just heard a clip of the announcement he was waiting for. "Car D is non-operational for pedestrians." He lowered back into his seat and raised his window. "The tube is coming."

"We running for it?"

"Just turn here. Back up near the platform." Will positioned Hope and undid his belt, preparing to get out.

"It's been a blast," said Will. Terry placed a restraining arm across Will's chest.

"We're not getting out. We're getting on."

"In this?"

"In this. Wave to the people." Terry waved at the crowd gathering, some waved back. "Here it comes. We're in Car D."

The tunnel rattled as the tube swept into the station. Doors opened. People exited the tube, some surprised to see the car and some missing it, wrapped up in the events of their own day. The descending police had nearly made the platform. Coach D stopped behind Hope. The doors opened. A bridge platform extended.

"Reverse in," said Terry calmly. "We'll fit. Don't worry." Will looked back, checked his mirrors, and reversed Hope in, positioning her in the middle of a cab which was empty of all furnishings, poles, and seats. Terry watched as the bridge retracted and doors closed with police running towards them. "They've been trialling this cab and that little bridge," he explained to Will. Terry waved at a copper who was trying to open the door to the cab. The tube pulled away.

Jack manoeuvred Faith towards his old lock-up where he stored his Gordon-Keeble. He had owned the garage for years which was in one of the quiet suburbs and was ideal for his needs. He parked up the 2CV and climbed out, stashing his mask in his pocket. Jack unlocked the garage, looked around and, seeing that nobody was about, entered. He pulled the dust cover from the vehicle and stroked the bonnet of the car smiling.

"Time for a long trip," he said as he climbed in. The engine started first time and he backed her out to the Citroen. Jack opened both boots, placed a wooden shelf as a bridge and started sliding loaded bags into the Keeble. *A free workout,* he thought as he transferred the heavy gold. With no on in view still, he drove the Citroen into the garage and covered it over, locking the garage as he left. He smiled as he climbed into the Keeble and started her up. His intention now was a gentle drive north where he could make a deposit at a safe location.

* * *

"That jet there," said Jane, pointing to a private plane with its engine running. A man stood at the top of the plane steps, beckoning them towards him. He appeared to be yelling. Charity stopped at the bottom as Tommy descended with a big grin on his face.

"Come on. We need to get going," yelled Tommy over the engine noise. Jane smiled and ran to the boot. Ted climbed out to assist. Aligned next to the steps stood a roof tile hoist. All three lifted and placed bags on the machine. Tommy and Jane climbed the steps and lifted them into the cab of the aircraft. The transfer took minutes. Both descended.

"Nice one, Ted," shouted Tommy, shaking Ted's hand. "Here, for your trouble." Tommy handed him a roll of cash. "We'll sort the rest when things settle. Can you ditch the car?"

"Anywhere specific?"

"It needs to be destroyed. Scrap it, torch it. Anything," Ted nodded. Jane leant in, kissed him on the cheek and gave him a brief cuddle. Tommy took her arm, guiding her to the steps. "We need to get going." They climbed, entered the plane and the door closed. Ted climbed into Charity and headed off.

* * *

"They're in the tube," said Debbie in astonishment. The door to the office crashed open and Selena strode in with two suited officers.

"What the hell's going on, Inspector?" she said looking at Smith. Smith didn't know how to respond. *Can I tell her?* He had no chance to reply. "Where's Harrison? Go and find him." Ali Smith made a swift exit, heading for Harrison's office.

"What tube station?" asked Selena.

"Bank," said Mary. "Northern platform."

"This needs to stop. Pull all the resources. Let them run." The room went silent, the staff were stunned. "I'm not joking. This pursuit is dangerous and not authorised. DO IT NOW!"

Unbeknown to the room, Selena had just received a call from her boss telling her that the bank had advised them that there seems to have been an error of judgement at their end, 'made in good faith of course', but for them today, was business as usual, 'no offences disclosed'. Selena couldn't wait to get hold of Harrison.

Ali Smith entered the control room with Harrison behind him. Serena turned to Harrison, ignoring Smith.

"I don't know what the hell you think that you are doing," said Serena, turning to the suited men. "Complaints and Discipline," she advised Harrison. She turned to the men. "He's all yours. Get him out of my sight."

* * *

Will sat waiting, engine running as the tube pulled into the next station.

"You ready?" Will nodded.

"You sure?" Will asked.

"Yes, they won't have a clue what's going on."

"We're slowing."

"Get ready." The doors to the platform opened. The bridge platform extended. Hope pulled gently out onto the platform and turned left towards the lift doors. Will parked directly before the doors. Terry stepped out, now wearing a guard jacket and cap, and turned to address people exiting the tube.

"This one's booked," he yelled. "There's the stairs, or this lift will be back down in a minute. Clear the way, clear the way." The engine of Hope revved, reinforcing his message. The lift doors opened. "Out you come." He directed the small number of people from the lift. "Round to the left of the car. Keep moving." The people automatically followed his directions. Terry waved Hope into the lift. The doors closed behind as he pressed the button for ground level. He tapped on the driver's window which Will lowered.

"Cut the engine, mate. I'm not dying of fumes after going through all this." The silence was deafening as the engine stopped and the lift ascended. "Nearly there." Terry ran to the passenger side and waited. The doors opened. The crowds stepped back and Hope slowly drove out of the lift to the main exit with not a police officer in sight. Terry jumped into the car and both men started laughing.

"Bloody brilliant," said Terry.

* * *

Six months later

Keith walked back from the bar carrying a large jug of lager in one hand and a cocktail in the other.

"Cheers," said Terry, accepting the jug from him. "What are you two having?" Jack and Tommy laughed in response. The four males looked well, with tanned complexions and cool summer clothing. Out in the bay waited Tommy's luxury yacht where they would all return later. Today they had business to attend to. A meeting to hold and decisions to make. Tommy had arranged a private meeting in the small taverna which he had hired from a friend of his.

"Sounds like a car," said Keith who still managed to wear his long coat in the warmth of the evening, with hair held solidly in place. The men listened to car doors closing. They turned.

A lithe young lady, wearing a loose linen dress and with short blonde hair, walked from the roadway. Jack smiled.

"Wait for me," yelled, a familiar accent as Veronica Pilcher appeared, tripping over a step as she did so. Veronica wore her familiar black clothing, dark sunglasses and had a sunburnt nose.

"Ronnie," Terry yelled standing up. "Well, I never ..." said Keith astounded.

"Told you I was bringing a surprise." Jack stood up and walked to the blonde woman, hugging her.

"Jane, it's been too long," he held her back at arm's length. "You look wonderful."

"Enough of that," interrupted Ronnie, slapping his arms away. "Where's the beer?" They all sat down, grabbed a drink and chatted like old friends. Food was produced and friendships solidified.

"Well," said Tommy, sitting back, full and satisfied. "You did it, Terry. You trumped me. Well done, son." Tommy raised his glass to Terry who was beaming. "Ronnie, is everything in place to send our donations?"

"Sure is. Shall I send it now."

"Go for it." Ronnie produced her phone and tapped into it. Numerous charities would soon be receiving substantial charitable donations from an anonymous source.

"What next?" said Tommy.

"What do you mean?" asked Jane. Tommy looked at Terry, who looked at Keith, who looked at Jack.

"Well," said Jack, "I know that The Sceptre of Dagobert, Tucker's Cross and the Irish Crown Jewels are still all out there." Jane looked confused.

"Maybe Fort Knox?" interjected Terry.

"The Bundesbank?" suggested Tommy.

"You are joking?" said Jane.

"Not at all," replied Terry. Ronnie lowered her pint and said.

"Well, wherever it is. I'm in."